GARRISON'S CREED

A TITAN NOVEL

CRISTIN HARBER

DEDICATION

For TeamCT

CHAPTER ONE

Sighting the target in his crosshairs, Cash Garrison accounted for all of the variables. Wind speed and direction. Distance and range. Now the world would be free of one more bloodthirsty warlord in less time than it would take for the walking dead man to finish his highfalutin champagne toast.

Hours had passed since Cash nestled into place, high-powered rifle held like a baby to his chest. A thousand yards out from the extravagant mansion, he'd burrowed into position, melting into the landscape, and waited for this moment. Antilla Smooth, dressed like the million dollars he made as an arms dealer and unaware of the grim reaper sighting his forehead, made his way past the French doors.

Cash caressed the trigger, knowing exactly how many pounds of pressure it would take to fire the round. He monitored his breaths and heart rate. When his entire body was still, in between beats and respirations, he'd take the bastard out. One less piece of shit strutting on God's green Earth. The world would be a better place, and Cash's job for the day would be done. He and the team could find a local bar, find some ladies, celebrate and make a night of it. *Good plan.*

He adjusted for a breeze, blinked his eyes, counted down his breaths, and—stopped. Stunned. Frozen in place. Heart pounding like a coal-eating locomotive.

A woman in a golden dress and sparkled-out jewelry that'd make royalty jealous wrapped her arm around Antilla. A soldier would sell his last bullet for a kiss from her lips. Cash saw her through his scope as though she stood a mere twenty feet in front of him.

She looked like... but it couldn't be.

His spotter spoke the direction in his earpiece. "Send it."

Cash spoke into his mic. "Stand by."

His spotter whispered again. "Eyes on your target. All conditions accounted for. Go. Send it."

Nothing. Cash didn't speak.

Earpiece again. "Go, goddamn it."

The woman slunk around his bull's-eye, her beautiful hair piled on top of her head, save for the loose pieces framing her face. Her smile slipped into a laugh. *I've inhaled gun oil fumes. I'm losing my mind right this second.*

"Cash, man. You there?" His spotter grabbed his attention, wrenching him back to reality.

"Here. Yeah, man. Here."

"Wind from three o'clock. Dropped to five mph. Hold. Target blocked." The woman draped over the man. This was a nightmare—his nightmare—blasting from the past and slapping him clear off of his prone position and onto his stupefied ass. The spotter spoke again. "Clear. Dial wind right, two mils. Send it… now."

Heartbeat. Breath. Heartbeat.

Fire.

And breathe.

Now, they had to move. Fast. He knew the spotter team should be slipping through the thick Maine forest. Cash paused and glanced longer than he needed to confirm the kill. Tuxedoed man on the ground. Kill shot. Dead. Panic attacked the room. People ran, most likely screaming. Security scrambled. Dogs loosed. Barks growing closer. But the woman. The golden silk-draped woman stood still, staring at the busted windowpane in the French doors. No expression. No emotion. Not a drop of anything.

Cash shook his head, clearing the ghost of her image, and focused on his job. One shot, one kill. Just the way he liked it. He cleared the shell and casing from his bolt-action rifle, policed his brass, and snapped to a crouch, erasing any evidence that he had spent hours in the spot. A half second later, he beat feet, sliding down the side of the wooded hill, leaving no trail.

His spotter buzzed in his ear, confirming their meet-up point. "Rendezvous at location A, twenty-two ten." He could do it. He should do it. He powered down a hill, sliding as dirt gave under his feet. Brush slapped him in the face. Vicious barking closed in. The main house illuminated day-glow bright.

Man, he was going to hear about it for this one. He told his spotter, "Location C, twenty-three hundred hours."

"Cash—"

It took a lot for Roman to break protocol and use his name over the radio frequency, but Cash knew his spotter, his closest friend, was pissed. And an upset Roman was as much fun to deal with as the dogs Cash was about to run back toward.

Not much to do except kill an hour. Cash pulled his earpiece out as Roman cursed again. Nothing good would come at the end of that sentence. Cash laughed. Radio silence wasn't the best road to take, but it was better than coughing up an explanation of the impossible.

Nicola glided around Antilla Smooth. His lifeless face stared at the ceiling, and his perfect hair hid the sniper round's entry wound. Given the crimson puddle painting the white carpet round the backside of his brain, the bullet was a through and through, and her night was ruined. Her operation ruined, completely FUBAR.

Chaos filled the room, and she was the calm eye of the storm. Everyone and everything swirled around her. Loud noises. Screaming people. Security moved fast, but what was the point? They'd failed.

She hadn't failed, but the last few months were now crap, and it was time to call the powers that be. They'd be interested in this turn of events. Nicola put down her champagne flute and pulled out her cell. She walked away, feeling her smooth silk gown train trailing behind her.

The phone rang once, and a surprised voice answered. "It's a little early for our chat."

"We should get together for ice cream." Nicola gave the phrase that told Beth, her handler, that this mission was dunzo.

Beth didn't miss a beat. "I have to run errands first. I'll meet you after you head to the dry cleaners."

Dry cleaners. Yup, time to turn into a shadow and slink away. It was the right move, pulling her home. Too bad she had nothing to show for the months spent playing to the dead megalomaniac's ego. She'd been so close, only one or two days away from locking down the international players in Antilla's arms network.

"You've got it. I'll be in and out first thing in the morning." She walked down the hallway, and a guard looked. Apparently, her saunter was too calm, given the way other women shrieked their horror. "*Ciao*," she said goodbye, keeping up her Italian persona and putting a hand against her throat.

She looked at her designer gown. No blood. At least there was an upside to this evening's party. That and she wouldn't have to feign interest in Antilla, the sick prick, then backpedal when he wanted to take her to bed.

Personal preference. Some ladies in the Agency did what they had to do without a second thought. She'd had second thoughts. And thirds and fourths. She'd wanted to screw Antilla Smooth like she wanted a root canal done by Kermit the freakin' Frog: choppy marionette hands flopping up and down.

"Gabriella?" Someone used her alias. "Gabriella, are you okay?"

Nicola saw a butler who had been friendly to her since they'd arrived at Antilla's Maine estate. Her name poured off his lips, imitating the Italian flare she used when introducing herself.

"Yes, fine. *Bene, grazie.*" He looked unassuming. Who knew why the man worked for Smooth Enterprises, but looks were deceiving. Trust no one. "I need to step outside. Fresh air."

Really, she needed to get out of Maine, but why elaborate? She slipped outside. The night was daybreak bright with the estate's security system fully engaged. Her hand caught her eye. The fluorescents made her olive skin look green, not complementing the dress she'd fallen in love with. Nicola weighed her lack of options, knowing she'd need transportation and, for the moment, not knowing how she'd secure it.

A chill spiked over her skin as a gust blew through the forest. Someone was still out there. The same someone who took out her mark.

Pop. Flash. Pop. The exterior lights died, and she was left to her thoughts in the moonless night. Another chill rolled over her shoulders. No wind this time. She pivoted, reluctantly ready and willing to ruin her dress and take it out of the ass of whoever was to blame. Her muscles tensed. Her eyes adjusted in a flash. A man. Large. Broad. Armed. Twenty feet away at the side of the patio.

He spoke, the baritone timbre coating her in a hurt she'd hidden years ago. "Nicola."

She didn't need to see his face. His voice shattered any semblance of strength she'd mustered. Nicola braced one leg back, prepared to attack. Ready to defend herself. But who was she kidding? If he laid one finger on her, it might be her undoing. All her suffering, pointless.

"Nicola," he said again. Still as firm, but this time knowing. "What the fuck?"

This was bad news of the worst variety. She pivoted back toward the doors, ready to go back inside and hash out an emergency extraction strategy with Beth. No time to wait for tomorrow's withdrawal plan.

Reaching for the doorknob, she willed herself not to run.

"It's you, isn't it?" he said.

Sweet Lord, why was Cash here? Why was the one memory she could never forget standing in the middle of her job? And why was he talking to her, armed and looking far more dangerous than the last time she saw him?

"Stop your sweet ass one second, and turn around, Nicola."

She spun on her stiletto heel, knowing she'd never be able to get to the subcompact gun tucked on the inside of her thigh. Even if she could, she'd never hurt Cash.

"No, sir. You're mistaken." She put on her best Italian accent, knowing it wouldn't fix this problem.

"Bull—"

The butler opened the door. "Gabriella, please come in. Everyone's gathering in the main hall. It's dangerous to be out here."

Cash stood in the shadows. She knew the butler couldn't see him. Yet, her pulse stuttered, and her throat tightened. She wanted to protect one man from the other. Nicola looked over her shoulder, and Cash was gone.

CHAPTER TWO

Cash ran through this mind-scrambling scenario as he pushed toward the semi-agreed upon location. He had two more minutes to scoot his caboose there before his spotter had one more thing to bitch at him about. Cash and Roman were tight. One hell of a sniper-spotter team, and best of bros. From boot camp to Titan Group, they'd been by each other's sides, watching backs, chasing chicks, and fighting in the trenches.

With fifteen seconds to spare, Cash rounded a moss-covered boulder and ran smack into Roman.

"How goes it, dickhead?" Roman scowled. "Your mic not working? Your earpiece burn out?"

A rumble of tires put the pause on their conversation. The armored Range Rover barreled around a tight curve, and they jumped in before it came to a stop. Two doors shut. The driver tore down the road as Cash and Roman righted themselves in the backseat. Cash ignored Roman and waited for the shitstorm he knew was coming.

As if on cue, Roman turned his camo-painted face and stared hard. Cash started to peel off his ghillie suit, unzipping the outfit of fake leaves.

"Hold your roll, Cash."

"Back off."

Roman lowered his voice. "The hell I will."

All the questions, all the confusions morphed into fury. Distrust. "Did you know?"

"Know? Know what?"

Cash lunged forward, wrapping his hand around Roman's throat. "So help me God. Did you know about her?"

Pressed against the window, Roman jabbed his knee into Cash's gut. Like two battling rams, they pounded and cursed.

The man at the wheel, Rocco, shifted in his seat. "What the fuck? Sit down."

Cash felt the Range Rover skid to a stop, knew he and his best friend were trading blows, but none of it clicked in his frontal lobe. He was all emotion and instinct. The back door opened, and Roman ducked out, pulling Cash with him.

Roman caught him in the jaw with a fist full of knuckles. Wet asphalt scratched his face. He righted himself, pulling an arm back. He'd kill Roman if it was the last thing he did. All that bullshit about loyalty and honor. *What a crock.*

Losing his balance, he fell back. Rocco clasped his punch-ready fist and pulled him off Roman, who pounced up into a fighter's stance, fists raised, knees bent. Rocco had killed the car's lights. No moonlight. Just the three men, two with sweat steaming off them in the cool night air and one level-headed, probably wondering what the fuck. Hell, maybe Roman wondered that too.

Shaking, Nicola walked into the main hall. Her fingers vibrated and her heart banged like she was one of Antilla's eight-ball snorting girls. It was a good look for her now that she'd been lassoed into the main hall with distraught women who were genuinely upset that the bastard was dead.

Sweet, funny Cash Garrison. She had no doubt it was him, though he must have a hundred pounds of pure muscle hanging off those long limbs. Could men in their twenties have growth spurts? She didn't remember him as tall. Certainly not as broad. And his voice was deeper than the bottom of the cliff she supposedly drove off of a decade ago.

Nicola looked from one woman to the next. She could identify all of them. Then she eyed the men. They too were catalogued in her memory, but she didn't know what each did for Smooth or how the money funneled in and out of his Swiss banks.

The CIA was right to be disappointed in her. Beth should put her on desk duty at the Farm until she was an old biddy talking about her days in the spy game. *Shit*. She really needed to talk to Beth.

In the corner, Antilla's head of security barked orders. There was no telling what that crackpot might do. Nicola needed to get the hell out of here. Patio escape plan, round two. The butler touched her shoulder.

"Gabriella, would you like a glass of water?"

Him again? He was always around, always watching. "No, *grazie*."

"May I get you a lemonade? The taste reminds me of sunset walks on the beach at night."

She went from ignoring him to pinning him against the wall with a stare. "*Scuzi?*"

He spoke slower. More deliberate. "I said. Sunset walks on the beach. At night."

Nicola processed his words. His look. It couldn't be. Could it? "*Non capisco*. I do not understand."

"Yes, you do."

Yes, she did. The CIA had someone else in here. The butler. She should have known.

"Yes, I do." She nodded, mapping out her next move. Did Beth know? The games. She hated all the games, and if this guy was here to make sure she did her job, she was going to lose her trademark cool. She hated being checked up on. Hated the doubt that she couldn't pull the gig off. Then again, she hadn't.

"I'll get you a lemonade, or would you like to come with me?"

Hell, why not? "Yes. Of course."

They made their way down an elaborate hall. Oil paintings of New England landscapes and native animals were framed in gilded boxes and lit by brass fixtures.

"They're bringing you in," he said as casually as if they talked about the change in the seasons.

"You?"

"No."

"Why me?"

"Not my call."

"Who else is here?" Or in other words, why was Cash here?

"Just the two of us."

"I didn't know about you. Maybe you don't know about someone else."

"Maybe."

Not the answer she wanted, though she wouldn't believe any answer he gave if it were a definite yes or no.

He handed her a drink and napkin from a side table. "Extraction directions are in your cocktail napkin. You leave tonight. Take this to the bathroom, and move as directed."

"This is because of the patio?"

"What?"

"I was supposed to go to the dry cleaners tomorrow."

"Change of plan."

"Why?"

"Not sure, other than Antilla was eliminated."

"What do we have on that?"

"Wasn't us."

"What—"

"You need to move. Go. Follow the directions. The extraction team is ready to pull you out in five minutes."

The butler turned and walked away, leaving her, drink in hand. Nicola sipped her lemonade and headed for the specified bathroom. She took in the empty lounging area and vanity counters and entered a quiet bathroom stall, closing the door behind her. She unfolded the edges of the napkin. It was blank. *What the hell?*

She held it to the light. Nothing. No ink. No code. No marks.

She'd been made. Confirmed it herself. Fucking safe phrase wasn't worth shit if someone unsafe knew it existed. Her pulse thumped in her neck. Her ears strained to hear the incoming attack. She was trapped, save the narrow window that opened two stories above a terrace. The window was tall but skinny. She might not fit. No time to overthink it, and thank God, she'd skipped dinner. Nicola chucked off her heels, lifted her skirt, and palmed her Beretta.

Despite grabbing a fancy, overstuffed pillow for use as a makeshift silencer, the shot was loud when she blew out the window. Hoisting herself up to the sill, she looked over her shoulder to see her extraction team, courtesy of the butler, blow through the outer door. No time to second-guess her next move, and oh, the landing would hurt. Barefoot, she sucked in a breath and pushed through the shattered frame.

Glass shards scraped her chest and back as she sidestepped through. Teetering for a hot second on the outside, she realized that the window frame was too narrow. She couldn't turn her head to look back at her attackers, but she felt hands grabbing at her dress. Before a hand could clamp around her calf, she leaped.

It felt like slow motion. Weightless, reaching for the sky, she floated in a sea of gold silk as her dressed billowed around her until she hit the manicured terrace lawn. Everything hurt. Her exit strategy wasn't strategic, and it gave her zero chance to position for a tuck and roll, but it did do one very good thing. It kept dangerous men inside the house.

Bang. Bang. Pop.

The men were inside, but their guns shooting out the window had a wide open range. She pulled up as fast as she could manage. Dirt spat around her. Their shots missed but not by much. Nicola hobbled as fast as she could. They were, no doubt, regrouping and busting ass to get her on the terrace.

As she half-limped, half-ran, she tried to assess her injuries. Nothing broken. Definitely going to have to make a chiropractor appointment. Blood had ruined her gorgeous dress, thanks to the window exit. Definitely a sprained elbow and wrist.

The thicket of the woods loomed ahead, and she closed in on it, praying she'd reach the dense cover. Only then did she realize that she still gripped the subcompact gun but had lost her purse, and with it her untraceable cell phone. How the shit was she going to call Beth?

First plan of action: get far away from this mansion. Maybe stumble all the way to another mansion, break in, and use their phone. She jammed her bare foot against the sharp side of a downed branch.

"Son of a bitch!" It hurt like an ice pick stab, shooting straight from her heel to her hip bone. She lost her balance, tumbling down the hill, head first, sprained arm next. Her throbbing foot screamed in pain.

Nicola came to rest at the bottom of the hill. Dress thoroughly ruined. Bleeding top to bottom.

"Get up, girl," she told herself.

Nothing moved except for her lips. No, she'd worked too hard, had too much to prove. A little thing like this wasn't going to take her down. She was too freakin' smart to stumble like a newbie recruit fresh off the Farm.

"Nothing that can't heal. Get up. Now."

Her skin prickled. She wasn't alone. In a heartbeat, she was on her busted feet, gun drawn, pivoting intuitively. She spun twice, focused her hearing, and took one step forward, her foot touching the gravel side of a rural road. A dozen yards up, an SUV idled in the dark. Three men the size of NFL linebackers stood frozen like oversized yard gnomes.

And they weren't the men who chased her.

She readied her Beretta. The slide echoed in the moonless night.

One man put his hands up. The two others straightened as if they'd been hunched, ready to throw down on a Maine backwoods road.

She took a step forward. Damn this pitch-black night. She couldn't see anything more than male outlines. After her run-in with Cash Garrison and then the men who'd shot at her... Lord only knew who else was in on this game.

"Turn around. Move away from the car. Now!" She needed their set of wheels. Maybe she'd strike spy gold and find a charged cell phone.

The man with his hands up took two strides back. Without communicating, the two other men took two steps forward. She did not have time for this. The men from the mansion might be driving this same road or trailing her through the woods. She limped forward, trying not to groan when her injured foot hit gravel again.

"I said move it." She shuffled toward the driver's door.

"Nicola?"

Not Cash.

Not Cash by a million years. Far worse. Far more confusing. She couldn't handle this. Nicola leaped toward the idling car.

David leaned against the wall as he heard the pop of gunfire in the bathroom. He loosened the god-awful uniform tie he wore in his role as a butler. Hopefully, Nicola was taken out in one shot, no need for it to get messy.

Tonight had been unexpected. The assassination caused several problems, but most importantly, it affected his retire-from-the-CIA plan. Smooth had paid David handsomely to keep him in the know about investigations into the gun lord's illegal activities and terrorist connections.

Evidently, David missed a memo. With Smooth and Nicola dead, his backup plan formed. He'd check in with his handler at the CIA, get his marching orders, and, until he could find another buyer of CIA secrets, he'd lift enough ammo and arms to pad his retirement account, and go back to his pain in the ass day job as a CIA operative.

And in the unlikely event that Nicola escaped, he would finish her off later. She hadn't figured out the central piece of information that could topple Smooth Enterprises, but why chance the risk? That one secret he'd kept from the CIA secured his future.

CHAPTER THREE

The woman ran to the open driver's door, actively ignoring the men, hiding her face. Too damn late. Cash and Roman sprang for the open rear door, pancaking one on top of the other on the backseat as the woman slammed the driver's door.

Pulling off of Roman, Cash slapped his hand around the car ceiling, searching for the dome light switch.

Click. Dull light illuminated the truth.

The gun pointed toward the backseat, but the woman still didn't look at them, avoiding their stares. He could easily disarm her. Roman could too. Neither did.

"Nicola?" Roman rasped again.

Her arm trembled, vibrating the gun as she flipped the safety into place, but her finger stayed at the ready. "Please get out. Just go," she whispered.

That was her voice. It had been her face. Cash looked at Roman. No, he didn't know. The man was as dumbstruck and hurting as he was. All they could see was the back of a bloody shoulder and arm and leaves sticking in messy hair.

Rocco approached the open door by Roman, perhaps not seeing the showdown. "What's doing?"

They ignored him.

"Nicola." Roman's voice cracked. "Am I going nuts?"

Cash looked at Roman and saw the confusion tearing his world apart, just like it had his. He wore the evidence on his hardened face.

Her unsteady arm lowered, placing the gun on the front console. Her ratty-haired head dropped, and then the face Cash used to adore eyed them both. Her bottom lip quaked, and her eyes spilled tears.

She closed them, and more tears cascaded down her cheeks. "I'm so sorry."

Roman busted out his door, knocking Rocco over in the process. He could have torn it off its hinges. The man wouldn't have cared. The driver's door flew open, and he wrapped his arms around her, pulling his baby sister tightly to his chest. Cash had no idea what words came out of Roman's mouth. It wasn't his place to listen.

Their tender moment was shut down when she pushed him off. "Are you here to take me out?"

No one breathed a word. Cash couldn't understand her involvement with Antilla Smooth and couldn't bear breaking it to Roman that he'd seen her all over the warmonger. It tore his heart apart all over again, just like the day they'd lost her.

But they hadn't lost her. She was alive and sitting in front of him.

Nicola spoke up again. "Who do you work for?"

What is she talking about?

Roman seemed to read his mind. "Nic, what are you talking about?"

"Why are you here?"

"You're alive. Let's start there."

"Go away, Roman. It's better this way. If you're not here to—"

"What are you talking about? You're alive. You're coming home. Mom and Dad... they, we buried you. We—"

"You have to leave. Now. If I can't have the car—" She tried to get past him, but he locked her against his chest. "Let go. Damn you, Roman. You don't understand. We can't be here."

"You're in trouble. We can help. We can fix this."

She moved before either Roman or Cash could react. Gun in hand, pressed against her brother's chest. "I love you," she sobbed.   "Don't   make   me."

Roman backed up, hands in the air. "Who are you? What's happened to you?" The tenor of his voice was clear. He'd moved on from shock to fury. At least Roman was catching up with Cash in the what-the-fuck department.

"Go away," she hissed, wiping at tears with the back of her hand.

"I can't. You're my—"

Nicola nudged the Beretta back toward him, groaning when she used her arm. "I need your car. Tell me how to contact you. I'll explain this. I promise. But I have to go. Now. I—"

"I don't think so."

"Goddamn it, Roman. If you're here to kill me, do it. Otherwise, get the fuck out of this car. You too, Cash. Move it."

Kill her?

Gone were her tears. In the span of a second, the emotion was gone. The steely eyed woman was in business mode.

Ten years had passed. Ten long-assed years. Who knew what she'd been doing? Clearly, bad things with bad people.

Cash spoke. "You're hurt."

She rocketed a glare at him. "I'll be dead if you don't leave."

Cash continued, hoping to make inroads even after Roman tried-and-burned. "We can help you. Whatever kind of trouble you're in—"

"I'm not in trouble. Get out!"

"No," Cash and Roman said in unison.

Click-click. The slide of the Glock turned them both to stone. Their third man, Rocco, had Nicola dead center in his close range sights.

"Get that fucking gun out of my sister's face," Roman said, cold as ice.

Rocco's face fell. He lowered the gun. "We need to get the fuck out of here. Work your family shit out in therapy. Buy some self-help books. I don't care. But go now."

Nicola dropped her gun again, pressing her head to the steering wheel.

Roman patted her snarled hair. "Nic, it'll be okay. Whatever's happened to you, we'll work through it. We'll protect you." He snaked his arms around his little sister and hugged. With an efficient lift, he had her up and in his arms.

A game of musical chairs ensued. Cash moved to the front passenger. Roman settled beside Nicola in the backseat. She groaned again when he placed her down. Cash eyeballed the driver's seat before Roc got in. There was a lot of blood in the front seat.

"We have to go," she whispered hoarsely.

"Roger that, hon." Rocco glanced at Roman. "Shit. Sorry on the hon. Roger that, um..."

"Nicola." Roman glared at Rocco.

"Right. Roger that, Nicola." Rocco gunned the engine, and they sped off.

Roman turned to his sister. "Nic, please start talking. Whoever had you, you're safe. Whatever the reason for the—"

"Stop. This isn't what you think. I left on purpose."

And that was all. She stared straight ahead. No amount of brotherly badgering or angry demanding changed her response.

Cash's head spun in circles. She was alive. Alive and armed, even though they'd buried her a decade ago.

His senior year of college, when they got the news, seemed like yesterday. But it was a lie. She was a liar. The only woman to steal his heart was a liar.

Liar, liar, girl on fire.

They eased into the driveway at the suburban safe house. Rocco hadn't breathed a word since they'd peeled out miles ago. Roman gave up his interrogation, looking distraught and angry and yet... hopeful. If there were seven phases of grief, how many for shock?

And Cash stayed mum. Hadn't done anything other than strip off his ghillie suit, wipe the face paint off, and pull his cowboy hat on. But hell, it hadn't kept him from watching her in the side view mirror.

Rocco jumped out and popped the trunk. He grabbed a bag and beat feet to the door. "Good night, good luck." He went inside.

The three of them sat in the car. Silent. Cash closed his eyes, remembering the last day, their last conversation, the horrible ache that ate him alive when he lost her.

"Cash?" she whispered into the dark.

Her voice made his spine tingle.

"Oh, screw that, Nicola. Talk to me first." Roman had every right to be pissed. And if he knew the half of it, he'd be pissed at both of them.

She opened her car door, and they did the same. Three doors slapped shut, one right after the other.

Suburbia was scary quiet. She took a step and tripped. As swift as he could, Cash stepped in, catching her. Nicola's body fit just the same in his arms as it always had. His muscles remembered how she felt against him. A shudder shivered up the nape of his neck and down the arms wrapped around her torso.

She locked eyes with him. Older. Wiser. And somehow more beautiful than ever. He should hate this woman. He did hate her, but until she looked away, he was stuck in a trance.

Relief and emptiness swirled in his chest. He rubbed his sternum with his free hand, wishing the feeling away.

Instead of focusing on the old Nicola, he needed to look at this one. "How bad's your ankle, Nic?"

She didn't answer, instead trying to right herself, smoothing the sexy dress that softly clung to her curves. Christ, he didn't remember a tenacious streak. But then again, he didn't really know the Nicola who pulled from his grip.

She hobbled toward the front door, the dress dragging behind her in a grand, out-of-place fashion, and turned to the stupefied men in the driveway. "I need a secure phone. Can either of you help me with that?"

A secure phone? On top of asking if they were going to kill her? Make that stupefied squared. Cash looked at Roman, who looked just as confused with a little "what-the-fuck?' painted across his forehead.

"Yeah, we'll help you." He looked at Roman, mouthing, "what's happening?"

The door shut. Cash and Roman stood unmoving in the driveway.

"That's my baby sister, and hell if I know." His voice trailed off. "We buried her body. There was a body. My mother cried for months." Roman's voice bottomed out.

They leaned against the Range Rover. Two men and too many emotions. Roman dropped his head into his palms, and Cash stared into the night sky.

No big brother should go through what Roman did, holding his mother's hand, consoling her alongside his upset father through a closed-casket funeral. There had been little choice when her body had burnt to smithereens. Check that. When they'd thought her body went up in smoke. Turns out her tall, lean body had just left them in the dark driveway.

Cash wanted no part in remembering that awful day. How he'd said he loved her, how they were going to tell Roman that his best friend was nailing his little sister. That's not what it was, not at all. Not even close. But that's how a dude would see it. Roman was gonna flip, and Cash was going to explain that she conjured up images of dum-dum-da-da and a poufy white dress.

Pushing away from the Rover, he wanted to knock off the mirror or kick the hell out of the side panel. Anything to burn off the acid churning in his gut. Shit, too much time had passed. Young love. What bullshit.

Cash eyed Roman. "You okay, man?"

Roman cleared his throat. "No. I'm not okay. My dead sister's alive and... working for Antilla Smooth?" He paused, as if looking into Cash's soul. "That's what happened earlier? You saw her? You thought I knew?"

That logic seemed so flawed now, but at the time... at the time, it was the only thing he could comprehend. And *working for Antilla Smooth?* That's not all she was to Smooth, but Cash would keep that tidbit to himself. It'd destroy his boy. Nicola in the arms of a decrepit arms dealer. It went against everything he and Roman lived for.

The Nicola he knew wouldn't touch a bastard like Smooth. But then again, he didn't know Nicola. He knew a liar.

CHAPTER FOUR

Nicola bunked down in the bedroom the farthest away from the guys. *Who am I kidding?* They were just the guys, like this was just another day. Roman and Cash. The two most important men in her life, even if it'd been an eternity since she'd felt their touch or heard their words.

The day she'd walked away from her loved ones had been the worst day of her life—until today. She pinched her eyes closed, remembering their stunned faces. The pain and anguish. And the anger. Who could blame them? She certainly couldn't. She blamed herself, though. She had no choice.

Yes. Today was officially the worst day, and the former was a helluva bad day to knock out of contention.

Her bedroom had a bathroom—well stocked with first aid supplies—like any good safe house. What the hell were Roman and Cash doing running around with guns and slipping into safe houses? Her mind raced. A million maybes skittered through her thoughts. Did they wonder the same about her?

Both men had Popeyed out since she'd last seen them. They were massive. Different builds, but no question, given her run-in with Cash's arms, they'd taken their passion for working out to a whole new level. Roman was stocky and square, broad top to bottom. Cash had some lank to him. Long legs, powerful chest. His chest had been sinful before, but now it was downright deadly.

She shook away the thought of Cash. No need to hopscotch down memory lane. Her cuts needed tending, and daydreaming wouldn't stave off infection. She cleaned them, dousing each raw mark in hydrogen peroxide. A smear of antibacterial ointment and she'd be okay.

Her elbow was another story. She'd have to wrap and sling it. Immobilization was key to recovery, but showing a blatant sign of weakness to three men who saw her as theirs to protect wouldn't work.

Another beautiful dress ruined. The wardrobe was a serious perk of her job, but the dresses never made it home. She'd known this one was headed for the dumpster when she'd wedged herself out the window. But damned if she hadn't hoped she was wrong, somehow. Nope. It was just a stupid dress anyway. But it felt like the only thing she could focus on without curling up into a crying ball.

A soft knock on her door stole her breath. Having no idea what to say or how to explain, she didn't move to answer it. The handle turned, and it slipped open. Cash stuck his beautiful head of blond hair—shower damp and face free of camouflage face paint—into the room. He looked older and harder. Tanner. Maybe a few lines around his eyes. The baby face was gone, replaced by something chiseled.

He held out a phone like it was a pass code and he was requesting entry. She nodded. As he stepped in, he held up his other hand. Clothes as another offering.

"Phone. T-shirt. Pants. Figured you needed to change." He sounded as unsure as she felt.

The air was heavy and the room much smaller than she'd realized. His eyes pierced straight to her soul, squeezing the soft part she'd tried so hard to hide. Nicola nodded again. "Can I have the phone?"

"You can have the phone and the clothes." He placed the items down on the dresser but didn't move.

"All right. Thanks." He took up half the room as he waited, expectedly, for something from her. "If you'll excuse me."

"Nope. Not how it's going to work. Our phone—I'll stay for your call."

"But—"

"You don't have much in the way of options here, Nic. Your big brother is raging or grieving upstairs, going through mood swings like a mental patient, trying to get his head on straight.

And I'm…" Pain shone in the deepest blue eyes she'd ever seen. He closed them and took a deep breath. When he finally opened them again, he cleared his throat. "I'm here to monitor your phone call."

His voice carried bitterness and torment. She was an evil bitch. Her eyes tingled with tears wanting to burst free. Again. Instead, she scooted across the bed, self-conscious that her trashed silk gown clung to her body. "Fine. You can stay."

"Like I said, you don't have much option."

She grabbed the items off the dresser and settled back on the bed. "Okay."

She was the devil incarnate, evil's bitchy step-sister. How could she have done this to the two of them? To her family? She wanted to call Mom and Dad more now than she had any other night. Mom would hate her. She should. But Nicola needed her mom, needed her hug. Un-spilled tears tried to escape again, and she breathed them away, focusing on Cash.

He leaned his hulking frame back, put one boot against the wall, and continued to watch. She turned around on the bed but kept an eye on his reflection in the mirror. Nicola punched the number into the phone, waited, and entered another series of numbers.

Beth answered on the first ring, as was her custom. "Hey, girl. Didn't expect you again."

"Gabriella was compromised. She avoided a hit. But not by much."

"You're hurt?"

"Minimal." Nicola never offered signs of weakness when she didn't know who listened. Her best friend would understand by the tone of her voice that minimal was bullshit, but nothing a bath in Bactine wouldn't fix.

"Gotcha. And who are you with?"

"Friendlies." *I think.* "The situation is… complicated."

"Why can't you give me more?"

"Because my friend—" She glared at Cash in the mirror. "—is too nosey for his own good. For now, I don't need an extraction plan. I'll make contact tomorrow."

"Do I need to be worried?"

That was the best friend asking, not her handler. The two components were often at odds, and Beth knew Nic would never answer in the affirmative, even if it were the case.

"I'll see you soon enough and explain in person. Night."

Nicola clicked off the phone and slid it behind her, not wanting to make eye contact with Cash. He ambled from the wall, one heavy footstep slowly following the next. The noise wrapped around her. She dropped her eyes. Her hands went clammy. The thump, thump, thump of her heart could've vibrated the safe house.

Cash's boots stopped, and she fought the need to look up.

A finger wiped away her resolve. It touched the bottom of her chin and lifted until he held her gaze. *Have mercy.* Sapphire eyes and a sad smile made her bleed on the inside.

"It's nice to see you again." His voice was hurt and husky.

"You hate me?"

"I might." He smiled again, taking the bite out of their reality.

"I had reasons." But with him standing in front of her and Roman upstairs ready for a riot, they didn't seem worth a shit.

"Seems like a lot has changed."

"I was thinking the same thing."

"Nice dress." His eyes wandered slowly down her neck, down the dress.

For the length of the look, she held her breath, unsure why or how his gaze made her skin blaze. She stammered to fill the silence. "I thought the only upside of this day was I could keep the dress."

He chuckled, breaking the heated glance. "How are we gonna do this, Nic? You want to just explain, or should I start an interrogation?"

"I can't."

"You can."

"But I won't." She stared at the comforter, smoothing a wrinkle. "You and Roman. You look different. You... I guess we all grew up."

"A lot of time has passed."

"I said I was sorry."

"So you did."

"I know it doesn't—"

"Enough with the apologies." The harsh change of tone surprised her. He pushed on. "You want to talk now? To me? Roman? Hell, to Rocco?"

"I already said—"

"And I don't care. The way I see it, you're having a bad day because boyfriend-dearest finally got what he deserved."

"What?" She recoiled. The words felt like a slap across the face. He couldn't possibly think she and Antilla were a thing. Then again, seducing the blood-hungry prick was part of her cover.

"Don't play me for stupid, Nic. You and Antilla Smooth."

"Cash, you—"

"I have no idea what you've been up to for ten years, so start talking, or you may need to classify me as something other than a friendly."

"He wasn't my lover."

"I don't care."

His face said otherwise, and the panging in her head shouted that he needed to know.

She tried to move away from the Antilla line of fire. She might've had a compromised operation, but she wasn't going to pass out details of a covert operation because of past feelings. Too many unknowns. "Why were you out there? And Roman? Both of you decked out like—" *Like snipers. Oh, holy hell.* He raised an eyebrow, watching her connect a few scattered dots. She'd been on an adrenaline cocktail, then shocked by their meet-and-greet, and now, the jagged pieces started to align themselves. "One of you took Antilla out?"

One of them ruined her operation? Everything she'd put in for months? The good guys finally had a chance, and they destroyed it?

His jaw gnashed before it set, and he spoke through his teeth. "What's it to you?"

That was confirmation enough. Cash and Roman blew up her mission, shattering any chance to further infiltrate Smooth's world, to take out illegal arms dealers. *No!*

She lunged at him. It was the wrong move, an amateur move, but she wasn't thinking like a trained agent. Screw her busted foot and arm. Nicola landed square in front of him. What was she going to do unarmed? Shake him to death? They'd already confiscated her only gun.

With her one good arm, she beat his chest, pounding out every frustration and emotion that ached within her. The bedroom door flew open revealing Roman and Rocco poised, ready to do... something. She looked up at Cash towering over her, his face cold. Emotionless. She realized she'd been screaming. Her cheeks were wet. Shit, fucking tears. Years of training with the best disintegrated in one night.

Roman looked at Cash. "What the fuck?"

"She's upset that I blew her boyfriend's brains on the carpet."

Roman's face fell until disappointment snarled onto his face. "Boyfriend?" He turned from her, muttering something to Rocco while walking back down the hall.

Cash whispered, "I can't believe I loved you."

God, no. This was all wrong. She didn't know enough about who they were or why they were there. Explaining her part could have exponential effects on the CIA's other operations.

Why had she run into them tonight? Aching to tell the truth, aching to remember his love, Nicola looked in the mirror as she collapsed onto the bed. Maybe she was too weak for the job. Self-doubt ate at her like she was back on the Farm, in her first week as a recruit when every man, and the handful of women, had eyed her like lunch. She hadn't been much, just potential, and she still felt the need to prove herself.

She could do this: act like the agent she was trained to be and stop reacting. Emotions shouldn't dictate action.

I can't believe I ever loved you. Don't react. Don't move. His voice clanged through her memory. Her internal orders didn't work.

"Wait!" Nicola jumped off the bed as best she could, and bounced on one foot to the door.

But Cash was gone, taking the phone and leaving her the clothes. She tore off the mess of a dress, moving as fast as she could, threw the t-shirt over her head and—

And, oh God, did the shirt smell like Cash Garrison. Clean soap and a masculine, peppery scent. On one foot, with one good arm, she balanced with the shirt covering her head and just inhaled, immediately transported back to college. She was in her second year, and he was finishing up his fourth. They lay in bed, naked. His balled up t-shirt served as her pillow.

This shirt smelled like her past. A distant memory. A deep hurt blossomed in her chest.

Oh, no. I'm going to break my cover.

She finished pulling it on but grabbed the collar and held it to her nose. Just one more time. Just enough to relive the memory.

Cash told jokes. Always made her laugh, but at that moment, in that memory, he was dead serious and unsure how he would tell Roman they were together. At the time, they'd said together forever, and it'd been time to tell her brother. After she'd walked away, she'd cried for weeks. It still hurt.

She shook her head. Time to get this over with.

Nicola hopped down the hall, limped up the stairs, and found the men at the kitchen table, passing a bottle of Gentleman Jack. Roman stood up, staring at her limp. Cash threw back a shot.

Rocco waved. "Not much in the fridge. Power bars on the counter. But if you feel like joining us, shot glasses are next to the sink. We're drinking to shitty days. Cheers." He downed a shot.

"Nicola." Roman eyed her. "Are you okay?" He smashed glare at Cash. "What's with the yelling? Dickhead said—"

"She's not welcome here." Cash scowled and poured another shot.

This wasn't going well, and she'd been in the kitchen, oh, two point five seconds.

"Shut your face, Cash." Roman glared at the table. "Are you ready to, I don't know, talk about this?"

"No."

Roman sat down. Nicola grabbed a shot glass and sat down at the square table across from Roman with Rocco and Cash on either side of her. The lights were dim, and the table's wood grain was suddenly very interesting. Instead of studying it, she grabbed the bottle of Jack, poured herself a shot, and threw it down.

It burned. It was perfect.

The kick gave her a shiver. God, she needed that. So she did it again.

When she looked up, Roman and Cash eyed her, maybe a little shocked to see her drinking like that since last time they'd seen her, she was all *hi, I'd like a pink drink with my pink paper umbrella*. Well, she still liked pink drinks. That hadn't changed.

Damn, could she handle three shots in a row with nothing in her stomach? Nope, probably not. She slid the shot glass back a few inches.

"Antilla Smooth wasn't my lover." She met her brother's eyes.

He coughed and squirmed. "Didn't know that was the discussion we were having."

Cash's face didn't register anything other than fury. If he didn't believe her, that was his problem. It didn't matter anyway.

Rocco picked up their slack. "Why were you running through the woods? Barefoot."

"Better yet, why were you all over him?"

So Cash *did* want to join in the conversation. He seemed to ping pong between hurt and jealousy. She couldn't blame him.

She studied Roman instead of answering because she didn't know what to say. His eyebrows bunched. Then she glanced at his bicep. *No, no.* A memorial tattoo. RIP. Her year of birth. Her year of death.

Sucking a breath, she breathed out, "I'm sorry."

Roman nodded. Nicola watched her big brother, who clearly hurt right now, but didn't know why.

"Sorry? You've made that clear," Cash said.

"Cash, stop." Her palms felt clammy. "I didn't freak out on you because I was pissed you killed him. It's... complicated."

"Yeah, today's the definition of complicated."

Rocco interrupted. "Dude, calm it down. She's not going to talk to us with you up in her grill. Nicola, go on."

"Who do you guys work for?" she asked, curious, but really buying time until her brain registered a what-to-say-now plan.

"Nope, not your turn yet." Rocco stated it like he was wrangling an out-of-line preschooler.

She closed her eyes, then blinked. "I don't know where to start."

"Try the day you died." Cash used air quotes around *died.*

Rocco knocked him in the shoulder, and Roman grumbled.

"Cash and I..." She stole a glance at Cash. An indecipherable flash in his eyes said that he'd never told Roman.

"You and Cash what?" Roman asked.

"Never mind. Simple version. Remember my job in college? I worked part-time for an accounting firm, translating international accounts. Unknowingly, I stumbled onto a money laundering scheme. I didn't know it, but one of our clients was a mobster who did a lot of business overseas. I'd been tracking cash-for-hire assassinations and hadn't a clue. Once I connected the dots, I couldn't believe the truth. Then I naively showed up and accidently saw a goon-squad massacre. Wrong place, wrong time. I'd figured out they were killers, but then I actually saw them murder a man. Too bad that they also saw me. I ran out as the FBI swooped in. A sting operation. Their timing was good for me, bad for the other guy." She shook her head, remembering the first time she'd watched someone die. "I was in federal protection by the end of the day."

"Bullshit. It doesn't work like that." Cash slapped the table.

"Sometimes it does."

"But you still go by Nicola?" Roman asked.

She nodded.

"Because?"

"I eventually left federal protection and took a job where I was... safe. I never got used to a different name. I'm Nic. It just worked."

Roman kneaded his temples. "You didn't call. Send a damn letter. Nothing."

"I thought it would be better. Safer. I had a hard enough time adjusting to life without you all. Mom's face if she got a letter from me? Dad would go insane trying to find me. You and Cash..." Remembering the decisions still hurt. "I had to."

"You walked away from your life to help prosecute some low life piece of trash?" Pain was evident in the scratch of Roman's voice.

"You walked away from us?" Cash followed up, and she knew he meant him and her, not their three musketeers.

"I walked away to stay alive. The mobsters knew me, knew what I was privy to. The FBI sting took out a few members, but not the whole organization. I had to disappear. My death had to be untimely and coincidental. If not, those same contract killers would've found me—our family—and made me watch as they hurt everyone I loved. The mob had to believe I'd died running away from them. What would you do, Roman? You'd endanger our parents? Me? No, you wouldn't. You'd do what it took to protect them. Just like I did."

Cash and Roman seemed lock-jawed. Rocco asked, "Wait? You were trying to protect them?"

"I did protect them."

"You didn't give us a chance. I'm your brother, for fuck's sake. You should've talked to me."

"I didn't have time. The FBI gave me thirty seconds to decide. They showed me crime photos and asked if I'd help them with the financial paper trail. All I could think was I'd been tracking accounts payable and receivable for murders. A lot of them. I wanted to keep you safe."

"Protecting these guys? Shit." Rocco tipped back on the back legs of his chair. "How ironic."

Nicola flashed him a glare. "Ironic? You want to tell me how?"

"Ah, nah. These fuckers can fill you in later. Why don't you tell us about tonight?"

"Can't."

"We've already done this song and dance, so let's cut to it so we can all finish getting drunk and go pass out." Rocco apparently wasn't taking any shit.

"My turn." She eyed each of them. "Who do you work for? Who sent you?"

Rocco bounced back down onto all four chair legs. "All right. Fair is fair. A company called The Titan Group."

"You work for Titan? All three of you?" The military, hell, the CIA, turned to Titan for jobs they didn't want on their books. How had Cash and Roman ended up on that payroll?

She shook her head out of the question cloud, and saw all three bright-eyed and interested as to how she knew Titan Group existed. *Damn it.* She was off her game. Little mistakes could be her undoing. She needed to tread with serious care.

Cash answered. "Yeah, all three of us. Roman and I joined the Army after college. We're a good team. We're still a team. We've been a team since day one. Grade school. High school. Sniper school. But you wouldn't know anything about that kind of loyalty, would you, Nic?"

"Lay off, Cash." Roman's defense wasn't that strong, but she appreciated it.

"What the fuck ever." Cash punctuated his words with another shot of whiskey.

"Christ, almighty. What is it with you two?" Roman glared from her to Cash. "You two used to be friends. Do you remember that? Shit."

Nicola traced the rim of her shot glass with a manicured nail. "You don't have to lay off. I can take it. I'm just one of the guys."

Roman rolled his eyes, but Cash pinned her with his stare. "Now it's your turn again. Why were you hanging off Antilla Smooth's nuts?"

She deserved that. They were with Titan, and they were her family, once upon a time before she walked away. She could trust them to a point. "I was on the job. Undercover."

Roman and Cash might have stopped breathing. They were frozen in shock, ready for a slight breeze to knock them away from the table. Rocco, perked up, more interested in that than the family drama. "No joke? Nice. Whose payroll you on?"

"Not going there." She shrugged.

"How long you been under?"

"Months. Since the start of spring—"

"So you *were* sleeping with him?" Cash interrupted.

He was going to out himself to Roman if he wasn't careful. Then the three of them would have that discussion to deal with.

Then again, Roman looked shell-shocked. He wasn't registering Cash's attitude.

"No. I wasn't." She smirked at him. "I was seducing him. Ignoring his advances made his interest in me grow. A manipulative game of cat and mouse. So no, Cash, I didn't fuck him."

Rocco laughed. "Cash doesn't know anything about women not fucking him. You might have to explain seduction to the man because they just throw themselves at him. He doesn't have to lay groundwork."

Roman laughed too. It was her turn for a flash-bang of jealousy. Cash glared at Rocco, who apparently took to heart the just-one-of-the-guys line she'd thrown down.

Cash was handsome, more so than when they were younger. His blond hair could use a haircut, but he was missing his trademark life-is-good attitude. She missed his smile, focusing instead on the width of his chest. All three men had muscles, but Cash was something to appreciate. Even his face looked strong with a hard jaw line that flexed when he tried to contain any number of emotions he had to be feeling.

Nicola continued. "My op was blown when you took out your target. I called in for an extraction plan. There was another team there. Not sure what happened or why, but they went after me. I did what I needed to."

Roman looked up. "And that was?"

"I shot out a window, jumped two stories, and ran into you assholes." She tried for a smile, a little humor, but got nothing. A-plus for effort though.

Cash said, "You shot a window?"

Roman followed. "And jumped out?"

"Hey, I'm not an asshole. Just so you know." Rocco laughed. Weird. Cash was always the one laughing in her memories, and now he was without jokes and zingers.

"Guess I'm not what you remember," Nicola whispered, stealing a glance at Cash.

Roman stood, rubbing his tattoo. It was beautiful, and it was a lie. How did she ever think it was right to hurt them?

"Nicola." He kissed her head. "That's enough for me. For now. I'm headed to bed, knowing you're alive. Best damn thing ever. And tomorrow, we'll talk about calling Mom and Dad."

She nodded.

Roman continued, "Cash, Rocco, good night, assholes."

Rocco stood, nodded, and bowed out without a word, leaving just her and Cash. Her and Cash and a bottle of Jack Daniel's. She nudged the bottle toward him. "Want another?"

Silence hung in the air.

She nudged it again. "How about this: do you need another?"

A smile cracked the thick tension on his chiseled face. "That would be a hell yes."

It wasn't a joke, but it was more his style. She wished he would smile the way he used to. Big and brawny, but so damn beautiful. Just once. "Me, too."

He poured them both a shot and watched her down the liquor.

"Down the hatch, like a pro. Like shooting Jack?"

"I'm pretty good at a lot of things now, but I'm more of a Jim kinda gal."

"You were before too. Good at things and a fan of sweet bourbon. But you dressed your drinks up frou-frou style."

"But I'm… a different person now."

"I think we both are."

"You saw me with Antilla." Nicola didn't ask. Just repeated what he'd already told her.

"Yeah, I did." He fidgeted with the shot glass, sliding it back and forth between his large hands.

"Why'd you come up to the house? That couldn't have been protocol."

"I couldn't not come to see. To really see you. I was having some scope-sighted nightmare. It didn't make sense. It still doesn't."

She reached for the bottle. Ugh, bad arm. An ache hit her throat and bubbled out. Cash looked at her, forcing her to 'fess up without uttering a question. "I landed on my arm. It's sprained. I need to wrap and sling it."

The thick tension couldn't have been sliced away with a machete. Seconds ticked by, and the shot glass pinballed between his fingers. Cash studied her arm, and she flushed. "You need help?"

"No. I think I got it. I'm just going to sit outside for a few minutes." *Because I need to cool down this absurd hot flash.* She hobbled over to the back door and peered at the deck. It had a picnic table, nothing else.

"It's good to see you again," Cash said.

"You said that already." She didn't know what else to say and didn't want him to go away. But that was exactly the reason he should.

"So I did." He breathed the words out slowly and stood. His broad chest loomed, and his beautiful blue eyes twinkled when he nodded good night.

Good night, Cash.

They were words she'd thought a thousand times since she left and couldn't bring herself to say aloud now. What was her deal? One second, she was feeling a little hot under the t-shirt when he looked her way, the next she wanted to sob.

It didn't matter what she did or how she felt, he was gone in a blink. Silent and all shadow. Just like a sniper.

CHAPTER FIVE

As safe houses went, this wasn't too shabby: nestled in some generic, upper middle class neighborhood, secluded from the neighbors by tree coverage, and packed with provisions like bourbon and protein bars. Cash couldn't complain. He couldn't complain, but he sure as hell couldn't sleep. Turning over in the bed again, the sheets bothered him no matter whether he kicked them off or tugged them back to his chest.

He flipped on the television, and despite the thousands of channels he skipped through, nothing held his interest. Well, nothing on the boob tube.

"I can't sleep," he groaned, looking at Betty the Shitkicker, AKA Miss Betty, his .50 cal high-powered rifle. Most of his guns had names, but Betty was the nearest and dearest to his heart. She wasn't the jealous type, though she was the only long-term girl in his life. Well, long-term since Nicola, but that hadn't been real. That was two college kids mixed up in each other.

He laughed, alone in the empty bedroom.

Hell. No reason to lie to yourself. Miss Betty exists because the real deal left you heartbroken.

Heartbroken. No other word could describe him.

He'd been far past puppy love with the flesh-and-blood girl. Nicola was far superior to the molded cheek rest that he'd been nuzzling and four-lb. pull trigger he'd been caressing lately. Nic was something special. He'd sweated their platonic relationship, chasing after her like she was handing out the secret to buried treasure. He knew damn well Roman would kick his ass for thinking of her as anything other than the kid next door.

And the kid next door she was not. Whoa, baby, the girl was a looker. Then and now.

Their hometown was small. Everyone talked. People assumed Nicola and Cash were destined to be together. Well, everyone but Roman. He'd wanted nothing to do with his little sister getting noticed by anyone. No Nicola. Not ever.

As far as Roman was concerned, Nicola should've found the Yellow Pages and looked up local convents. He would've signed her up for nun duty if it had kept every man on campus from chasing his younger sister. Cash was surprised he hadn't called up 1-800-CHASTITY-BELT.

Man alive, did that girl get chased. How he was lucky enough to have her bat those beautiful chocolate eyes at him, Cash had no idea. None. But she did. So innocent. Him, so caught up in the shouldn't-but-couldn't-help-it moment.

Best day of his life, when he'd picked up the phone and seen her text. *Come on over, pool party.* He'd arrived at the house she shared with some girlfriends, and it was just her. Her in a teeny, tiny green bikini holding an open bottle of wine. Half empty.

He'd watched, hoped, and thanked God for the brim of his always-there cowboy hat hiding the desire in his gaze.

Another bottle later, she sat on his lap in the shallow side of the pool, and he thought he'd been pushed into the deep end.

"You don't want to kiss me." Nicola blushed as she said the words, one arm draped over his shoulder, as they hovered on the line of can't-change-it-once-we-go-there.

"I don't?"

"You don't?" Her flirtatious blush threatened to turn embarrassed.

"Oh, hell. Yes, I do."

And then he did. Cowboy hat pushed off into the water, floating away, his arms wrapping tightly around her slim shoulders. Even now, it fired his blood. Hot, slow burn. They'd kissed for hours, breathing each other in, floating in the water, bathing suits on, maybe clearing second base. He wouldn't have changed a thing.

"All right, Betty. I need to go for a run." He looked at the rifle, and she didn't say a word. That was good because he thought he'd already lost his mind. If Miss Betty chimed in with something to say, he'd have to call up his boss at Titan and put in for some sick leave.

Cash jumped out of bed and threw on his Nikes, sweatpants, and a muscle shirt. He grabbed an ankle holster and the .38 that wasn't a pain to run with, then tucked it in. Making his way through the dark house, he moved past the kitchen and caught sight of Nicola sitting outside. It'd easily been an hour since he'd left her.

He opened the back door. She looked lost and alone, but so much stronger than he remembered. "You on sentry duty?"

"Couldn't sleep."

He looked at her arm, free of bandages, and at the sling next to her and the bottle of Jack. No shot glass. "Did you try?"

"Nope." Her feet were planted on the picnic table's bench, and she sat on the table top. "You were asleep?"

"I tried and failed." He sat down next to her, opened the bottle, and took a long swig. The liquor's fire coated his throat, so he took another. Propping his elbows on his knees, he hung his head and passed the bottle, not looking at Nicola.

Their fingers brushed, sending a cascade of awareness from his hand to his chest. She took the bottle and swallowed a Nicola-sized swig. And then again. "I'm scared to close my eyes. Vivid memories. You know?"

Yeah, vivid described that green bikini. "I was thinking the same thing. About to head for a run. I needed to clear my frontal cortex."

"What were you thinking about?"

All night long, the moon had hidden beneath a blanket of clouds, but that moment, it decided to peek out a sliver, just enough to paint her in a gauzy, milky light. She was beautiful.

He sighed. "It doesn't matter, Nic. Does it?"

"Guess not."

She took another pull of Jack and handed it to him. Cash did the same, embracing the thought-pausing sear of liquor. He didn't know what to think about her sadness-tinged voice.

"Give me the wrap." His run was never going to happen if he sat there making excuses to stay. Still, he took the bandage from her hand.

She didn't look at him, keeping steady watch into the woods. "I'm not weak."

"Never said you were."

"I can do my arm myself."

Cash shrugged, starting the process of binding her arm into a secure position. Her skin was silken, her arm toned. The girl had muscles, but not in a bulky way. A little deceiving. He liked it. Different from what she had been before: a little skinny, not flabby but no definition. Reaching behind her, he grabbed the sling and bent her arm in, careful to adjust the strap.

"Done."

"Why are you being nice to me?"

"Shit, Nicola. I don't know. I gotta figure you're fucked in the head right now, as much as Roman and I are. True?"

She nodded. "You never told him?"

"What? About you and me?"

"Yeah."

"That'd be a hell no. Hey, sorry your sister died, and, oh yeah. I was doing her on the side."

"We were more than that," she whispered.

Cash stretched his arms over his head, trying to alleviate the discomfort in his chest. Didn't work. Instead, he leaned back on the table top and stared at the sliver of moon teasing the dark night. "Yeah, we were."

A light breeze picked up. An owl hooted. Time floated by, until she also lay back on the table. He turned his head. Nicola was as stunning now, staring into the night sky, as she'd been in that pool years ago. "Life's thrown a few curve balls, huh?"

"Did you ever think about what if?"

"Did you?"

"I did for a while. And then I drowned myself in work."

"You going to tell me who you work for?"

"CIA."

The CIA? Well, shit. Color him flabbergasted. "Not what I thought you were going to say."

"You were thinking more like, FBI. Linguistics department?"

He laughed. "Yeah. Truth is, well, yeah."

"I guess Uncle Sam thought I had too much to offer to stick me in a middle of nowhere Podunk town in witness protection when they found out I was fluent in, like, eight languages."

"Eight? Come on, slacker. I thought it was more like twenty."

She laughed. "Oh, now you're counting dialects."

It felt so familiar it made him want to tear his hair out. "You could say the same thing about me and Roman. Drowning ourselves in work. He never questioned why I was just as torn up about you as he was."

"We'd been inseparable, the three of us, since we were kids."

"True." He took her hand in his and leaned them both up. The heat from her touch stayed with him after she drew her fingers away.

"I never told you this, but I actually had a crush on you way before college. Like sixth grade."

He heard the smile in her voice. "Now you're just making shit up. You need another favor? Cell phone privileges again, huh? Maybe you want the cute little gun you pointed at my head?"

"Maybe I am. Maybe I do."

God, he hurt again all of a sudden. "I never told you this, but I had a ring."

She bolted straight up. "Excuse me?"

Cash pushed up on his elbows, unsure where the fuck that honest tidbit materialized from. He laughed, not all that shocked that he'd confessed the truth, and stood up. "Good night, Nicola. Hope your arm feels better."

"Oh, no you don't," Nicola yelled from the picnic table.

He walked into the house and shut the door before she was even upright. Hopping and hobbling as fast as her good and gimp feet would move her, Nicola tried to balance with an arm in the sling. He couldn't throw a bomb like that and just run. Hell no.

She threw open the door and hollered, "Get back here."

"Night, Nic." He was halfway across the kitchen, not looking back. "Have a nice life."

"Cash Garrison. Stop!"

He pivoted and looked at her in a way that tore her emotions into bits of shrapnel. "Why? What does it matter?"

"You can't say you had a ring and walk away."

"Why not? You walked away. You left, remember?"

"I left everyone!"

"You left me." Cash laughed. "You know what? I don't care about everyone. I never even cared about me. I cared about you. I mourned you. I died that day alongside you. But ain't that some shit?"

"Cash—"

"Yeah, yeah. You had your reasons. But it was a good thing. Never would be here, where I am now, if you hadn't walked away."

She hopped two steps forward, and the pressure in her chest nearly debilitated her. "You're a son of a bitch."

He met her in the middle of the kitchen like they were squaring off for a round of celebrity death match, operative-style. "You're a goddamn liar."

The lights flicked on. Roman stood in the hallway, gun in one hand, other hand still on the wall. "What the fuck are you two doing? Nic, are you okay?"

"Yeah, what are we doing, Nicola?" Cash's glare locked on hers.

Silence.

She had nothing to say. Nothing except for… she narrowed her eyes. "I hate you, Cash."

"You hate me? Jesus fucking Christ. If that's not the best line you've had all night, I don't know what is. The CIA feed you those beauties?"

Roman cleared his throat. "CIA? What's the Agency got to do with this?"

They ignored him. "You think you can keep your mouth shut about anything? Mister Let's-sit-and-talk-under-the-moon?"

"At least I'm solid to those I care about."

They were nose to nose. Well, as close as they could be with him towering over her. She breathed hard through sealed teeth, angrier than she had ever been, and she didn't know why. She shoved him with her good elbow, attempting to push past him. He grasped her bicep, pulled her close.

Inches. She was inches from his face, and for some reason, all she could think about was how he smelled like soap. Soap and Jack Daniel's.

"I mourned you too, Cash." Her voice broke. "Don't you know that?"

Eyes locked, they stared. She felt bleeding pain down to her soul.

And suddenly, it wasn't just them. She came back to reality and the voices in the background. Roman was saying something. She drew her eyes away from Cash, dimly aware of how close, how heated she and Cash were. Cash seemed to notice also, releasing his grip on her arm. But they stayed in place, close enough she could still smell him.

By the look on his face, Roman must have repeated himself. "What is going on between you two? You've been at each other's throats for hours. Christ."

With all the emotion required to play *Grand Theft Auto*, Cash turned from her to Roman. "Sorry, man. I was doing your sister on the side. Beat my ass later. I'm going to bed."

He ambled out of the kitchen, throwing a finger up in a fuck-you goodbye. Roman, the brother she'd once known so well, stared at her. Unreadable.

He opened his mouth, but it just stayed open. Nothing came out.

"I should have told you."

"I don't really know what to say." He shook his head. "Cash? How did I not know about… you two?"

"I'm sorry," she repeated for what felt like the hundredth time. It didn't do any good for all the lies she was tangled in now.

"You've got that on repeat tonight, huh?" Roman rubbed his face, digging fists into his eyes. He sighed. "Look, sorry. I'm not trying to be a bastard. It's just, that's Cash. *Cash.* I'm a little shocked. He's a piece of shit in the womanizing department. I mean, I love the guy, but shit. I wouldn't have wanted you with him."

"I don't know if he was back when I knew him."

"Cash has always been Cash." Roman paused. "This is just a lot to take in. You're alive. You were with Cash. You're avoiding Mom and Dad. Heavy shit, Nic."

"You should probably disown me and go back to thinking I'm dead. Everything was easier ten hours ago or so. Hurt a lot less too."

"Nicola Beatrice, you're my little sister. I can be angry at you. I might be furious or shocked or simply fucking confused, but I will never turn my back on you. You're blood. You're family, and for whatever fucked-up reason, you're back. We need a sit down with Dr. Phil or some couch doc like that, 'cause I think my head's going to explode. But I'll deal."

She nodded.

He wrapped her in a bear hug. "Promise me you won't run off in the middle of the night?"

Nicola shrugged into his embrace, nodding. "Promise. Besides, I don't have wheels, and my boss is going to question my ass for blowing my extraction plans."

"The CIA, huh?" A proud grin snaked across his face.

"Uh-huh."

He hooked an arm around her as they walked out of the kitchen. "Well, how about that, baby sister?"

"Don't give Cash a hard time. It was years ago, and I made the first move."

Roman stopped walking and looked down the hall, clearly uncomfortable that the conversation had continued. "The last thing I want to talk about is the details of you with him. He and I will hash it out mano a mano."

"That's stupid."

"Now you sound like my kid sister, not some operative spewing extraction plan bullshit."

She nudged him with a playful elbow. "Leave him alone. It was more than ten years ago."

"I'm not having some guy *do* my sister and not have hell to pay. You deserve something, someone special or some crap like that."

"It's not like he was my fir—"

"Do not finish that sentence." He shook his head, then all but covered his ears.

"Roman, I wasn't a—"

"Shut it. Now."

"I was a sophomore in college, for Christ sake."

"You were my innocent kid sister."

"I think we've already established that nothing I do, or have done, has been that innocent."

"Cash is a slut. You need to stay away from him. I should've told you that in college. I just didn't know. Or realize. I thought we were all buddy-buddy."

"Cash is your best friend. Was mine too."

"Dudes don't have best friends. No BFF necklaces and shit like that. There's a code, and there's repercussions. You two might've been tight. Best friends or whatever, but he and I were buds."

"I loved him."

Well, that shut up the banter. Roman's jaw hung to the ground. He threw his hands in the air. "That I'm not touching."

"I did. Love him, I mean, and I think..."

He turned back to her, almost pityingly. "'Cause you've known him your whole life. That's not love. That's like... brotherly affection or something else."

"No, Roman. You're wrong. I fell in love with him the day he let me ride his dirt bike in grade school. Again the day he took that girl everyone in high school picked on to the prom when he was Prom King. And the day in college he tried everything to keep me from kissing him."

"Whatever you two were, it wasn't much if he tosses out *doing you on the side*. He deserves a beat down, if for no other reason than leading you on. That piece of shit."

"You don't know what you're talking about."

"Neither do you. Stay away from him. He's my bro, but he's a man whore with indiscriminate taste. Hell, I don't even know you anymore, but I know you deserve better than that."

This house had shitty insulation. For middle-class suburbia, it could have used better interior construction because, for everything he did to ignore the brother-sister convo, Cash failed.

He *was* a piece of shit, and Roman was right. He was always down for a fuck, but damned if that busted-up beauty hobbling in the kitchen wasn't the cause of it.

At least brother and sister were making amends. He and Roman would duke it out in the morning. Wouldn't be the first or last time they'd throw down. It worked for them, and truth be told, he felt like a beating might kill off the emo bullshit bouncing around in his brain.

Cash took off the ankle holster, laid the gun under his pillow, and looked at Betty. "Looks like you're the only one in my life. Glad you can't hobble away."

Then again, he wouldn't have Betty the Shitkicker if things hadn't gone down with Nicola the way they did. He'd be married, kicking it with a white picket fence somewhere out in Small Town, USA. No idea how he'd earn a living. It sure as shit wouldn't be traveling all over the world, blowing the brains out of other POS. And his wife wouldn't be up to her cute nose in the CIA.

"Night, Betty."

But saying goodnight didn't accomplish his sleep-focused end game.

I fell in love with him… And again. And again…

Well, that was enough to drown him in memories. They'd been on the same page from day one. How he waited so long to kiss her, he had no idea. She was an adorable brat when they were neighbors, always wanting to play with him and Roman. No tea parties for that girl. She wanted in on cops and robbers. Maybe he should have seen the CIA coming.

He laughed about prom. Every high school dance, he'd taken someone other than the girl he wanted. Except for one time, when Nicola's date came down with the chicken pox. Homecoming his senior year. Yeah, he'd been Homecoming King too, and dancing with Nicola in front of the school had been the best moment of his high school career. Not the state championship winning touchdown. Not any other single memory.

He didn't care that he'd ditched the Homecoming Queen two seconds into *their* dance. He had eyes for one girl, and since he was her stand-in-date for the night, Cash had used it to his advantage.

Yeah, he needed Roman to beat his face in tomorrow. Maybe that would knock out all these shitty memories.

CHAPTER SIX

Nicola needed new clothes and a pair of shoes. Cash's shirt and sweats made her finger-tapping, mind-spinning anxious. They smelled like him. It was as if the ghost of boyfriends past wrapped its emotional arms around her and hugged her all night long. The morning was a long time coming, but now she faced dawn. Time to go.

Glancing in the mirror and deciding her makeup was a lost cause, she scrubbed it off in the bathroom. Still not better. A shower was the better option. Using all the shampoo and body wash in the travel-sized containers she found, she did her best to clean up. With a quick towel dry of her hair, she put her clothes back on, and was off, limping toward the kitchen.

Raucous male voices bled down the hall until she rounded the corner. Their conversation faltered as she entered.

She smiled. "Morning, boys. I'm praying Roman still knows how to make a killer cup of coffee."

There. She'd addressed the elephant in the room. *Her very presence.* She was still the evil, abandoning sister, but she was also still Nicola. And just that easy, they went back to bitching about something from the sports page. She watched the dynamic: Cash spoke to Rocco. Roman spoke to Rocco. Rocco spoke to everyone.

Maybe it was one hundred and eighty degrees from easy, but at least they fronted well.

Roman eyed her arm. "Where's your sling?"

Nicola tried to straighten her bandaged elbow but flinched at the tenderness. "Don't need it."

"You're Super Woman?"

She shrugged. "Can I borrow that phone again?"

Cash didn't look at her. "Yup. But same drill as before."

"That's fine."

"Someone will get it for you after breakfast, unless you need it now."

Someone wasn't lost on her. He certainly wasn't volunteering. "No, that's fine."

Half a dozen types of protein bars, individually wrapped cookies, and crackers served as breakfast, spread across the granite countertop. Tasty and typical as a gas station buffet. She grabbed a bar and a cup of coffee, taking a scalding sip.

Nope. Not made by Roman or Cash. It was military mud, and she assumed Rocco had joined up and been discharged just like the other two. "Delicious." She smiled.

Rocco smiled.

No one else smiled.

After she'd added about a pound of sugar and powdered creamer, the coffee was bearable. Caffeine was a requirement to function. She did what she had to do and downed the sludge. "Yeah, I'll be downstairs. Let me know when I can use that phone."

Rocco smiled again. At least he was of the friendly variety. A half hour later, she'd had her Rocco-supervised phone call, and an hour after that, she still needed to kill thirty minutes until a CIA extraction team arrived to bring her in for debriefing.

Finding nothing better to do, she hobbled up the stairs. The guys were kicked back watching the television.

"I'm leaving soon. Just wanted to say bye. Maybe see if I can call you later? We can hook up and do lunch. Catch up. Something."

Roman stood and turned to face her. "Shit, yeah. Whenever you want to, I'm there."

"What the hell happened to you, Roman?" Her eyes widened at the sight of her brother.

Roman's swollen lip was split in the middle. He had a black eye forming, and his knuckles hung at his side, raw. Cash turned from the TV, looking just as messed up. Both of his eyes were swollen.

They'd thrown down because of her. The two most important people in her life—whether they knew it or not—had beaten the crap out of each other. All because her op went bad, and they knew about her. How did she not hear them fight?

"Goddamn you both."

"What?" All three men played stupid. An urge to smack each one across the head tickled her palm.

"You all are morons." She hopped to the kitchen, wrote down her contact info, and continued. "Should you care, here's how you can get a hold of me. Grow the fuck up."

Rocco interjected. "Nicola, they did what they had to do. They're fine."

"They're assholes."

"They're men. And it's done."

"I'll be down the block, at my pick-up location."

Roman walked toward her. "You're barefoot."

"Maybe stupidity runs in the family."

"Let me give you a ride." Her brother shrugged.

"No. I'm not compromising the safe house, and I'm not compromising you."

"You can stop with the 'I'm-going-to-protect-you' bullshit. I'm more than capable of watching my ass, kiddo."

"I'm done with you two today. You can call me later." She turned for the door, and looked over her shoulder. Roman remained in place. Rocco was back to watching television, but Cash remained silent, watching her, still breaking her heart. "Bye, Roman, Rocco." She paused, trying to swallow the pain. It hurt to walk away from him again. "Cash... bye."

Ouch. Maybe Nicola should've let Roman give her a ride. This sidewalk had way more gravel than her busted foot needed. She hopped over another stone. In the land of manicured lawns and matching Range Rovers, someone should really take care of their gravel issues.

She rounded the corner and waited on the park bench. No cell phone, but at least Rocco had given back her gun. Like a thugged-out gangster, she tucked it into the waistband of the men's sweatpants. Everything she wore smelled like Cash. Sitting there, ignoring the previous night's events, it was the only thing she noticed.

Her first stop would be the nearest Target or Walmart for footwear and clothes. There was no way she was going anywhere dressed like the aftermath of a one-night stand with a gym rat.

A blacked out SUV rolled up, a little early, but fitting the right description. The window rolled down. A pleasant looking woman Nicola had never seen before smiled.

"Gabriella? So nice to see you again after our play date with Beth."

Code words, ding, ding. Play date and Beth. Nicola smiled and responded as directed by her handler. "My car broke down. Could you take me to the service station?"

Ding, ding again. The woman unlocked the door, and she crawled in. Thank God her traveling companion was a woman. Maybe there would be some camaraderie when she asked for a clothing related pit stop.

"Gabriella." The familiar voice made her skin tighten. The butler. He was in the backseat. Nicola jumped forward, her breath punched from her lungs. The door locks secured.

"Why are you here?" she demanded. *How is this happening?*

The butler's face smiled. "What happened last night?"

Nicola's hand went to the door. "Pull over. Now!"

The driver stared at her like she'd spouted purple slime from her ears. "What?"

"Pull over."

"Gabriella? Are you okay?" the butler asked. "My name's David. We're the team pulling you out."

Nicola pulled her gun from her waistband, and pointed it at the soccer mom lookalike. "Stop the car."

The woman eased off the gas pedal and pulled toward the sidewalk.

"Now unlock the door."

"Gabriella, you've got this all wrong," he said.

"My name's not Gabriella."

"And I'm not really a butler. Your handler sent us."

She moved the gun at him, point-blank range. "You walked me into an ambush last night, jackass."

"Wrong." He looked smug despite her finger on the trigger.

"No directions on the cocktail napkin."

"Yes, the—"

"Open the car door now." No move from the soccer mom. Nicola swung her aim back to the driver's seat. "After last night, I'll have no problem saving my ass and explaining why your skull's in pieces. Open. The. Door."

The woman blanched like Casper but unlocked the door. Nicola jumped out, landing on her good foot. The back door cracked open. "Drive away, soccer mom. David, don't try it."

He got out of the SUV, hands up. "Gabriella. You need to come in."

"Like I said, I've got no problem with paperwork. And there's going to be a ream's worth if you don't get back in that car. I'll leave you bleeding out in the streets of suburbia."

Soccer mom moved fast in the corner of her eye. Worst case scenario was the woman moving for her piece.

Bam! Nicola fired, shattered the window, warning shot style, and pivoted straight into the barrel of the butler's Smith and Wesson. *Fuck.*

Nicola heard the slide on soccer mom's gun. Two against her one. Her odds sucked right now.

"Get in the car, Gabriella. I don't want to kill you," David growled.

"Just like you gave me extraction directions."

"Whatever you think you know, you're wrong."

"I know if you're on CIA payroll, you're a fucking double-dipping dick."

"You want a showdown on fucking Main Street? Some minivan's going to drive by and call local cops. Then we're all screwed."

They were in suburbia, but suburbia in New England. Large McMansions, tons of trees, and land between each house. She stepped forward an inch. If she could ping a round off, then drop, she'd take out the butler, and soccer mom wouldn't have a shot.

Nicola smirked. "The last thing I want to do is—"

Bam!

CHAPTER SEVEN

Roman held the remote, but after their fucked up morning, he could keep the clicker. If the dude wanted to watch The Today Show, that was on his conscience. The constant drone of Hoda and Kathy Lee made Cash's head spin. Wine-Day Wednesday. There was probably a lot of morning drinking happening in Happyville, Maine, where everyone had matching houses and cars and their requisite, matching children enrolled in travel lacrosse teams.

I'd have to have a bottle of wine by 10 AM if that was my paint by numbers life. Then again, neither Kathy or Hoda looked like they'd actually survive the boredom of identical houses and PTA competitions. They looked good for downing a bottle of vino.

He should've followed Nic. He should've tried to apologize. Or jumped up, asking to see her again. Whatever the cause for the sick twist in his gut, a heavy feeling of *should've* burdened him.

One of the talking TV heads said something funny, and he caught himself laughing. *Damn you, Roman. I don't need to enjoy this show.* Cash pinched his eyes closed, though the bruises were doing a good job of keeping his lids drawn for him. He pulled his cowboy hat down low, blocking the flat screen from his swollen, narrowed line of sight. Roman and Rocco commented about something ridiculous one of the babbling heads said about butt-lifting jeans, and—

Bam!

All three men jumped to their feet. Gunshots ringing out in Kathy Lee and Hoda country wasn't a good thing.

Bam!

Son of a bitch.

They were out the door and into the Range Rover. Rocco squealed tires, reversing out of the driveway. Roman and Cash shut their doors as the tires spun from reverse to forward.

Nicola hadn't been gone long. There was no telling what the woman was up to, but her plans hadn't worked well in the last twenty-four hours. Those gunshots couldn't have been planned.

They screeched around a corner. Rocco murdered the brakes. The smell of burnt rubber filtered into the vehicle before they came to a full stop.

A blacked out Explorer, missing the front passenger window, idled at the curb. A woman dressed like Miss Suburbia USA held out a Glock, bouncing her aim between a man and woman pummeling each other. Nicola and a man, and that motherfucker threw solid punches. She took one and ducked another. Cash was out of the Rover and ready to kill. He ignored the Glock. His fists balled, his blood rushed, and he was ready to end the brawl. No man would ever live after—

Whoa.

The tide turned fast. Nic was on top. Her left hook struck hard, not flinching when her knuckles landed on a cheekbone. The man reached his hands around Nicola's neck. Enough of that shit.

A glance to Roman, and the plan was set without words. Roman slide-tackled the standing woman and disarmed her. The lady hit the ground hard, and the Glock skittered out of reach.

One gun down.

Who knew where Nic's .22 was during this melee. Who knew what dude-about-to-die packed. All Cash knew was he would kill him for punching Nic's pretty face.

The man made a swift move, flipping on top of Nic. Cash threw himself on the man, spearing him away. He heard Nicola breathing hard. Panting. Saw Rocco out of the corner of his eye pulling her to safety. She fought him, trying to jump back into the fight. Too fucking bad, this asshole was Cash's to take out.

He straddled the man, raining punches on his dome. Right fist. Left fist. Over and over, on repeat. Cash was in the zone, wanting blood. This wasn't a fight anymore, just Cash on a mission of destruction. Sweat poured off of him, biceps and knuckles screaming for a reprieve.

Reality came back. Arms wrapped around him. He couldn't breathe, couldn't move, couldn't focus on anything but the broken nose and bloodied mouth in front of him.

"Cash."

The sounds of his name pulled him out of his trance. He shook. Someone was shaking him. He didn't want to get vertical, but someone pulled him upright. Rocco slammed him against the black Explorer. "Get your ass in gear. We gotta roll."

Cash looked around. He'd fucking gone nuts. "Is he dead?"

"Almost, dude. Almost."

Cash lunged forward, but slingshotted back against the Explorer, thanks to Rocco. "Chill."

"I'm cool man. I'm good." Cash nudged out of Rocco's grip, rolling his shoulders.

"Walk it off. Get in the car. Nic's in our Rover. She'll drive you back to the house. These two fuckers—" He pointed to the KO'd dude and the none-too-fazed woman. "—will go with us in their car. Move. Now."

Roman pushed the lady into the backseat and did a once over of Nicola, making sure she was okay. They did some brother-sister nod that made his gut twist in what could be labeled a jealous swell, but was really more a pang of nostalgia. A connection had been severed that he missed in a way that tightened his airway and clouded his judgment.

Rocco could've used a spatula to scoop the dude off the street, but used his hands instead, then hopped back to the driver's seat. He pulled a U-turn, leaving Cash standing alone in the middle of Mayberry-frickin'-Avenue.

"Cash. Let's go." Nicola was in their Range Rover, waving him in, as cool as if it was just another day for her to man the getaway vehicle.

He snapped to attention and jumped into the SUV. God, he'd lost control in a bad way, and he didn't need to be near that dude for a while. His white-hot temper was so far past boiling that he was surprised the guy was still breathing.

Nicola hit the gas. Their tires spun. They'd been on scene for five minutes, tops. Nicola had been gone a short while prior to the bam, bam. The whole thing had gone down in less than twenty minutes.

Stupid suburbia.

"You okay?" Nicola asked, driving past identical black mailboxes with little red flags.

"Fine."

"Yeah, totally looked like it."

"Back off," he snarled and immediately hated himself. "Sorry. I flipped. I just... lost it." No reason to go into why, though his motives were clear.

"Yeah, you did."

They were three driveways from the safe house. "I need a minute. Keep going. I'll kill that dude if I see him right now." He saw the red welted handprints around her neck. "Fuck that. Turn around. I'm going to kill him."

"Cash."

"Turn around. No, I'll get out."

"Cash.

"Pull—"

"Cash, look at me!"

The welts on her neck hurt him. Damn, he couldn't breathe. He needed to catch his breath.

She pulled her shirt up, unsuccessful in her attempt to cover the red marks. "I'm fine. Promise."

Bullshit. She was hurt. Dude left marks on her. "You're not—"

She slapped the center console. "Yes, I am. I've got a problem, and you killing him isn't going to help."

"He attacked you."

"You don't know that."

He turned in his seat to glare at her. "What?"

"I've got a problem, and I don't know who I can trust other than Roman, who's seeing me as his kid sister. I want to trust you, Cash."

"You can trust me."

"Can I?"

Good question. He'd about murdered a man in the middle of the street for the operative equivalent of picking on an ex-girlfriend. He was a flippin' loose bazooka. "I'm sorry about saying all that to Roman last night."

"That's not what I'm talking about."

"I know."

"I'm in it, earrings deep. I need to talk this out."

He took a breath and ran a hand around the nape of his neck. "'Kay. You keep driving, and I'll shut my trap." *At least I'll try.*

"The man you just beat within a hair of his life was the butler at Smooth's estate. After you bagged and tagged Antilla, he found me, said he had extraction instructions that superseded my handler's. But he turned me over to the men I avoided with my flying window trick. My handler made arrangements for me this morning. Voila! Hello, butler."

"So you're thinking… "

"He's doing double duty."

"He's CIA, and he's… on the clock for Smooth?"

"Maybe." She shrugged.

It seemed possible. "Why not take you out long rifle style?"

"They want to know what I got first. My job was intel. Map out Antilla Smooth's network, his high rollers and big players."

"You debriefed yet?"

"Nope."

"What's your handler know?"

"Little to nothing."

"You seriously think this dude is stupid enough to fuck with you CIA folks?"

"It's been done before. He must've thought I was weak."

"Well, you schooled him, didn't you? I saw that left hook. Killer, woman. Killer job. For real."

Nicola looked at him with a half-cocked smile. The most honest look he'd seen on her since she stumbled in front of their car. "I've got a few tricks. But truth is my right arm is too sore to use."

How different their lives could have been. She could've been at home, or at least at a job that didn't require knowing any tricks, though the woman could take a punch. Nicola, all schooled in hand to hand. Never saw that coming. Too bad it had almost killed him. This CIA bullshit was damn hard for him to understand. He needed a subject change and quick.

"You got a boyfriend or something at the Farm?" *Not exactly a subject change that would lessen my urge to kill.*

She laughed. "Um, that's a big no. You?"

Thank fuck.

He cracked a grin, which hurt his busted face. "Got a boyfriend? No."

"I missed your smile."

And I miss your laugh. Shit. Nothing warm and fuzzy should be tingling anywhere in his body, but he was all loosey-goosey at the moment.

"Nah. No girl for me."

"Why not?"

"Really, Nic? This is the convo you wanted to have after I just went all WWE on your colleague back there?"

"You started the let's-talk-about-our-love-life chat, and he wasn't my partner. He— Never mind. Can I use your phone? I've got to call my handler."

Cash shrugged, handed her his phone, and thought about the guys back at the house who probably wondered where he was, but knew it was better for him to cool down.

Nicola finished dialing numbers, then entered more numbers. She waited with the phone next to her ear.

"Hey. Yeah, didn't make my pick-up. We've got dirty laundry to deal with."

She nodded her head. Gave a few uh-huhs, and nodded some more as if her handler could see her.

"No. I'm coming in on my own. I'll have my Bonnie and Clyde extraction team brought—"

More uh-huhs. Then one nu-uh.

She rolled through a stop sign. "If he's still breathing when we get there, he's all yours. I've got a theory or two."

More nodding. *Hello, Nicola. Only I can see the head nods.*

"Yes, when we debrief. See ya. Oh, wait—"

She looked at Cash, paused, then looked back to the road, making turn. "What do you know about Titan Group involved with Antilla?"

Son of a bitch.

More uh-huhs.

She clicked off the phone and looked at him with those warm, chocolate eyes. "I need a favor."

Oh boy. Here it comes. "Depends."

"I'm headed back to Langley on my terms. Bringing the other two with me. You know who hired Titan on this project?"

"Yeah."

"The CIA?"

"Yeah."

"Why didn't you tell me?"

"Not my place. You know their section chiefs don't talk. All that one-upmanship bull crap."

"I know their games well, but I try not to play."

"So what's the favor?"

"Bring Bonnie and Clyde in with me?" she asked with a face she certainly knew he couldn't say no to. He needed reinforcements around her, ASAP.

"That's not a decision I can make on my own. Despite my protocol-ignoring ass last night, I can't just fly by night to Virginia."

"Where are you based out of?"

He laughed. "Virginia."

"Well—"

His phone rang, cutting her off, and she handed it back to him. How long would that drive take? Hours in a car with her. He might not live through it without doing some serious, pansy, emo outtakes. Whatever. He looked at the caller ID. Jared. His boss. Not necessarily what he needed right now.

"Yeah-ello," Cash answered, slowly and intentionally, just to screw with Jared.

"What in God's name did you three do up there?"

Well, hello to you too, dick. "The job."

"Why's the CIA burning up the wires, trying to nail a commitment out of me? For something I know nothing about?"

"Last night… we had an unexpected complication."

"Last night, you three stumbled upon a compromised female operative and wanted to play hero? That's not a complication. That's you boys getting ready to fucking sword fight over some pussy."

"Watch yourself, boss man."

"You—"

"She's Roman's dead sister. My dead… ex. But the girl ain't dead. So, like I said. Complicated."

Mark this one down in the record books. Crystal clear phone clarity and Mister Big Bad Balls was radio silent.

Which lasted less time than it took to order a Big Mac, but it was still a record. "Fine. Complicated. I need updates on all complications." He paused, clearly working something out in his head. "CIA knows about you two?"

He looked at Nicola. "Does your handler know about me and Roman?"

She shook her head. Cash went back to Jared. "Nope."

"And where's her extraction team?"

"Near dead at our safe house with Roman and Rocco."

"Because?"

"We may or may not be dealing with a double agent."

"Goddamn it, Cash. I'll hit you back." And the line went dead.

As convos with Jared go, that was smooth and productive. Nicola was driving laps around the sprawling upper-middle class neighborhood. Cash needed to make sure he saw the forest, away from the one big tree in the driver's seat he kept focusing on.

Before he could say anything to her, his phone rang. Jared. Again. That was fast.

"Yeah?" Cash said.

"Private airstrip about an hour from your safe house. A Titan jet will be there in three hours. You boys are headed to Langley with your three friends."

"Not exactly going to be a friendly ride back with two of my three friends."

"If you've got what you think you've got, I don't care if they ride home in black hoods and hog tied. As long as they make it back alive. The Farm will handle their own. Have no doubt."

He didn't either. They water boarded the way some offices doled out demerit write-ups.

"Got ya." Cash clicked off the phone, and looked at Nicola. "Looks like your favor is granted. Titan style. We're jetting it back, babe. All six of us."

"Great. Two guys I can't take my eyes off of in one plane."

CHAPTER EIGHT

If Cash hadn't been seated in the passenger seat of the Range Rover, he'd have fallen on his derrière. His face must have read like a billboard. Either that, or she could see that his stomach jumped into his throat, and he'd lost his breath for the teeniest of seconds.

"Sorry. Just messing with you," she said.

She'd said sorry, but she didn't look repentant as she maneuvered around another turn. Nah, not sorry by an inch. *Can't keep her eyes off me?* He mumbled something incoherent, trying to mask that she was under his skin.

"Look, I need to get some clothes. Do we have time before we're wheels up?"

Why was it endearing when she said 'wheels up' like one of the guys instead of some boring civilian verbiage like *take off*? No, her jargon slinging shouldn't be endearing. It was a warning with bright flashing lights. She'd seen too much, done too much, and didn't have someone like him or Roman to tell her to keep her butt safe.

He nodded, not ready to jump into that argument. "We got time. Not a lot. But enough."

"Good. Fire up that GPS, and show me the closest Walmart."

"Can do." He paged through the list of shopping centers and saw Midland Galleria. Anything galleria had to be nice, right? "Let's go here." He selected their destination, and the direction-wielding lady in the GPS scolded them to make a U-turn at the nearest intersection.

"That's not Walmart. I need quick, cheap, throwaway clothes."

"Come on. We have some time. Let's explore."

"We should shop and get back to the safe house."

"You turn in your woman card or something? You don't want to shop?"

"I don't want to—"

"Look at it this way: I still need time to cool down. You don't want me to pop your buddy, do you?"

"You're calm, Cash. Cool-collected-Cash. It took you about fifteen seconds to power down to lazy cowboy."

"Lazy?" Nothing about this morning had been lazy.

She laughed and tossed her hair over her shoulder. It looked as soft as he remembered. Her laugh warmed him from the inside, as if they were sitting fireside under the covers.

"You know what I mean. Chilled out, nothing's ever wrong," she said. "But seriously, we need to head back soon."

"Relax, Nic. Dude will be there when we get back, and if we're running late, well, they can't leave without us."

Fifteen minutes later, they pulled up at the Galleria. It was everything he wanted, though he didn't know why he cared. Signing up for a shopping trip would be classified as out of character. Hell, maybe he did know why. Taking care of her wasn't out of character, even if he was years out of practice. It once topped his list of favorite activities, and what a list that was...

She parked and waltzed in, not noticing anyone noticing her. She rocked his sweatpants and gym shirt, making them the sexiest things he'd ever seen. Even barefoot with a limp, the woman carried her head high, walking straight into the hoity-toity store.

Catching the raised eyebrows of sales clerks as he followed Nicola in, Cash gave them I-see-you-watching-me waves of his hand. No doubt, he was a sight to see. Black eyes. Swollen lip. Gun holstered on his hip. Sure as Kathy Lee and Hoda were about their Wednesday wine selections, he knew they flavored the water cooler gossip with a shot of, "oh my god, did you see that?"

Nicola bee-lined it for the shoe department, and he trailed behind, watching the tsunami effect of her presence. Nicola grabbed a pair of overstuffed, pink bunny slippers, walked over to the clerk and said, "I need these now. I'll be back for different shoes in a minute." She looked over her shoulder, pointed, and smiled. "And that beauty of a man over there plans on paying."

That he did. He smiled his split lip. It stung as the fresh scab ripped open. She could have called him a lot worse than a beauty.

Decent shoes and a well-fitting outfit did more for Nicola's mental state than she cared to admit. Cash glancing sideways a couple times to check her out was even more of a boost. Problem was, giggling like a school girl didn't fit the persona she'd created at the CIA. Nope. Those who knew Nicola thought she was married to the job and needed to get out more. At least she assumed that's what they thought.

Leaving the mall and heading to the airport was easy. Overthinking what Cash and Roman would say and do—that was a headache.

Not a lot of women did the whole intel operative routine, and fewer did it out in the field. Men assumed she played the game for a rush and that they'd swoop in to save the day just like Cash did, though, true enough, she had needed a hand in the Main Street rumble. Barroom brawls, even in broad daylight, weren't her forte. She might be tall and strong, but she wasn't oblivious to her physical limitations. There was a difference between knowing what might bring you down and being strong enough to say, "Fuck it. Let's try anyway."

Cash wasn't keen on her doing field work. She could tell. He hadn't said it word for word, but she got the gist. Every time his eyebrows hit his hair line, she translated it to, "Nicola, go home and watch *Jeopardy!*" Roman would be even worse. He didn't like her to take out the trash at night. Well, ten years ago, he didn't.

They breezed onto the private airstrip, sidled up to the plane, then Cash gave her a look. She foresaw an intervention in her future.

Nicola made a point to walk up the staircase in front of Cash. Roman and Rocco were already on board with Bonnie and Clyde. She wanted them to see her first, to show her extraction team that she wasn't hiding behind a man. To show Roman that this was her job too. All good reasons, but she'd be lying to herself if the thought of Cash behind her in these ten-out-of-ten fitting jeans hadn't crossed her mind.

God, no. She needed to erase him from her thoughts. The giddy school girl routine was going to get her into trouble.

Two steps before she passed through the door, Cash snagged her belt loop. He pulled her to a quick stop, his hard body catching right behind hers. A shiver licked down her back and tingled where he pressed against her. Her body vibrated, needing to push back against him. Mind over body, she only managed to freeze.

"Nic. One sec," he whispered in her ear. He was way too close, and it felt familiarly amazing. His breath warmed a spot behind her ear and rippled down her neck. The thump, thump of her pulse might have been loud enough for him to hear.

She shifted to look at him, balancing on her good foot, more than aware that her insides were spinning. "What's up?"

His hand stayed at the base of her back, the heat of his touch warm through her shirt. "Goddamn, you're gorgeous. Just thought you should know what I'd be looking at on the flight home." Then he patted her bottom, scooting her up the last two stairs and into the cabin.

Good thing he did because telling her legs to work—right and then left, repeat—would've been a chore. Her fuzzy mind spun, trying to let autopilot take over. His touch seared from her ass and spun out of control to the tips of her fingers and toes.

Somehow, she rounded the corner and slammed into Roman. Great. Autopilot disengaged. He eyed her, doing a quick assessment, then stared at Cash. "You okay, Nicola? You're looking... sick."

Sick? Try flush with flippin' pheromones. So much for her grand plan to act big, bad, and in charge. "I'm good, Roman. You need to chill out."

Roman's eyes bounced to Cash. "Everything kosher?"

"Everything's as you like it." Cash pushed past both of them, pulled the brim of his hat over his eyes, and sat down next to Rocco.

Nicola saw Bonnie and Clyde cuffed and secured in place. Roman gave her another overprotective glance, then gave a thumbs up to the pilot. They were airborne by the time she got comfortable in her seat. Bonnie's angry face said she was going to raise all kinds of hell once they got to Langley and figured out this headache. Clyde—AKA David, AKA the butler—was a blank canvas. Anything she tried to read on his bruised expression was a figment of her intel-seeking imagination. The guy gave her nothing. Damn CIA training.

Whatever. If they were both in on it, she was coming up aces. If it was just the butler, then she owed Miss Bonnie a sorry-I-almost-shot-you card and a fruit basket carved up like a flower bouquet. Or maybe just a gift certificate to Guns R Us, because Nicola was sure Rocco wasn't handing Bonnie her piece back.

The flight to Virginia was fast. They deplaned, jumped into waiting government vehicles and were sped away to Langley. Arriving at CIA headquarters, their group was separated and, she assumed, all waiting to be debriefed. Nicola had to explain the little problem of why she'd gone all berserker on her extraction team. Beth would believe her.

Maybe...

Well, of course she would. Beth was her best friend, the only person she trusted inside Langley and maybe outside as well.

It's not that Nicola had proof, per se. It was more of a gut feeling, but there were facts that couldn't be denied. Blank extraction instructions. Gunfire after she jumped the window. The butler saying he didn't *want* to kill her. Little things like that.

As interrogation rooms went, this one was standard. Nicola shifted in the uncomfortable chair, wondering how many sets of eyes watched as she sipped a Sprite.

Patience.

She needed a barrel of fortitude. The analysts and behaviorists were always looking for signs of... everything. She needed to send off a vibe of complete professionalism.

The door cracked, and Beth walked in. "Hey, girl."

"Hey." Nic smiled, not feeling it, but knowing the watchers in the wall expected it.

"Let's debrief and go get a drink, though I have a feeling a few beers isn't going to do it tonight."

"I'd be okay if we sat in your office with a couple bottles of wine and straws."

"Nice. Classy plan to match those nice threads you're wearing." Beth nodded approvingly at her new BCBG getup.

"Yeah, little shopping trip was required. So it goes. Designer label souvenir, I guess."

"All right, start from the top. Antilla was shot. Go."

Nicola recounted everything from that moment until she'd landed ass first in front of Titan's Range Rover. Beth nodded encouragement, smiled like a supportive handler should, repeated a few things, but didn't clue Nicola in on her thoughts. Nicola chatted her way right through the adventure until they were wheels down in Virginia, arriving at Langley.

Beth sat back for a minute, then pushed a pad of paper and a pen to her. "Smooth Enterprises. I know it's earlier than we'd planned to break down the network, but map out the players you know."

"I don't know everyone. Antilla was everywhere at once, so it was hard to track who he was with and what they discussed. But I'll give you what I know." It took an hour and page after page of notes. Her hand cramped. She knew analysts would study her handwriting, looking for clues, deceptions, and unvoiced revelations. When she was done, Beth took the papers and left. At least she'd been supportive enough to sit there while Nic wrote.

Her Sprite was empty. She spun the aluminum can on its side. The hum of florescent lighting started in on her nerves.

How much time had passed since Beth stepped out? An hour? Three? It could've been all damn day, for all the sense of passing time that she had.

I wonder what Cash and Roman said. I wonder where they are. The opening door pulled her from that thought tornado. Beth sat down, a tight smile marring her normally expressionless face. Shit, Nic didn't need to be a facial expression expert to recognize that tension.

"Nicola, there's nothing to suspect David—"

"What? BS, Beth. Bull—"

"Not my call. Not yours either. And to make matters more complicated, the powers that be need you to partner with him and finish up some loose ends in Antilla's file."

"No."

"Don't make me change that request into an order. We've never gone down that handler-agent road, and I sure don't want to start now. Work the system, but trust in me."

"Beth—"

"You've got no choice, but I'm not giving you this crap assignment by itself. Here's a side project to keep you happy." Beth slid a folder across the table. *Eyes Only.*

"Eyes only? Why? Nothing's been eyes only on this assignment."

"There's not much on the inside other than a couple of notes. I'm hoping you can change that for me."

Nicola opened the folder. One slip of paper. Handwritten. *Assignment JW. 7:30 PM blind date. JW Marriot. Washington, DC.* Creative, naming the op after the location. She stifled a chuckle. She'd have to tease Beth about her lack of titling ingenuity. This one lacked the one-two punch that would interest her in the job. Who would she meet? At least she didn't have to bring the butler with her. "Back to the butler."

"David."

"Fine. David. The guy's a pr—"

"Honestly, I don't care if you make up, hook up, or fight it out. Get rid of the hostility and tension between you two. And so you know, it's not like he's looking forward to hanging with you either. The man's pride is more than a little wounded with those shiners." Beth winked.

"I couldn't care less about the butl—about David."

"Here are your instructions to meet David." Beth handed her another piece of paper, but she didn't look at it. "Seriously, Nic. Soon as you come to terms with this, then you can get the hell out of here and go home. I'm trying to be a friend."

Trying to be my friend? You're supposed to be my best friend.

Nicola cracked her knuckles and rubbed her neck. She picked up the slip of paper and turned it over. Blank. She took a moment to look at it, as if reading. *Someone's always watching.*

Beth looked at her. "Got it, girl?"

Pocketing the paper, Nic said, "No problem. Consider it done." The only thing crystal clear was her confusion. "Am I free to go now?"

"Sure thing."

Nicola waved to the cameras and left.

CHAPTER NINE

Each passing minute in this godforsaken coffee shop irritated David further, both because the couriered package from his contact—code name: Mister Mars—was late, and because he'd smell like coffee grounds for the rest of the day. He tapped his manicured fingernails in annoyance.

A teenager with unkempt hair and neon yellow shoes clomped through the door, sweeping from table to table with a searching gaze. What passed as fashionable for today's youth was atrocious. When the kid's eyes landed on him, the yellow-footed courier scurried to his side.

"You're late," David scolded, his bruised face hurting from the scowl.

"I'm sorry. I got—"

He shook his head. The kid hadn't confirmed who he was, and his hands were already opening the delivery satchel.

"Do you have something to ask me?" David harrumphed. *Amateur hour.*

"Uh, yeah. Yes. I'm supposed to ask you for a special word."

"So ask. Don't suggest. Ask." He hated teaching in the field. It was another reason he couldn't wait to leave the CIA. This teenager acted as though the delivery was as benign as a flowers and balloons delivery. Did he look like he'd just had a baby? Just graduated from college? No. David didn't. He looked like a man who wheeled and dealed with high paying arms dealers.

"Er, um. Yes. Sorry. Can you please provide me the security word?"

David shook his head again in disgust. He cleared his throat. "The word is valor."

The kid frowned and followed up as he'd been directed. "And you are?"

"My name is Mister Nero." David thought the Mars-Nero code names were unnecessary, but Smooth Enterprises had always obsessed over ancient Roman history. They were the client. The paranoid client, even if they had reason to be after the assassination.

The kid deposited the small box on the table and skedaddled before David could tell him to get out. He opened it and took out the charged cell phone. Turning the screen on, he found the directory and selected the only entry.

It rang once, and David's client, Mister Mars, answered.

"You're late." Mister Mars's Austrian accent was smooth and slick as the spilled blood that had brought them together.

"And you should hire more qualified couriers. That kid wasn't qualified for delivery positions."

Mister Mars ignored his suggestion. "The CIA has no concerns about you?"

"None. They're so sure I'm a team player that they've forced Nicola to work with me on an assignment. We're to make up." David laughed. "I'll show her how good a Farm boy I really am."

"What is your assignment, and how will it affect our work?"

"It will enhance our business relationship. I've been given my choice of operations, as a sort of apology from Langley. She and I will orchestrate an assignment in Turkey, while providing back cover assistance for an asset. I'll have access to chatter on Smooth Enterprises, solidifying my role as a reputable agent, and you'll not only get Nicola, but have new details on the Turkish arms market. Consider it a bonus."

"Excellent. But, Mister Nero, don't forget. She's mine. She must pay, and the revenge is mine."

Nicola walked past the gift shops pushing White House memorabilia and monument-adorned post cards. She breezed by the valet manning his wood and brass podium at the front driveway of the JW Marriot.

A bellhop opened the side entrance as she avoided the revolving door. Nic had never been a big fan of glass containers. They just seemed like an ideal place to trap someone and take them out. Clear shot. Nowhere to go. Nowhere to hide.

She clacked heels across the gold-flecked marble floor and studied the people milling through the lobby. Business folks talking on phones. Tourists with fanny packs and maps. Nothing noteworthy, but then again, that was always the point.

As she entered the elevator, Nic saw a man pick up his pace, intent on making the elevator before the door closed. She threw him a smile that said, "come on I'll hold the doors," but reached for the close door button and held it. As the doors slid shut, she shrugged faux confusion and mouthed apologetically. There was no way that man was her blind date. He was too obvious.

Not wanting the doors to open again, Nicola hit the RB button. Rooftop balcony. She had no idea where to meet her blind date, but thought she might as well start where the view was the best. Classical music played overhead and—lucky her—the elevator didn't stop on her ride up. The doors opened into the sunset light, and she stepped out into a warm summer evening, surrounded by impressive buildings. *Yes, this is a magnificent view.*

A few people looked over the rail at Pennsylvania Avenue, taking in the downtown DC vibe. A man leaned on the railing. He was as large as Roman and Cash, but he looked meaner. His aura growled, and he hadn't even said a word. *Oh, fun.*

She walked up to him, offered her hand and waited. They stared each other down. Who would break first? Him or her? Him or her? Well, sure as the sun was setting over this swamp town, she wasn't dropping her extended hand if he remained standing there. He could be the asshole who moved away.

"Nicola." He spoke as if perhaps expecting a round of applause. Men and their egos. This man in particular looked impressed with his I-can-kill-you-with-a-paperclip attitude. He shook her hand, and though she expected him to wrench it off, he didn't. Just a firm shake. A little anti-climactic.

"And you are?" she asked.

"Jared Westin." *Oh, JW.* He must've seen the connection in her eyes. "Yeah, I like fuckin' with you CIA types. You play your games, and I poke fun at them."

All righty then, a jackass with a sense of humor. If he only knew how little she liked the Farm's games. "Right. I'm exhausted. Rough couple of days. You mind telling me what this all about so I can go?"

"You got somewhere more important to be at than—"

"Your secret game of mess-with-the-CIA? Yeah, I do. It's called home, where I have a nice bottle of wine waiting for me."

"You want to order a glass of wine?"

"No, I don't. You're missing my point. I'm exhausted and bitchy, and I want to know—"

"I might as well be talking to Roman right now. Jesus H. Christ." The man ran his hand over his close-cropped hair, looking none too pleased that his big tough guy attitude hadn't fazed her. But dropping the likes of her big brother into the conversation would get her attention.

"Roman?"

"Yeah, Roman. The jackass who runs his mouth like he's an alpha dog on 'roids. Though you seem to be a classier version."

"And who are you again?" Her eyes swept the DC cityscape.

"Jared Westin."

"We've established that, Einstein. You work together?"

"In a manner of speaking."

"Oh, cut the shit, Jared Westin, Jackass to the Spies."

His laugh sounded like a grumble bouncing off the walls of a cave. She got the idea he tossed barbells for fun and spent too much time at the gun range. "I like you."

"Spectacular. At least one of us is feeling the other." She gave him a smile that moved the dial from sarcastic to snarky.

"Want to do a job with us?"

Then again, if he wanted to talk about a job, she'd listen. "You're with Titan Group?"

"In a manner of speaking, yes. I'm with Titan."

"Well, in a manner of speaking, explain a little more, or I'm gone."

"Roman works for me. As does Cash. As does everyone at Titan."

For him? Crap. This was the big boss, and she wasn't on her best behavior. "You could've just said that."

"And miss all this fun? Not on your life, princess."

What? Princess? "I'm not a princess. Why am I here?"

"I want the butler, and the candlestick too, if you think you've got it in you." For the first time, Nicola was willing to let him play his game. He tilted his head. "Got your attention, didn't I?"

"The CIA sent me to you because of the butler?"

"The CIA doesn't trust him either. You've been partnered with him, and you and I are going to smoke his ass out."

"And why aren't the Farm boys doing that?"

Jared smirked, maybe as impressed with some of her co-workers as she was. "It was better to outsource this one. They already had us working on Antilla Smooth anyway."

"Yeah, found that out."

His smile was half-cocked and fully-loaded with a snarly comment. "You're just like Roman. Bet you're a pain in the ass too. Aren't you, princess?"

She rolled her eyes. "I'll partner with you if you don't call me princess."

"Why are you negotiating when we both know you can't wait to gut the fucker?"

He wasn't at all stupid, was he? "Fine."

"Fine. I'll be in touch." He turned toward the elevator. "Have a good evening."

Of all the people this blind date could have been, Titan's head honcho wasn't someone who'd crossed her mind. Nicola's phone buzzed in her purse. Unknown caller ID.

"Hello."

"Hey, Nic." *Cash.* A deluge of questions flooded her mind. The only one that bore noting was why the deep timbre of his voice caused a shiver to cascade down her shoulders. "What ya up to?"

Where to begin?

"Not much. You?"

"About the same." This had the makings of a boring conversation if neither of them were going to tell the truth. Cash cleared his throat. "Actually, not true. But nothing I can burn up a phone line about."

Maybe they were on the same page. "Cash, I, um—"

"I want to see you."

Her breath caught, and her heart picked that moment to have a palpitation. Oh, behavioral analysts would have a field day with that reaction. She nodded instead of speaking, but it didn't do any good. Why couldn't she string two syllables together? *Okay. No prob. Me too.*

"Nic? You there?"

"Yeah. Sorry. I'm… tired."

"Tomorrow night, bunch of us are getting together for a cookout. You down to go? You know, catch up with us for old time's sake?"

She nodded again, and this time managed two syllables, one word. "Okay."

"Good. Pick you up tomorrow night. See ya." He hung up before she said she'd drive herself. Damn it, being stuck in a confined area with Cash spelled trouble.

Nicola swirled the plastic soda cup, not stifling a giggle. She'd been tired and toeing the edge of a swan dive into a drama abyss, but Beth had called, promising a girls' night. Nic needed one, badly, because the last thing she wanted to do was go to her apartment and have a conversation with her roommate about things she couldn't discuss.

Nicola met Beth at an apartment she kept in the city above a convenience store, which was, indeed, convenient in that it sold all kinds of mixers and had a supply of plastic cups at the self-serve drink station.

"Tell me again why you have this place." Nicola hiccupped and giggled, putting her hand over her mouth. Another one escaped.

"Came in handy tonight, didn't it, Nic?"

Hiccup. "I need a refill."

"Me too." Beth snorted and poured way more Ketel One than she needed into her plastic cup. "Pink or red?" she asked, topping off her own.

Nicola studied the cranberry and pink lemonade mixer options. Tough decision. "Um, red this time."

Whoopsie. Splish, splash. They were making a mess.

"Alrighty." Nicola may have slurred that word. "Tell me again how this happened. How were there two teams on the same project?"

"Okay, the hot one—"

"What?" Nic recoiled, laughing. "Hot? Who?"

Beth grinned. "Well, they were all kinda hot."

Nic shook her head, whipping her hair back and forth. "Um, no. No how, no way. One of them was my brother."

"Nic, you're a show-stopper. You don't think your brother can be hot? Cause, girl, he is. But anyway."

"Well, Jared's *not* hot."

"He is until he opens his mouth."

"Maybe." Yup, words definitely slurring. Hiccup and a laugh. Did Jared look hot on the rooftop? Eh, maybe... "But Cash's hot-hot."

Beth nodded, eyes wide open. "Hm-huh. Cash's hot." She took a long sip of her drink. "So you and him, huh?"

"Past tense." Nic worked hard to enunciate her words. Her lips tingled.

"I'm totally cool with sloppy sec—"

"Beth, you—" She threw a balled up paper bag at her. "Off limits. You can't have him."

"Then I'll take Roman."

"Ew." She wrinkled her nose.

"Jared's too mean."

Nicola agreed. "Amen to that. Who does he think he is?"

"You should talk to Cash. Tell him what you're thinking, feeling." Beth ditched her straw and swallowed the rest of her drink. "What will it hurt?"

Don't say anything. Nicola repeated the thought two more times. It didn't work. In wine—or at least vodka—there was truth. "He doesn't know me anymore."

"Get to know him again."

"I don't want to."

"You never want to. What's the deal, anyway? That tech guy was flirting with you a few weeks ago. But he was a no-go. I know for a fact that analyst Bill or Bob or whatever asked you out. And don't forget your FBI bomb tech. He *was*— probably still *is*—completely obsessed with you. He's inhaled too many fumes if you ask me." She giggled. "I get paid to know these things."

"All those men are boring. But Cash... that's complicated."

"Nope. It's really easy. If it gets serious, I have a form you can fill out. Same form you filled out when dating your—"

Her phone buzzed. It was her roommate—talk about timing—and she sent the call to voicemail. "We were never serious, and I didn't fill out paperwork."

"It's simple. It says I'm sleeping with what's-his-name and promise not to divulge national secrets during pillow talk. Oh, and I give my handler permission to pillage through his personal life without him knowing."

"I've worked so-o-o hard to get here." Yup, too many Os in that so. Very professional. Oh well. "I want them to respect me." Respect sounded funny. She mouthed the word a couple of times.

"Them?"

"All the men we work with." She tried to mouth respect again. It still felt off.

Beth pulled her hair back into a ponytail. "They do respect you."

"No, they don't. They all think women at the Agency want to be saved by a man, whether we know it or not. That they're supposed to be our superhero saviors, and I'm just waiting to see who gets to save me. Everything's a game." She shook her head, slurring her words together. "This is probably a game.

You aren't my best friend, but some analyst doing a psychological, behavioral workup on me right now. Shit, this will end up in my file."

"Nope. Promise."

She laughed, shaking a finger at her handler. "I don't believe you, Miss Beth-the-Handler."

"Pinky-swear. Nothing leaves these walls." Nicola shot her a look. "Nothing's transmitting from these walls. How about that?"

"Hmm, maybe a little better."

"How about this? In January, I totally had a thing with Michael."

"Oh my God. He's our boss. He's your boss. He's like super-duper, everyone's boss. And, have mercy, he is so hot."

"Right?"

Nicola nodded like her head was on marionette strings. "I can't believe you never told me!"

"And I didn't report it."

Nicola finished the last sips in her plastic cup. "We should have found bigger cups. These little drinks go too fast."

"Or we're drinking too much."

"I don't know. I think we're drinking the right amount, given my day. Pink this time, please."

Beth topped off her vodka. At least Nic's hiccups were gone. That was a bonus.

Nicola took a sip. "Okay, my confession. I don't want to leave my job. I love it. Yeah, you can note that part in my file, please. But Cash doesn't see it. He doesn't know that me. And if I fall in love with him all over again, and he hates this me, I won't be able to take it."

"That's ridiculous, Nic."

It might be, but it was her fear. She took a huge suck on her straw. Pink might be a little better. Sweeter. "He loved college me. I liked me then too, but now I'm run-around-the-world-with-a-gun me." A quick gasp of a hiccup made her squeak. "Damn it!"

Beth laughed then snorted.

Nicola pointed. "I heard that!"

They both laughed. Another snort. Another hiccup. More laughing.

Nicola's phone rang. Beth wagged her eyebrows. "Maybe it's Cash."

She focused on the numbers on the screen. "Nope. Jared."

"He's hot too. Let me answer." Beth reached for the phone. "Everyone's hot. Is that the only word we know? Hot." She made a face, twisting her lips. "That sounds funky. Hot. Hawt. Hottt."

"No." Nic batted Beth away, hiccupped, and answered, serious face on. "Yes, hello?"

Beth fell on the floor, laughing. Her drink spilled. Nicola hiccupped, covering her mouth with her palm to hide her own giggle.

Jared grumbled. "Nicola?"

Beth snorted. Nicola tried, but couldn't stop laughing. "Hold on one minute." She put the phone in her lap, two fingers to her mouth to shush Beth, and tried again. Serious face back on. "Yes, hello?"

Was that a British accent? Beth ran toward the bathroom, shouting something about peeing on herself.

"Nicola, what the hell is going on?"

"Nothing." Yes, her I'm-very-sober voice featured a British woman with a nasal problem. "Can I help you, Jared?"

"Have you been drinking?"

"Have you been drinking, Jared?" Oh no. Why had that come out?

"Good Christ."

"Did you need something? I have something on the stove." *What? The stove?* "And must go." The last part came out with a definite accent. Beth came out of the bathroom just in time to hear her. She doubled over, wiping at the tears running down her cheeks.

"Titan's having a cookout tomorrow night, which you're invited to. But I'm changing it to a retreat. We've got shit to work out. Be there. Bring a bag. You'll have a room. I'll text you details."

Oh, that was sobering. "What?"

"Be a good little princess, finish your cocktail, and get a good night's sleep. We start work tomorrow."

Nicola hung up. Beth wiped the last of her tears. "What's Mister Hot-and-Grumpy want?"

"I have to spend the night with Cash."

"What? He said *what*?"

"Um, well." Nicola's thoughts waffled. Beth erupted into a laughing, snorting mess. Nicola smirked and poured another drink. "This is an emergency. Stop laughing. He said I have to stay with Titan this weekend. Under the same roof as Cash."

"You two should totally hook up."

"No way! I have to be professional. I have to prove to him that I can do my job." Prove sounded more like proof, maybe poof, but Beth didn't seem to notice.

"He's so hot."

"Beth, you aren't listening."

"And you're whining. Hot guy may or may not have feelings for you. Same hot guy was in love with you once upon a time."

"He loved someone else. Not me."

"Blah." Beth tossed her hand like it was no big deal.

Nicola smiled. Maybe she was making too much out of it. Maybe she needed more girls' nights. "We need to get out more."

"We need to do this more."

"Deal." She took another swig. "I have no idea what I'm going to wear."

"Bring something lacy. You never know."

Hiccup. This retreat had the potential for serious mistakes.

CHAPTER TEN

Nicola had sleepover anxiety. Spending another night under the same roof as Cash would be hazardous to the uninterested, uber-professional charade she was trying to pull off. But here she was, next to a chilled out Cash in the too-tight confines of his heavy duty pickup truck, on the way to the cookout-turned-retreat.

"We're here," Cash mumbled to himself, barely audible.

They rumbled off the paved driveway, veering away from a large, up-lit white house, and rolled onto a beaten path in the grass. In the distance, a raging bonfire danced in the night. Several trucks and SUVs were backed toward the fire on one side. Nic assumed the black abyss was the lakeshore that Cash mentioned. Laughter and good times drifted through his pickup's cracked windows.

Her overnight bag shifted as the truck bounced down the road, reminding her again that she'd be caged with him around her new co-workers. *Please don't let them see me as just another girl he's bagged.*

Cash's cowboy hat was pulled low over his shaggy blonde hair, hiding his eyes from her. Nicola glanced in his direction any time he looked off the road, but mostly, she sat in silence, not trusting her voice to not give away the spark that flared each time he gave a not-so-innocent smile or whoops-I-meant-to-do-that touch. He made her dizzy. She placed a hand on the oh-shit bar.

"I'm not driving *that* bad, Nic."

If he wanted to believe holding herself in place had to do with his off-road driving, fine by her. Whatever kept him from knowing too much.

She tried for another deep breath. Every time Cash looked at her, it sucked the wind out of her lungs, and whoosh, the words out of her brain. How was this going to go down in front of the Titan boys? Um, bad. Very bad.

I need a beer.

Cash turned down the radio, shushing George Strait and his song du jour about lost love. "You've been awfully quiet. You lost in that pretty head of yours, daydreaming about something?"

Um, yeah. You. Maybe I need two beers. "Just thinking."

"Right." He eased up on the gas, and they crawled toward the massive bonfire. "Yeah, me too. Just a thinkin'."

"About?"

He stretched. His shirt might well have been painted on. "Just thinking that I'm down for a few drinks and some barbeque. But I'm worried that, put a little booze in us, and we're going to face off again. Our little bout with Roman probably had more to do with the Jack Daniel's than it did with us wanting to clue our boy in about us."

"Then you should air your grievances with me now." She smoothed her wrinkle-free shorts for the fifth time in as many minutes.

"Actually, not sure my issue is a grievance." He stared at her, big blue eyes locking onto her before looking ahead.

"Oh." *Oh?*

"You're breathtaking, you know that?"

Nicola felt her cheeks heat, and she looked out the window. Cash pulled the truck off the worn path, and they drifted to a stop. Panic started in her stomach and climbed into her throat. "What are you doing, Cash?" *Shit.* Did she sound panicked?

"No idea." Putting the truck into park, he raked a gaze over her.

She'd never heard him sound anything but Rocky Mountain strong. "Cash—"

"I've missed hearing you say my name." His arms draped over the steering wheel, his head pressed to its twelve o'clock.

"Nic, I'm having a problem keeping my head around you, so why don't you shut your pretty mouth and give me a minute?"

What? There was no way he had the same issues she did. He hated her. Hadn't forgiven her. "Wha... why?"

He still faced the steering wheel, but slid his hands to the nine and two positions, and hung on like he was strangling Cupid. "I'm forcing my hands to stay put. Physically willing them away from you. One move, one too-sweet word, Nicola, and I'm done for."

"I don't understand." *I thought I was the one holding back.*

He peered up from his steering wheel pillow. "What's not to understand?"

"You're mad at me."

"Angrier than I've been in my entire life." His eyes held her in place, riveting her to him.

"You said you might hate me." God, it hurt to say that out loud.

"Yeah, I might."

"So what else is there?" she asked, scared and hoping at the same time.

"If that isn't the question, I don't know what is."

"You mean..."

"I mean, I'm confused." He sat upright, straightening his broad shoulders. "I mean, I don't do this whole soap opera, back from the dead thing. And it's been so long. But..."

"But?" Her head circled, lungs went on strike, blood pounded in her ears.

Her phone rang. Loud. Killing any confession that may have fallen from his lips. Words she'd die to hear. If she could've thrown the damn thing out the window and begged him to continue, she would have. But she couldn't and checked the caller ID. "Jared."

Cash shook his head. "Jared?"

She glanced at him and accepted the call. Cash hardened, seemingly not thrilled that Jared had called her. Jared grumbled in her ear. Something about making sure she made it to his Titan get together. She nodded as if he could see it. Bad habit. "Yeah. Almost there. See you."

Nicola clicked off the phone, then dropped it into her purse.

"Why's Jared calling you?" Cash looked pissed.

Fucking Jared. He hadn't talked to Cash yet. "You know why I'm coming out here for your boys' retreat?"

"Dunno. You're going to fill us in on Smooth Enterprises? Have more to tell us after we debriefed?"

"Fucking Jared," she repeated, but aloud this time, then finished another slew of curses in her head. She didn't want to act crass in front of Cash.

"What?" No, now Cash looked pissed. Whatever that look before was, it was clearly a warm-up to this face. "Talk. Now."

"Someone needs to read you in."

"Nicola, you have two seconds. Then I get pissed."

Hmm, not pissed yet? Could have fooled me. "Me and Jared."

"You and Jared?" He stared hard. "You and Jared, what, Nicola?"

"We're working together on this one." She shrugged like it wasn't a big deal. It wasn't. Why was he acting like this? See, this was the problem that scared her, that kept her from wanting to get too close to Cash.

"The hell you are."

"I already told the CIA and Jared I'd do it. We're going after the butler."

"No," he growled.

"Yes."

"Fucking Jared." That's what she said. Wasn't he listening? He slapped the steering wheel, then threw the truck into gear.

"Cash, calm down. Why are you mad? This is my job! This is my assignment."

"Nic, you can't do this shit. You can't go running around with guns and spies and infiltrate fucking arm dealing networks. You cannot. End of discussion."

And there it was. He didn't trust her to work for no other reason that he didn't think she should be in the field. She knew it. Tears stung behind her eyes. Her throat was raw, and she tried like hell to swallow the boulder, but couldn't. "Why?"

It came out as a whisper. He hated her. He didn't trust her. Now, he wouldn't respect her on the job. Her mind and her body hurt from the rejection. Her biggest fear and the truest love slammed together. Pain overwhelmed her thoughts.

If he was speaking, she didn't hear it. She only noticed that they'd started toward the bonfire again. Cash parked, jumped out, and left her alone in the truck with all of her insecurities.

This is what it would be like to hang out at a superhero convention? Nicola nursed her beer and watched. They were all dressed head-to-toe in varying versions of tactical gear. Tight shirts, pants with too many pockets. She was sure there was enough firepower to invade a small country stashed in their vehicles.

Roman hovered over her for a while, checking in and presumably fending off anyone who might want to talk to her. Typical overprotective Roman. It almost felt good, familiar, to have him breathing down her neck, glaring at anyone with testosterone. Cash worked the crowd with his lazy laugh, ignoring her, and the rest of the Titan men filled their roles by shotgunning beers and chowing down on barbeque.

Jared walked over to her with two beers in his hand. Her butt was numb from sitting on Cash's tailgate, and she was a tad lonely. Yeah, she'd talked to Roman. But there was very much an invisible line drawn around her. No one approached her without what looked like an okay from Roman, although Jared didn't look as if he'd asked for or cared about the Roman go-ahead.

Maybe she was the problem, looking like she held a sign that said *Beware: I bite.* Or maybe, *I came back from the dead.* Who knew?

"How goes it, princess?"

"How goes it..." She needed a name for him too, and dickhead wasn't going to work in front of his men. "Twinkle Toes?"

He would have reacted, she thought, but he was too alpha to show the flicker of surprise. "You got jokes. Beer?" He held out a fresh one.

She raised her beer. Its label had long ago been peeled off. "Still got this one."

"So finish it."

Jared was growing on her. She turned the bottle up and drained the last drops of the warm beer. She'd had it in hand too long. Yuck. A chilled longneck would be good. "Done."

"Good girl. Here."

She nodded her thanks, appreciative for anything that would lessen the buzzing feelings in her head. If Jared had handed her a horse tranq, she might have tried to kiss the grumbling jerk. "I needed this."

"I see brother and sister are reunited and acting brotherly-sisterly. You and Roman cool?"

"Of course. He's pretty forgiving or, at least, not as much of a bastard as you might think."

"Good. So what's the deal with you and Cash?"

"Why?"

"Something came up. I can't partner with you on Operation Smoke-'Em-Out, and I need a man working with you."

"I don't need a man."

"Not what I meant. All I got is men. I need a *person* working with you."

"I work fine by myself."

"I'm not a work-on-an-island kinda guy. You get a partner, or you lose the job."

"Fine. Whoever will do." She shrugged like she really didn't care and looked over his shoulder.

"Actually, not fine. No one will work with you."

"Like I said—"

"You're hard-headed like Roman. Great. Fuckin' fantastic. Roman doesn't trust himself to work with his little sister. I talked to him. He won't do it."

"He's a moron."

"Right. And Rocco must have spread the word, 'cause him and two other guys I wanted to partner you with won't. Hell, they won't work with you to save their lives."

"I'm a good agent—"

"It has nothing to do with that. It has to do with Cash. So spill it, woman. What do I need to know?"

"We dated before I left."

"You loved him?"

Nic rolled her eyes toward the bonfire, taking in Cash's amazing silhouette. "And how is that your business?"

"Everything's my business when it comes to my ops. Let's try this. You love him now?"

"No. Of course not."

"Can you keep it in your pants?"

She shot her gaze back to him. "Christ, Jared."

"That wasn't an answer." He laughed.

"He and I are fine. We're not jumping into bed. Not confusing the past and the present. But I'm not working with him."

"Yeah, you are." He looked so certain.

"Nope."

"No choice." He laughed again, and it was more irritating each time he did the cough-grumble thing he used as laughter. "You don't partner well, do you?"

"Cash won't do it either."

"I have a feeling he would jump at the chance to—"

All right, that strategy went down fast. Try, try, try again. "We'll distract each other. Not a good idea."

"So, you're walking away, princess? Didn't take you as a quitter."

"God—"

"That works much better. God. It has a good ring to it. Better than Twinkle Toes."

"Jared—"

"Okay. Jared or God. Your choice."

"Would you shut up?"

"I like you, princess."

"Fine. Cash. I'll do it. Go away."

"I knew you'd see it my way. Don't forget to grab some potato salad. Mia Winters can cook like you wouldn't believe."

CHAPTER ELEVEN

Jealousy. It wasn't a logical response, but Cash fought back a growl, wanting to physically remove Jared from Nicola's proximity. She sat on the tailgate to his truck. Her long legs dangled, and the bonfire light danced across her skin. No doubt about it, Cash was jealous. His fists bunched in his jeans pockets, but he knew he wasn't hiding his reaction from anyone.

He threw a piece of meat to Winters's dog. The pup had been running around the fire soliciting donations like he was starving to death. Winters swore he fed the mutt. Cash laughed. He knew better than to think that Mia, Winters's wife, would let the dog go hungry.

"Hey, asshole. Don't give the dog any more food." That'd been Winters's line all night long. Too freakin' bad. He should feed his dog.

"Call me asshole again, the pup gets beans. And Mia told me the dog sleeps next to you."

Roman sidled up to Cash and joined him in throwing scraps to the dog. "So Nicola drove out with you?"

"Yup." This wasn't a conversation he wanted to have with Roman in front of the guys. Hell, he didn't want to have it at all. The girl was throwing him an ice-cold shoulder, and he wasn't at all sure why he cared. Except for the whole maybe he still cared for her thing. But other than that...

"I've calmed down about you two back in the day. It was more than what you said? You know. The other night."

"Yup." He picked up his beer and drained it. Maybe they were standing too close to the bonfire. He started to sweat a little.

"Huh." Roman genuinely sounded at a loss for words, which was unlike the guy.

Cash grabbed a fresh beer from the cooler behind them. "You going to ask more questions or something? Or are we done talking about me and her?"

"You two really done?"

Well, shit. If that wasn't the question, he didn't know what was. "Not sure I want it to be."

"Huh."

Cash cracked half a smile. "Yeah, how about that?"

"Well, then maybe you should do something about boss man leaning into our girl and her giggling. It's enough to make me sick."

It didn't take much of a push. His boots were moving before he realized he was closing in on her. Why? Something to prove? Something to say? Who knew? Maybe he wanted to be closer and make sure no one thought she was a free agent. But then again, she was. Shit, he had no claims to her. Even if there was a flicker of interest in her eyes.

What he felt was more than a flicker. Too bad he still couldn't catch his breath.

He walked up as Jared said his goodbye. "What's up with you and boss man?"

"Shop talk."

"Great." His brows furrowed. Not what he wanted to hear, but it was better than Jared throwing lines, 'cause he'd have to throw punches. It wouldn't be good for his employee review. Well, if they had things like that. "What would you do if life hadn't pushed you toward the CIA?"

"What do you mean?"

He perched beside her on the tailgate. "Like, if you finished studying linguistics in college. Maybe you'd be a teacher or something? A professional translator?"

She laughed, a beautiful sound that churned his guts. "What's funny?"

"Cash, I'd be here. Doing the same thing."

"No—"

"Yeah, I would. I love this. I'm good at it. There's nothing else I want to do."

She was almost finished with the beer Jared'd brought her. He should've done something smart like that.

"But you're—I don't know—home, for lack of a better word."

"I wasn't lost. I'm not the prodigal daughter returned."

"But you're—"

She rolled her eyes. "I'd be doing the same thing, whether I stumbled upon you and Roman or not."

"Why didn't you call us? Once you knew everything was okay? I mean, come on, you live so damn close. Why not—"

"It's not worth all the questions. I wasn't allowed. I don't have the same last name anymore. I don't have the same Social Security number or background. It's all manufactured. There are a million places I could be in the world. Just because I'm based near here doesn't mean that's where I live."

"What's your last name?"

She paused, then took a long draw off the bottle. "Garrison."

Sucker punch to the dome, and he was almost lights out. "What?"

"I'm embarrassed, if you want the truth. I got to pick. It was the only other last name I ever wanted. I didn't think I'd ever see you again. Certainly not have to explain it to you."

His mind ran round, his thoughts speeding like a car chase. "You're killing me."

"Look, Cash. Don't worry about me. I'll do this job and be out of here."

He stood and leaned back against the side of his truck, wrapping his arms over his chest, trying, willing the words to stay in his head where they should be. "I don't want you doing this, Nic." He said it. A little louder than he intended. *So much for keeping private thoughts private.*

"Big surprise. But it's never been your call, and it's not now."

"It's not safe." That was the most important reason he had in the quit-your-day-job arsenal. She needed to walk away from the gun play.

Her body language clearly didn't agree. "It's not safe for you either," Nicola countered.

"I'm trained. I can—"

She recoiled. "You think I'm not?"

"No." His voice rose, frustration igniting his words. She wasn't having any of his reasoning. "I don't."

"You don't know me."

"Not my fault, is it?" God, she made him want to shake her. Or pin her against the wall. Either would do right now.

"We're throwing down in front of everyone again." Nicola gestured to Rocco, who tuned in like they were a reality show in the making. "Should've aired your grievance earlier, when I gave you the chance in the truck."

He glared at the guys, tugged on her good elbow. "Come with me."

"No way."

His hands itched for something to do. He gnawed on the inside of his cheek to keep from saying something he'd regret. It wasn't killing off the urge. He threw a handful of Altoids into his mouth. Still no help. "Nicola, I don't have time for this."

"Guess what, Cash. Jared just partnered you and me together. You'll get to see how good I am."

He froze, cemented to the ground. "Excuse me?"

"You heard me." She laughed. "Now what are you going to do?"

"Fix it." There was no way she was going out in the field with him.

"Oh, hell no."

"Watch me."

"Cash, stop it."

Cash looked at Rocco, who was now flanked by his buddies Winters and Brock. They all smiled, enjoying the hell out of this. *Good Christ.* "Let's go. We have to talk. In private."

"Don't feel like it."

He scooped her off the tailgate, threw her over his shoulder, and stalked off. The background noise was littered with laughter and jokes. It didn't matter. He was sick of this BS. Nicola wasn't going to get herself killed on his watch.

He rounded the hood of his truck, and her hands wrapped around his neck, digging a grave into his carotid artery. Her bad arm had a helluva grip.

Damn it.

He had her at a bad angle. The only way he could pull her loose was to slam her against the truck or drop her to the ground. She wasn't playing nice either. She was out to prove her point. He twisted his neck, testing her handhold. It was strong. Maybe she *was* trained. Trained *well*, for that matter.

Nicola hissed in his ear. "Think again, if you think I'm not. You embarrass me, I'll embarrass you. I'll drop your ass in front of all your boys. Give me six more seconds, and you're lights out."

Truth was, she was right. Unless he pulled some kind of defensive measure, her vise-lock on his neck would take him down.

Here goes nothing.

He dropped forward, cradling the back of her head before they slammed to the ground. He absorbed the impact with his other arm around her back, pressing her to him. They crunched into the grass. His knees were on either side of her thighs. Her breaths were fast, and her hair splayed in the grass like a blonde halo. Her cheeks flushed, and she was the most beautiful woman he'd set eyes on.

Years ago.

Right now.

It made no difference.

Cash leaned over. Nose to nose, eyes locked. Lavender and flowers were all he could smell. She was all he could see. The electrified air zipped and zapped around them, pushing them together. Heat poured off her long frame. Her quick breaths kissed his lips, the way he so desperately wanted to kiss her.

Never had a woman grabbed hold of his spinning world and stopped it cold. Just him and her, suspended in time. Never had he focused on wanting a kiss like the one he was about to take.

Her chocolate eyes didn't blink. She watched, waited. Anticipated.

He pushed through the minute fraction of charged space between them, brushing his lips over her plump bottom one, instantly drawing his eyelids closed to savor her. Soft velvet, tasting like sugar.

The brim of his cowboy hat sheltered them. His mouth opened and caressed her top lip. Her mouth parted on a breath, and his tongue dipped into their kiss, living the daydream that had stolen his mind.

She sighed into him. An eruption of goose bumps trailed down his spine, tapering their descent at the small of his back and rushing blood to his groin. Every muscle tightened as if awaiting a command for action, but all he could do was repeat: bottom lip, top lip, both lips together.

Nicola relaxed, chin reaching up, tongue stroking his. Her hands slid up his neck, and she clasped his cheeks in her palms, pulling him to her. Sweet and hungry.

She was familiar, flared with something exciting and new to be explored and relished.

He nibbled her soft kiss, then paused. "I never thought anything would feel like that again."

His lips were still against hers, and he felt the smile melt onto the face he memorized years ago. The girl next door, turned into the woman who promised his dreams could come true. He knew every facet, every expression. Even if it had been years, her smile was pure warmth, soothing the animosity that confused him.

"Kiss me again," she whispered.

As if she had to ask. He rolled them to the side, running his hand through her hair, letting the silk slide through his fingers. The grass was cold, tickling and biting his skin, momentarily reminding him they laid on the ground at his buddy's house. But fuck it. They were far enough away, and nothing could have stopped him from kissing her at her command.

Cash wrapped Nicola into his embrace. She nuzzled, kissing up his neck.

"I missed you, sweet girl." He took her mouth, possessive and entirely focused on the little sounds she purred. She clung to him, a long leg kicked over his thigh. The whip of her tongue shocked his senses, ricocheting his nerve endings to the tips of his toes. Her breasts pushed into him, and his mind fast-forwarded to where they could be, how they could be.

"Stop." She pushed back hard, surprising him straight out of his kiss clouded mindset.

What just went wrong? Floored. He was floored. Literally on the ground, as she dusted herself off and jumped upright, and figuratively, dumbstruck.

Never. Ever. Not once had a woman walked away from him when they were warming up. Not that much could go down in the grass and in front of God and co-workers, but still. He hadn't a clue.

Instead of jumping up, he rolled back onto his back, propped up on his forearms, not particularly caring who saw his hard-on, and pulled his hat over his face. Neither embarrassed nor hiding, he was just plain confused. But her footsteps didn't walk away. She stood there. One pointy-toed shoe bouncing in a pissed off allegro.

No way was she pissed at him.

No way.

They'd kissed. It wasn't all him. She was there with him, every lip lock, tease, and torture. She'd been game.

He murmured, "You're standing there 'cause you want me to ask what's the matter. And I don't feel like it. So scurry along, Nic. You have your reason not to work with me. Jared will give you a pass."

"I want to work with you. You're the one who doesn't want me." Tap, tap, tap of the toe. She wanted him to keep guessing.

True enough, he didn't want to work with her. He deflated an exhausted breath. "I don't know what you need me to say. Help me out, or go away."

"Challenge me."

"What?" He picked the hat off his head, catching a good stare at her.

"Test me. Ask me to do something you think I can't do."

"I'm not playing games."

"I'm not either, but if we're going to work together, you have to believe I can keep up with you."

"No—"

"I'm not playing, Cash. Try me. Challenge me. I want to earn your respect."

"I respect you. Promise. I'm sorry about this whole kissing in the grass thing." He paused. "Actually, no, I'm not."

"It has nothing to do with—"

"Then your timing sucks. As usual." He knocked the cowboy hat back into place. It hung on a tilt, but he didn't bother to fix it.

"Cheap shot." She put her hands on her hips, and the foot bounced, bounced, bounced.

"Blue balls. What can I say?"

"Classy, Cash." She smirked, her face reading sky-high on the bitch-o-meter.

"I'll tell you what. You want to spar, we can do that. But here's the deal, and it has nothing to do with working together. You win, you get whatever you want. I win, I get to finish that kiss."

The foot stopped bouncing. He jumped up and walked away before she could rain a storm of excuses on him.

CHAPTER TWELVE

"Best two out of three." Nicola swore he'd let her win that one. She'd hooked an ankle above his knee and shoved a hard hand against his chest. He should've been able to roll out. He should've done anything, but nope. Pinned beneath her, Cash looked pleased, sporting a hi-how-ya-doing grin on his handsome face.

Didn't he want to finish their kiss? Or did he want to see what she wanted? Oh, this was frustrating and confusing. *I've been hanging with CIA folks too long.* The guessing game and lack of trust permeated every question and situation, giving her a constant headache.

"You're on. I'll go two out of three." His sly smirk said he *wanted* to get pinned.

Nicola jumped up on bare feet, and he followed. She waited for him to move, then charged.

Attack. Block.

Counter-attack. Block again.

She rocked back on her bare heels. "Come on, Cash. This is too by the book."

He put his hands on his hips. "You started out textbook. I'm taking your lead."

Shit. She was so concerned about displaying what she knew, that she'd left the heart out of their battle. She'd anticipated, shown off, and lost focus, all of which sucked the fight and emotion out of her natural moves. Proper footwork wouldn't impress Cash. Heart would. She knew that. She knew him.

Nicola breathed in, centered, and readied her launch. He was taller, stronger. Speed and quickness were on her side. She needed to get in, get close, and get out. Faking a throw, he jumped away, then stepped into her spinning back kick.

She set up high, struck low. Cash grunted with the blow, and a smile of pride slipped across his face. *Hell, no.* She wasn't here to impress him. She was here to take him down.

Jab. Jab again. He caught her hand before it fully extended. He took a side step and countered. A leg hooked behind, and down she went. Cash was over her, hovering so close, so sexual. Broad arms trapped her. His heavy weight held her in place. He smelled like masculine effort. Salt from her sweat teased her lips. The air was charged. Hair stuck to his damp forehead. The scent of fresh perspiration tightened her stomach. His beautiful sapphire eyes shone, pinning her to the ground. The air vacuumed out of the gym, and she was done.

She tapped the mat.

Once.

Twice.

Released, Cash rolled off her and lay next to her on the blue athletic pad. She studied the ceiling. He had the win. He'd earned his kiss. Their kiss. Her body tingled, not from the body slams and mat burns, but the vivid flashback of the grassy field interlude. She shivered, despite the warm temperature and the hand-to-hand workout.

Nicola turned her gaze from the ceiling lights and crashed headfirst into Cash's gorgeous gaze. Her heart squeezed ripcord tight and forgot to beat. Sweat dampened his cotton shirt, and his mesh shorts stuck to the rippled muscles in his thighs. Not an ounce of fat. Nothing but lean, mean, 100% Grade A Cash.

He would look spectacular naked. Sculpted and tan. Blonde chest hair and cut muscles. Memories raced. A fresh round of shivers skipped down her neck and chest, hardening nipples under her tight spandex shirt.

"You're good, Nic."

She mumbled a response, not even aware of its meaning, and looked past him to the row of equipment. Free weights. Treadmill. Heavy bag.

"Feel   better   now?"   he   asked.

Nicola propped up on her elbows, but her head hung back. She didn't want to see him answer her question. "Better question is, do you?"

"Meaning?"

"You thought I hadn't been trained."

"You're CIA. Logically, I know you've undergone the best that the best has to offer. But it's hard to connect the woman I knew to the woman with roundhouse kicks and evasive maneuvers, catching her breath next to me."

Now she looked at him. She couldn't help it. "Do you like her? I mean, me? Who I am now?"

He propped up on an elbow. "Yeah, Nic." He pushed a loose strand of her hair behind her ear. "I really do."

She was suddenly aware of her thumping heart—the same heart that went on boycott a tense moment before—and her nerves responding to his smoldering look. She had to change the subject to something, anything else. Sitting up, she dusted off her hands. "I need to thank Mia for the clothes. I didn't think I'd log any gym time this weekend and didn't pack anything for a workout."

He chuckled. "Are you nervous around me?"

Maybe. "Of course not. You're so damn cocky, Cash." She jumped up, ready to run. Cash stayed on the floor, eyeing her, knowing her far better than she liked to admit.

"'Cause you seem to do just fine when we clash, but given a quiet moment, you smooth your clothes or pick a fight."

"How very observant of you." She tried very hard not to fidget with her shirt.

"Right there. Hear it in your voice? That's a fighting tone." His voice drawled, hinting at their Virginia roots. "I observe. It's what I do."

"You're a sniper. That's what you do."

"Nah, sweet girl. That's just my specialty. I observe. I conclude. I react."

"Good for you. Night." She had to get away from him. It was confirmed, without a sliver of hesitation. She wanted Cash. Needed and craved him. Desperation would take her down, and he'd see her come apart. Her pulse raced, but her fingertips ached to run across his lips, just to take in their softness again.

"Nic, wait." She heard him slap the mat. Halfway to the gym door, she turned around. No other man on Earth could sound so distant and still mean so much to her. "I'm sorry."

Sorry for what? He had spoken the truth. No surprises there. Her chest ached.

"No prob," she lied, still needing to get away from him. A flick of a wave and she was out the door. It slammed behind her.

The caged, florescent lights above his head were set on motion detectors, and one by one, they blacked out. Click. Click. Click. Surrounded by darkness, Cash sat with his thoughts. It made for a lonely moment and summed up the last decade. Granted, he hadn't physically been alone, but he sure as shit felt that way.

And I have no interest in being alone now.

He jumped up. Two flights of stairs later, he was at a guest room door. He knew Mia would give Nicola this one with its fancy private bathroom. Jared would get the other with the same layout. The rest of the grunts could share the hallway bathrooms.

The sound of footsteps padding on the carpet caught his attention. He looked over his shoulder to see tiny Mia with her big pregnant belly smiling as if she knew what clamored around in his head. She was a therapist, after all, so maybe she understood this maze of emotion.

She nodded toward Nicola's door. "Are you going to knock?"

That was the question, all right. He hadn't mapped out what he'd say. Or if he'd knock. A compulsion had brought him to her door, but it hadn't clued him in on the next steps. "Not sure."

"I think you should."

"You don't know—"

"I know enough, being that I'm a military therapist. Jared has no problem bouncing concerns off me."

Cash laughed. Mia Winters might be the only woman in the world who would square off against Jared. It happened a lot, even more now with her crazy hormones, though he'd never say that to her face. Watching Mia take on Jared was better than watching a Saturday night barroom brawl. And Mia won almost every time. She was the odds-on favorite.

"Oh, I moved your stuff to the room next door. Adjoining doors, by the way." Mia winked.

He choked when he tried to swallow and didn't know what to say. There was no way he'd sleep tonight. He'd been sweating another night under the same roof as Nicola. Now one flimsy door separated him from her bed. No way. No how. He wasn't going to survive the night knowing she slept mere feet away.

What would she wear to bed?

Time to find out.

Knock. Knock.

No answer.

Cash wasn't going to let her ignore him, especially not when her clothing options, or maybe lack of, were on his mind. He knocked again. No answer. Cash turned the knob and walked in.

Nicola emerged from her bathroom in a cloud of steam with a tiny towel wrapped around her chest that barely reached her thighs. Her cheeks were fresh and rosy, and her blonde hair dark and shower-wet. He choked, again, and whatever he wanted to say dissolved into the steamy air. She looked like a heaven-sent angel.

"Cash!"

"Sorry." He put his hands up in surrender, but didn't retreat, freezing in place, mesmerized by long legs and a scrunched-up, pissed-off face. The scent of lavender filled the room.

He lowered his hands. "Can we chat?"

"I'm in a towel."

"Don't I know it, darlin'." She clung tighter to the towel, as if Cash could will it off of her.

"I need to get dressed. Get out of here." She tried to shoo him away without releasing her grip on the towel.

"Or I could get undressed. Even things out." *Whoops, probably not the right thing to say.* He tilted his head, praying for her grin, knowing damn well he'd shed his gym threads quicker than she could say, "go ahead."

She smiled and gave a tame laugh that said he wasn't a dead man. *Thank God.* "What do you want?"

"You. Nicola Garrison."

Her hesitant smile faded, but her warm eyes spoke with a fire and sparkle. She didn't move. Didn't speak. Didn't give him anything to work with other than the brightness in her glare.

"Stop with the last name."

"No."

"I don't want to be just another notch in your belt. I'm not one of your many conquests." She smirked, and he made a mental note to give Rocco another round of hell for telling tales. Maybe this honesty bullshit would be the only way to figure things out.

"No, you aren't a conquest. You were my first love, and I'd thought you'd be my last. Anything after you was just killing time."

She turned away from him, fidgeting with a pair of earrings on the dresser. Her body looked strong, and the towel wasn't hiding much. She cleared her throat. "Killing time until what?"

"I had no idea." He scrubbed a hand over his five o'clock shadow. "But now I know." Silence. She didn't say a word, and his heart combusted, falling to the hard floor in a fiery explosion.

Her head dropped back, and she stared toward the crown molding. He took one step, then another. He had to save this moment. Had to save them.

Cash placed his hands on her warm, freshly dried shoulders. She smelled delicate and felt silky, satiny, and so much better than he remembered. He slid his hands, shifting her hair over the spectacular slope of her neck and thumbed the nape, rubbing her muscles until a soft sigh drifted into the humid air and hung between them.

Shivers erupted under his touch, and goose bumps rose. Chasing their path, he caressed her neck until she released another sigh.

There was no hiding his arousal. He thought about it too late as she leaned back into him. Hell. He'd tell her—he'd show her—the truth. He was consumed by her.

"I don't want to be just another girl."

"You weren't, and I promise, you aren't."

"I'm confused. Concerned."

"Why?"

"You hate what I do, and what I do is who I am," she whispered over her shoulder.

"That's your hold-up?" He trailed a finger down her arm.

"It was hard enough to walk away from you before, Cash. I can't get mixed up with you again. It's a recipe for heartache."

"I loved you once. You think I can't again?"

She sucked in a breath. His thoughts raced, dying to say something more, but having no idea what more there was to confess.

Nicola's towel dropped like it was lead lined, taking with it any coherent thought left in his brain. Seeing her gorgeous back trail down to her perfect ass, all he could do was feel the smoothness and strength of her body. He fanned his fingers down toward her waist. Hands on her hips, he spun her to face him. Studying every inch of her body, one thought detonated in his mind. *Never just another girl.*

He traced her jaw, tilting her head up. Trusting eyes met his. She fingered the hem of his shirt, and he shrugged it off.

"I need a shower. I should've..." He should've done a thousand things.

"I'll get in with you."

"You just—"

"I don't care—"

He hushed her with a kiss as promising as he could make it. His hands knotted into her hair, and her mouth welcomed his. Cash tasted her sweet lips. A step forward and he crushed his body against hers, needing nothing but her.

She sighed into the kiss. "Shower?"

Taking her hands in his, he walked them into the bathroom. The fog on the mirror had started to fade, but the humidity and heat enveloped them. She turned the water on and stood naked by the cascading water, his image of perfection.

Cash was suddenly aware of himself, of his history. His unworthiness. She deserved better than him. Rocco and Roman were right.

"Cash?"

"Yeah."

"You okay?"

"I'm feeling guilty."

"That's my line." She smiled, warm and caring as an embrace.

"It's just…" He gestured toward the bathroom counter, like that was supposed to mean something.

"Let's take a shower. Kiss me like the years weren't missing." She stepped to him, pushed her bare breasts against his chest, and he almost moaned. He considered bartering for a ten second shower, then a long dive under the covers, but her lips met his, she hooked an arm around him, and they kissed into the shower. No bartering or negotiating needed.

CHAPTER THIRTEEN

Heat surrounded her. It wasn't the hot water pouring down that made her feel wash-cycle dizzy. The granite-tiled wall of water jets and the rain showerhead added to the mind-reeling moment. Cash was naked, gloriously large, broad, and overwhelming. His rolling pecs and biceps rippled as he moved. His muscles barely hid under the layer of golden, water-flecked skin. He locked her with a gaze that made her legs tremble. The knowing and depth in his eyes told the story of their past and made her heart bleed and her hands heavy.

In this impossible moment, she existed in the midst of deliberate, tender kisses. The minty taste of his kiss flooded her mouth and melted away her hesitation in the way only a promise and a hope could. As Cash explored her throat, his stubble tickled the underside of her chin. This was more than she remembered. Deeper. A grown man on a mission. She teetered on the devastating edge of a Cash coma. She'd dissolve and slip down the drain, a puddle of the liquid fire burning through her veins.

"Sweet girl," wet lips whispered against her neck. Vibrations buzzed inside her, and her body responded with a desperate wetness that only Cash knew how to command.

Nicola swayed forward, her hand finding balance on the rigid plane of his abdomen. Cash cupped her jaw, thumbs skimming over her cheeks.

"You still with me, Nic?"

Absolutely. She nodded, a lust-drunk smile slipping onto her face. "Still here."

"Good."

"Wait." Pulling back, reaching for reality, she grabbed the shampoo bottle. "We're in here for a reason."

"Nah. I'm here 'cause you're the sweetest thing I've ever seen, and then you smiled."

Oh, the things he said to her. Heat flared in her cheeks, and she focused on action, rubbing a dollop of shampoo into a lather. She reached for his hair. Caring for him felt as natural as running kiss-first into the shower.

Her fingers massaged in the soap. Lathered hair feathered under the water. Zips of sensation spiraled from her fingertips. Cash's eyes closed. Sudsy, soapy water ran down his chiseled cheekbones and straight nose. All hints of the bruises were gone. His face was unmarred and unhurried.

"I missed you, Cash."

The corners of his mouth turned up, not quite into a grin, just an acknowledgement of this perfect moment.

She rinsed his hair clean, watching the last of the bubbles slip down his chest and over his torso, past the light dusting of hair that rolled down his stomach leading to his hardened shaft. Nicola felt twenty years old again. All she could do was stare. Each time she brushed and moved against him, shockwaves of excitement pulsed to her core.

Startling blue eyes caught her staring. Her breath hitched in her throat, a rare mixed reaction of nervousness, interest, and eagerness. His finger ran over her lips, then he kissed her mouth.

"Come here."

Water cascaded down her face, dripping off her eyelashes. Cash thumbed the droplets away and carefully lowered her down onto the massive shower's built-in ledge. The cool tile was a welcome contrast to his warm, strong hands. Cash knelt in front of her and nudged between her knees with his large hands. He was a massive man. Built powerful and beautiful, and his laser focus made her feel like the center of the universe.

She wanted him. Wanted them. Nerves and doubt could disappear. She had no interest in second guesses. Right now, they had the opportunity to make things whole again.

"In your truck tonight—I swear." Nicola cradled his chin in her fingers, holding his gaze to hers. "I trembled for your touch."

Honesty. It was the only thing she could offer. The only thing she knew might heal the aching, gaping hole. A hole just like hers that every deep breath in his arms helped to repair.

He took her hand in his, put her palm to his mouth, and kissed. His tongue stroked each finger. Nicola moaned, whispering his name. Steam danced around them. The heat of his touch swirled with memories. Thank God for the warm waterfall protecting them from the outside world.

Putting one word after another was too hard a task, and his kiss said that it was all right. She would be okay.

Cash leaned forward and nuzzled the valley between her breasts, then turned his attention to one stiff nipple. He drew it into his mouth, and the tip grew tighter against his gentle suction. Her sex ached for contact.

He moved to her other breast, repeating the action. She arched forward, needing to be against him. Needed to feel him covering her. Her hands threaded into his hair, moving with the lazy motion of his kisses. Lips, mouth, and tongue, he teased her. Heat bloomed within her, a magical feeling both intoxicating and addictive.

He whispered in their waterfall. "I'd wait a decade for you again. For this."

Her bottom lip quaked. Cash smoothed his hands over her stomach, gliding between her legs. His lips followed, creating a sensual trail her body craved. Nicola tightened her grip in his hair, shifting toward him. She swayed in place when his tongue licked her hip bone.

"Yes?"

She nodded, scared she'd given him a reason to stop.

Following the water's path, his mouth crept across her, inching toward her sex. A kiss captured her breath as he molded his lips and tongue against her heat. A curse slipped from her lips. Cash lowered the width of his shoulders between her legs, relaxing into place, spreading her legs further apart.

Her legs flexed around him. He kissed until she moaned, eyes closed. Water misted around her. One of his fingers teased and tested her sweet spot. He found her willing and wanting, then eased forward, retreated back, and started his seductive torture again. She couldn't catch her breath. She didn't want to. This was the beginning of exquisite madness.

The strength and restraint he showed was as much an aphrodisiac as seeing the man so intent on her climax. She wanted to watch, but couldn't. Her head drifted side to side, his name escaping on each gasp.

Teeth rasped over her. Cash's fingers speared her as she pushed toward him. A thrilling build started. Feminine muscles tightened. The tight bud of nerves praised his loving attention. An internal, slow pulse started deep within her body, that she knew Cash would drive straight to an explosion.

He growled sweet words against her and thrust his fingers each time she rocked into him.

Nicola cried out as she unraveled, pushing for more and rocketing away almost as fast. An internal supernova— heat and energy—blasted from deep within. Her climax exploded from her core, vibrating to her hands that clung onto the granite and her toes that flexed against the tile floor.

A deep breath rolled into her lungs. She sighed, and he stilled, catching her with his sapphire stare. Watching him was bliss.

Cash leaned back, water rushing over him and framing his face. His smile looked like she felt.

"Hi." It was the only thing her brain could manage.

He hitched a one-sided grin. "Hey." He grabbed her purple shower poof and sudsed it up with foaming bubbles. "Give me a second."

Whatever you say.

He'd smell like a flower and didn't look like he cared. From shoulders to kneecaps, he covered himself up in bubbles. He snagged a handful of bubbles and put them on her nose.

"You're adorable."

No one had called her adorable in years. Warm, fuzzy compliments tended to evaporate in the wake of castrating looks. Funny, she didn't mind it from him.

"Let me take you to bed." He turned off the water and leaned over. "Wrap around me."

Nicola bear-hugged his sturdy body, and they eased out of the shower. Cash grabbed a handful of towels, put one on the counter, and set her on it. He started with one foot, drying her. Methodical as he was tender, he worked up her leg to her shoulders, then back down to the other foot.

She was speechless.

No one had ever paid that much attention to her, and his face said this move was a first for him too. She kissed him a thank you and kissed him again because no moment had ever been sweeter.

He picked her off the counter and sent her world spinning counter-clockwise. Her blood rushed to life again at the sight of her bed. Sex with Cash had been spectacular before, and the anticipation of him holding her, being in her, made her stomach twist into a thousand excited knots.

Cash pulled back the covers, placed her under a sheet, and slipped in next to her, pulling the comforter over their heads. Cocooned away from the world, it was just her and him, and everything felt as it should.

"My sweet girl." He'd left the lights on, and they could see each other under the bedding canopy. "Hope you know you're not leaving this bed until sunup."

"You've said worse things to—"

Knock, knock, knock.

She giggled like they'd been caught breaking a rule and whispered the obvious. "Someone's at my door."

His fingertip traced down her nose. "Do not engage the enemy."

She giggled again.

Bam, bam, bam.

Both hands were over her mouth, losing the battle with an attack of the giggles. "Cash, we have to answer."

"Why?"

"What if it's impor—"

A voice growled through the door. "Nicola, I know you're in there. I need to talk to Cash, and I can't find him anywhere."

She lost the battle, laughing out loud, eyes watering. "We're so busted."

And Jared was so killing the mood.

Nicola sat up, pushing the covers off of them, and Cash looked ready to kill his boss. She could only imagine the things Cash would say once the two men were alone.

Cash-the-sniper, not the man from the bathroom, lumbered out of her bed, grabbed his gym shorts, and stepped into them, cursing Jared with every passing step.

He opened the door and leaned his elbow above his head on the doorjamb, blocking any view inside the room. Good, it gave her a chance to watch without Jared seeing her wrapped in the comforter. It also gave her one hell of a view of Cash. Those gym shorts might as well have been made for his body.

"Better be good, boss man."

"I thought you two were old history." She could hear everything Jared said, and maybe that was Jared's point.

"What do you want?"

"Hey, princess, I thought we talked about keeping it in your pants."

"Watch yourself, Jared," a woman's voice warned from the hallway. Mia Winters. It had to be. No other woman was around, at least that she knew about. From what she'd heard, Mia was one hell of a firecracker. Maybe Nicola could hang with her some this weekend.

"Hey, Mia," Cash said. "Still wandering the halls?"

Jared ignored Cash, responding to Mia. "Just 'cause you're all cute and pregnant doesn't mean you get to talk to me like that."

"My house, my rules, big boy. Play by them or go home."

Jared spoke back to Cash. "I need high explosive, incendiary tipped, green tracer .50 caliber ammunition by oh eight hundred. I've got nothing armor piercing. Can you and Miss Betty hook me up?"

"Nothing at home. You ask Roman?"

"He's got nothing incendiary. You two are worthless."

"Brock normally keeps a stash of—"

"We're all dry. Fuck special requests from governmental bureaucrats. They want to start picking the color of tracers? They've played too many games of Call of Duty."

"Sorry, man. Don't know what to tell you."

"Find a shirt. You and Roman have to head over to HQ. Check everywhere, I need that ammo."

Hard pause. Nicola almost felt his jaw drop to his bare feet. "What?"

"Not kidding. Get your ass dressed, Cash, and get to work."

"Fuck you."

"More like fuck no one tonight, buddy."

Jared would pay for this stunt. Jerk. She'd have his ass if Cash didn't.

Cash didn't move from the door. "You can't be serious."

"Never more," he said with a grumpy laugh.

"Fine, and a big fuck you."

"Like I said—"

Cash slammed the door. Nicola sat up in the middle of bed. He turned. Brooding. Intense.

They stayed silent, looking at one another. The tension hadn't slipped out when he'd opened the door. The air was just as charged as before the shower.

"I'm not going anywhere."

Was the room too warm? It felt too warm and too small with too many pillows. Just the two of them in a tiny room with a ginormous bed. She tried to catch her breath.

Cash's jaw flexed. The blue in his eyes sparkled. Every tight muscle looked ready to pounce.

Nicola shifted under the covers. The fabric swished. The pulse in her neck thumped faster and again faster, and she hoped he'd ignore any protest. "But—"

"Do you really think I care?"

Nope. Didn't look like he cared about anything outside of the bedroom. She shook her head slowly, her stomach launching into her throat. Potent sparks zinged around the room. Cash was coming toward her to take her right here and now, and nothing short of her saying no would stop him.

Holding her tightly with a virile gaze, he stalked forward. Then took another step. The heavy weight of anticipation wrapped its fists around her chest, squeezing. Her breaths compressed. Her mouth watered, but she didn't move. She couldn't.

Excitement warmed between her legs. Cash approached as if on a mission to devour and destroy his target. And then he was bedside, broadside, leaning over her, caging her against a wall of pillows with just his arms.

"But?" He took a deep breath and let it out against her skin. "You don't want me to stay?"

No way would she speak. No way could she try. Her body had abdicated control to him in the shower, and her mind was one sensual touch away from waving a white flag. He knew it too. His eyes danced, knowing that she was only his.

Cash nudged her hair away from her ear and whispered, "'Cause I can leave if that's what you want, babe."

"Don't." Yeah, her voice quivered and trembled with the acoustic equivalent of her stomach's reaction to his whisper.

His lips skimmed across her cheek, hovering over hers. His breath tickled. Fire exploded under their lazy, brushed kiss. "Say that again. Not sure I heard you."

Her head dropped back. Sensations tingled in her cheeks and slalomed down her back. Slow, heavy breaths purred out, the warmth crashing against his very close face. "Don't you dare leave this room."

His body eased onto the bed, forearms above her head. Pinned in place, Nicola lifted her chin and closed the distance. His mouth took hers. His temples slid to her cheek, and he pulled her into his kiss. He groaned, and deep within her belly, Nicola needed him all the more.

The covers shifted, and he lost the shorts, sharing with her the bulge that fabric hadn't hidden. Heavy and hard and hungry. Cash swaddled the covers around them, drowning her in a fury of deep kisses. Her legs shifted, and his body fell into place. The silky smooth glide of his shaft rolled between the vee of her legs.

The taste of mint remained in his mouth. She probed with her tongue, needing and searching for more of him. Pangs of desire flushed through her. He cupped her body to him, tenderly caressing her breasts, thumbing her nipples. With each delicious flick of pressure, she readied for him. Silky moisture dampened her sex.

Her hips reached for more contact. Her pussy ached, rocking against his bare shaft. The build-up was too much. When it seemed like her desire couldn't jump any higher, his talented fingers slid between them, over her mound, and into her juices. He danced over her nerve endings, driving her to the edge of sexual insanity.

Sweet Cash. "I need you," she said on a gasp. "I don't want to wait any longer. It's been too long."

She felt his torturing hand fall back and position his erection against her, stealing her breath. She wanted to beg and fought to move, but in that moment, she could only stare at his perfect face.

"Nicola." He breathed out her name, eyes closed, body pressed against her wetness. The blunt head of his erection tested entry. She was ready for him, wanted him more than she could understand. He whispered, "I missed you."

And I love you.

Her mouth shut to make sure she didn't say that aloud. He didn't jump away, so *love* was only in her brain. His hips rolled forward, inching into her. Her opening parted for him, muscles melting away at his command, starting the luminous ecstasy that only he could create.

Love. Love and sex were confusing. Love and sex were often mixed up. Cash withdrew his shaft from her, and her mouth hung open. Gasping for breath, she prayed for his return. Her hips flexed. The need for him to fill her again overwhelmed her. He did. Again and again.

He thrust and kissed, and everything became clear. She loved him. Always had and never stopped.

Her fingers laced into his hair, and she smiled from the inside out. Her legs wrapped around his waist. He moaned into the curve of her neck, biting and kissing. His blond stubble scratched and marked her. A tornado of nerve endings twisted alive from her flesh to her core, starting the unmistakable build she craved.

Nicola mouthed his name. She thrashed for more, needing his strength and power to push her to climatic heaven. She felt the rhythm of their perfect dance. Sapphire blue eyes locked onto hers, Cash took her hands in his, threading their fingers together.

They drove in sync and on fire, deeper and farther than Nicola remembered possible. Her building ripple of muscles tightened around his erection. She cried out, he pulled away from her, and she fought it, needing him. *I won't ever leave again.* And she held on tightly, pushing into him. Her orgasm exploded. Her body vibrated, every muscle taking its turn, clenching and releasing around him.

He came with her, in her, reviving her climax.

One breath, and then a longer one. Her eyes opened in lazy satisfaction.

Panic.

She saw wide-eyed, mouth-open panic. He'd turned to stone, unmoving, breath held. The color shattered from his beautiful face.

"Cash?"

"Oh God."

"Wh—"

"I wasn't thinking. Then I couldn't—"

What?

Oh. She hadn't been thinking either.

Nicola framed her hands around his cheeks, still catching her breath. "We're fine." She'd never heard him like that before. He was terror-stricken. "You're okay. Birth control. We're okay, Cash."

He didn't move, frozen, cemented, stuck in time.

Oh no.

Her stomach dropped. "Are you okay-okay?"

"Yeah. Yes. Of course." Well, that snapped him to attention. He sucked down a gasp, then a calmer breath. "So we're okay."

She smiled, nodding, and he moved. A sensitive flash of nerves reminded her that she was more than okay. Cash's forehead dipped down, touching hers. He relaxed and, finally, a deep breath fell from his lips.

Cash rolled to her side. Strong arms gathered her up, her back to his chest, and held her close to him. A powerful leg locked over her thigh. He tugged the blankets around them and smoothed her hair.

"I'm sorry, Nic." His voice was heavy and low. He twisted a strand of her hair around his finger.

"Why?"

"You deserve romance and flowers and stuff, and all you got was Jared hitting the fast forward button and me freaking out."

She stared at the mocha-colored wall, feeling Cash stroke her hair. "That was both of our faults. But it isn't a problem. Right? So we move on."

"I should've—"

"Stop." She turned to him. "We're not that couple on a first date. We're not playing by the normal rule book."

He smiled. "Very logical, Nic."

She gave him an I'm-super-clever grin and laughed. "Nope. Just observant. I observe. I conclude. I react. You might say it's my specialty."

They laughed together, and she turned back to the wall, snuggling into his hold once again. He kissed the back of her shoulder. "Smartass."

"I thought it was sweet girl." She looked over her shoulder with a smile and wrinkle of her nose.

He kissed her softly. "Smartass. Sweet girl. Perfect woman. Whatever works—"

Knock, knock, knock.

Go away, Jared.

"Nicola, don't make me ask if Cash is in there." The muffled voice bled through the door.

Nope, not Jared.

Go away, Roman.

Cash kissed her again. "I think that's my cue. I'm sorry, Nic."

She shrugged a naked shoulder. "It's part of the job. I'll see you tomorrow sometime. Morning meeting, I guess?"

He shook his head. "My morning would be a hell of a lot better if I woke up next to you."

Bam. Bam. Bam.

Go away!

"But I gotta run. Go to sleep. Soon as I'm done, I'm crawling back into this bed."

"I sleep with a gun under my pillow. That might be a bad idea."

"So look before you shoot."

"All right." She laughed, snuggling down in the covers. "I'll look first."

He snagged his shirt and shorts off the ground, threw them on, and loomed over her in bed. "Night, Nicola Garrison. Sweet dreams."

CHAPTER FOURTEEN

Nicola woke up to the scent of her shampoo and the heavy weight of solid muscle draped over her. *Cash.* A warm rush swirled in her stomach, and a blush heated her cheeks. He'd sneaked back into bed during the night without waking her. Then again, he was a sniper: an undetectable liquid shadow.

"Morning, Nic." Arms that had caged her to the bed last night pulled her against his warm chest. *This is a deep-sigh kind of nice.*

"Morn—" The alarm clock read thirty-three minutes after it should have gone off. Had she set it? Shit. "Oh my God, I'm late. We're late. We have to—"

"We don't have to meet for another half hour or so."

Nicola sprang up and out of bed, tearing through her overnight bag. "I have to get ready."

"Throw on some clothes."

"I can't just throw on clothes. I have to get ready. It's a chick thing."

"It's just a bunch of dudes. No one to impress."

She smirked at him. Grabbing a brush, she combed her ragamuffin bed-head into a bun.

"Cash?"

He relaxed against the headboard, and his eyes twinkled as he enjoyed the show.

She moved around like a woman on speed, desperate for her missing makeup bag. "What are you looking at?"

She was still naked. Running around, naked and crazed. *Clothes. Must find clothes.*

His smile said it all. He didn't have to open his mouth. "Just watching. Better than a cup of coffee."

"Get up. Get dressed. We're late." She tugged on fresh panties and a matching bra. They were a little flashy. Maybe subconsciously, when she'd packed them, she'd hoped to wear them for him. Well, he saw her now and looked thrilled. "Cash! Come on."

"All right, all right. I'm up."

He stood up, just as naked as she'd been. And he *was* up. *Oh, Lord.* Her stomach dropped to the floor. Every womanly part of her body screamed for her to hold him. Whoa, that was a hell of a reaction.

"Nic, you're staring. Not complaining, but you should know I'm down with going back to bed and earning a slap on the wrist for rolling in late." He winked at her, and her stomach jumped, only to fall back down.

No. Concentrate. For all intents and purposes, this was her first day at a new job. Even though the CIA still owned her, she was on loan. New co-workers. New people to size up and make an impression on. Rolling in late, when everyone surely knew her history with Cash, would be catastrophic.

"Put your clothes on. I can't be late."

"You can be whatever you feel like, sweet girl." Cash stretched, and every muscle in his body rippled.

"Well, I feel like holding on to my reputation." *Ouch, that was harsh.* She knew his standing with ladies well enough. He didn't flinch, though. "Sorry, that's not what I meant. I've tried hard to make every man I work with see me as capable. Just one of the guys."

"Nah. I get it. I'll leave you to get dressed. You show up when you do, looking however you do. Gorgeous, I'm sure. And I'm gonna mosey to the great room, meet up with everyone, and get some coffee."

Her shirt hung in her hand. Cash scooped his clothes off the floor and turned for the door to the adjoining room.

"Wait," she said, causing him to pivot. "You like?" She modeled the lacy red bra with a spin.

"I   like."   He   paused.   "Come   here."

She was in his arms in a second. Wrapped against his bare chest, his fine chest hair tickling her skin, she found a good argument for running late. He slanted his mouth over hers and ran his fingers into her messy bun. The tender touch elicited a sigh. This was definitely a lets-run-late morning kiss. His smile broke the intensity as he pulled back. His fingers petted her cheek. "Do your thing. I'll see you downstairs."

She continued to stare after he'd shut the door, wondering how this was possible and if it was too good to be true.

Rocco, Roman, and Brock were kicked back on the large leather couch, wolfing down steak and eggs. The smell alone was almost enough to drag Cash out of Nicola's bed, but when she gave him the final push, he'd high-tailed it downstairs to get some Mia-style cooking.

Voices in the kitchen drifted into the room. Winters. Jared. Some of the other guys. Breakfast was set up family style on a large table in the great room. Big, juicy-looking steaks. Heaping piles of scrambled eggs, knowing Mia, filled with sharp cheddar cheese. Biscuits and a bowl of gravy. *God love Mia Winters.* Holy hell, she could cook.

Plate piled high, he perched on the oversized chair and chowed down. Jared grumble-laughed from the kitchen. At least the bastard wasn't in a terrible mood. Maybe someone had been able to find his stupid, flippin' ammo. Green tracer and all. He and Roman hadn't, and they'd searched while Cash had been away from Nic's bed. It was almost eight in the morning. If Jared was still here and laughing, the morning meeting wouldn't be as bad as Cash'd guessed it might be.

Nicola rounded the corner. A freakin' vision of tough girl beauty. She didn't overdo the makeup, didn't show off the lacy bra that had almost brought him to his knees. No, she rocked a tight pair of jeans over those skyscraper legs. He noticed a small bulge at her ankle. Ankle holster. That was hot, no questions asked. And that shirt loved her curves. Cash looked at the guys. All of them but Roman noticed too.

Roman lifted his chin to her. "Morning."

She said her hellos, joked with the boys, and grabbed a plate and some coffee. She was perfect, the picture of ease, and gave the impression he was sure she wanted. Smart. Stealthy. And lethal. She had the I-can-kill-you-with-a-toothpick look. Dead sexy. Whether she tried or not, wanted others to notice or not, the woman was an attention grabber.

"Cash." She nodded, treating him just the same as the others, as if they were a secret. This was fun. She was fun. He could handle this game.

He played along. "Nicola."

Roman rolled his eyes. Rocco watched today's version of their reality show unfold. Brock watched Nic. More curious than interested, but Cash would have a talk with Brock about that later.

Jared and Winters walked into the room. Jared looked like the grumbling asshole he always was. Winters looked like he could use a shave, the way he always did. Same old thing, just another Saturday morning when half the guys were shipping off somewhere for some job that required a green tracer, and a few others were readying a plan to smoke out a CIA mole.

Jared interrupted the breakfast chatter. "Morning, assholes. And lady." He nodded to Nicola, who nodded back. "Those going with me, we leave soon as that fuckin' ammo arrives. Fucking desk jockey, wannabe commandos, and their color requests. The rest of you are working with Cash and Nicola, who's from the CIA."

Cash liked the sound of them working together. In the last twenty-four hours, his opinion of her in the field had changed. Slightly. He still wasn't thrilled. He hated the reality of it but, hell, she was doing it with or without his permission. With or without him by her side. So fuck it. Better to be on her side.

Right?

Maybe?

She could shoot. She could hold her own at hand-to-hand. She could throw down with the toys and the training the CIA gave her. She was good. Impressive. He liked the calculating, sparring Nicola, the adult Nicola, the woman who knew what worked for her and wasn't afraid to embrace it. And spy games worked for her, so he'd deal. Kinda.

He stood up to stretch and put away his plate. Something to concentrate on besides Nic.

Jared continued, "So who here hasn't met Miss CIA-herself? Nicola Garrison. Anyone?"

Roman shot coffee out his nose. Whoops. That probably didn't go the way Nic had planned. Roman was on his feet. "Excuse me? Garrison?"

Cash felt his cheeks catch fire and stole a glance at Nic. She wasn't fazed. Didn't respond, other than a roll of her eyes.

Roman stepped toward Cash. "What the fuck? I thought you said you weren't sure about her. That sounds pretty fuckin' sure."

Oh fuck. He told Roman he hadn't been sure if they were really done because he didn't know what was going on with her. Damn it, he was sure that he was interested in finding out. Then he had found out, and everything fell into place. Shit was working out. But coming from Roman's lips, it sure sounded like he wasn't sure about Nicola.

Her face was tight. Imperceptible to anyone but him. He knew that face too well, and she was hurting. Goddamn Roman.

"Why is it that I'm always refereeing high school drama with you guys?" Jared growled. "Princess, explain yourself. Roman, sit down. Cash, I don't care what you do. Keep standing for all I care."

"CIA gave it to me, Roman. Cut your shit out." That Nicola sounded pretty damn tough and to the point. Props to his girl. *His girl.* That sounded good.

"So you aren't…" Roman gestured.

"What, Cash and I ran off to Vegas last night? Give me a flippin' break."

"Oh."

Yeah, jumpy asshole.

Rocco threw a handful of biscuit in his mouth like he was at a movie theater munching on popcorn. Winters laughed, looking confused but loving the drama. *And I want everyone to mind their own business.*

Winters's cell went off.

Jared smiled. "That'd be my ammo. I can't wait to get away from you assholes."

Winters answered his phone, telling the delivery boy how to get through the NASA-like security gate and to his front door. He ended the call with, "—and the door is open."

Good. Get Jared the hell out of here so they could map out Operation Catch-the-Butler with less of a headache.

Jared's cell buzzed. "What the fuck? Hold on." He stomped out of the room and slammed the door.

Clack. Clack. Clack. Heels clicked down the hall. Bright lipstick and fuck-me hair rolled around the corner carrying a big box marked EXPLOSIVE.

Fuck me.

Her trademark Girls Love Guns shirt was pulled over a set of fake tits he knew too well. Painted on leather pants were held up by a belt buckle of dueling silver pistols. Pretty much her uniform of a guy's wet dream.

Sugar.

Fucking Sugar.

Well, fucking Sugar was the problem. Damn it.

Cash looked at Winters and whispered, "What the fuck, man?"

Winters shrugged, obviously not having a flippin' clue. "When you guys came up empty-handed, I called Sugar."

Cash had once tried to set Winters up with Sugar, but not really. He knew the guy wouldn't take the bait, and Winters was being such an asshole that someone had to show him the only woman in the world he wanted was Mia. Cash did that for him. They should name their first baby Cash—boy or girl—because he pretty much considered their make-up and marriage his doing.

Maybe Sugar would behave, although that wasn't one of her many talents. She'd never met Jared before and had always wanted to. Of course she'd behave in front of Jared. She wanted more of the man's business at her gun shop. The woman could build the hell out of a high powered rifle. Titan would be the gold standard of clients, the way they went through guns and rounds.

Winters stood. "Sugar, girl. Thanks much. We owe you."

Her smile was as sweet and fake as her name. "That you do. Where's my boy? Why didn't he call me?"

She pivoted on the heel of a stiletto that might as well have been a pointed dagger. She snagged Cash with a stare, and he stood helpless, not sure what the fuck he should do. Extend a hand? *Shake the woman's hand.* It was a plan. He stepped forward with every intention of a proper hi-how-ya-doing, but she snaked a pink painted nail through his belt loop and threw the other arm around his shoulder. *Fuck.*

"Cash, baby. No call, no show. What's the deal, babe? Our boy, Mister One-Woman-Man, has to call. Tsk, tsk, baby. Tsk, tsk."

The first lesson in sniper school was controlling the mind and body. Controlling breaths. Slowing the heartbeat. Acting and reacting perfectly in the worst possible situations. Well, this might be the worst possible, but there was no way his heart was listening to his commands. For every "slow the eff down," it sped up. Right now it was going through a bang, bang, bang crescendo.

"Sugar." He coughed a hello and shrugged out of her perfumed embrace. Nicola slammed them a glare so powerful, he was surprised to find his feet still on the floor.

Sugar took in the room. "I'm not sure that I know everyone." Who knew Sugar could do anything understated, sarcasm included? "Cash, introduce me please, darh-ling."

This sucks.

"Sugar, I don't believe you've met Nicola. Nic, Sugar owns a gun club I belong to. Gun range, shop, stuff like that."

Sugar purred, "Yes, stuff like that. Nicola, was it?"

"Nicola *Garrison.*" Nic for the point. That was good. He'd take it.

"Sister?"

"Not a chance, Sugar." Nicola smiled, cold and frosty for the win, at least against Sugar. Nic still looked homicidal.

A door down the hall banged open. Jared walked in a second later and slammed to a stop. "You're Sugar?" His mouth hung open. "Cash's Sugar?"

Sugar made some sort of hell-yes noise. There was no Cash's Sugar. The two of them were casual and occasional, nothing that allowed for possession, and all about blowing off some pressure, when it was needed. And it hadn't been needed in a while.

Jared slapped his thigh. "Well, fuck—"

"Shut up, Jared." Cash didn't have time for this shit. Sugar needed to get out. Fast.

Jared looked at Nic. Sugar looked at Nic. Everyone but Cash looked at Nic. He was content to shoot daggers at Jared. Rocco choked on his biscuit. Winters's eyebrows rose as he caught on to Cash's nightmare. Goddamn it.

Sugar sized Jared up, combat boots to jarhead cut. "You're Jared?"

"I'm everything. Jared will do though."

"Humble, I see."

"You look like your name."

"I look like a lot of things, Jared. Doesn't mean you're right."

They squared off. Everyone was tense. Pissed off women were trouble. Pissed off at him was a disaster, as far as Cash was concerned. "Alrighty, Sugar. We have to get started." If Jared wasn't going to wrap up this meet and greet, Cash would. Sugar needed to get gone. Now.

"Soon as someone pays up, I'm outta here, cowboy."

"Right. Let's do this. Come with me." Jared walked out, probably expecting Sugar to follow. He needed to learn a little more about her before he could make those educated guesses. Sugar did what she wanted, no matter who was looking or ordering.

"So, Cash, baby. You coming over after this job's done?"

"He's not. But thanks for inviting him." Nic was on it, spitting sweet sarcasm. All Cash could do was watch.

"Not sure I was talking to you."

"Not sure I care."

"Sugar! Get out here," Jared yelled from the hall. "I do not have time for this shit."

Sugar walked over to Cash, and his stomach turned. Nothing good was about to happen. She went up on tiptoes and kissed his cheek, only because he took a step back and avoided the lip press. "Bye, cowboy. See ya later."

Jared grumbled from the hall. "I told you assholes, no chick problems. I'm about to make it part of your contracts."

Damn. Faster than Cash could take out a target with Miss Betty, this day had gone from for-the-records-book awesome to knee-in-the-nuts awful.

CHAPTER FIFTEEN

That woman, all sex-in-heels, rolled out of the room. All the men save for Cash waved goodbye. At least he had some smarts.

Nicola sipped her coffee and ignored the male tongues hanging to their combat boots. Mia'd have to get the place wet-vacced for all the drooling they were doing. For the moment, it didn't seem as if anyone thought about Cash's girls being ready to knock knuckles. As for acting professional and making a good impression on her first day with a new team? Nicola's morning had gone down in messy, gossip-worthy flames.

At least she'd tried to look nice this morning. She could have used an extra few minutes, but she didn't look bad. Not perfect. Certainly not let's-run-into-an-ex good.

Sugar was all va-va-voom and then some. Was that what Cash liked? All plumped up and plastic?

Maybe her opinion of Sugar was a tad too harsh, and Nicola did like that Girls Like Guns shirt. The way it was poured over Sugar, Nicola bet Cash and every man in the room liked it too. Well, except for Jared. He'd need a two-by-four to the brain to notice anyone but himself.

Jared droned on about tactical this and strategic that, all very important. Too bad she wasn't listening.

"Princess." Jared's raspy voice pulled her from her pity party of one.

"Hmm?"

"You and me and Cash. Dining room. Now."

Great. Where was Cash anyway? Chasing after his Sugar? What the eff? It didn't matter. They were on two completely different paths. How had she not noticed that? Here she was, choking up over nostalgic thoughts from last night. And there he was, searching out a woman made for fantasies, who threw herself at his boots. Ugh.

Sugar could have him. Nicola knew better. Her job was her life. One game was enough. No need to play two at a time, and Cash was the player king, just like Rocco had said. Freakin' awesome. She'd either misread Cash, or maybe hoped she hadn't heard the truth.

"Princess, move your caboose," Jared called from the hallway.

Yeah, yeah. Coming. She followed his steps to the dining room, strangling both her hands around her coffee cup. No one would notice that they shook if she didn't let go. Her adrenaline after the quick-flash Sugar-showdown needed to wear off.

Cash stepped over the threshold. Sapphire eyes caressed her, and she vividly remembered clinging to him last night. The memory made her ache.

"Nic, I need to talk to you for a sec—"

"No, you don't." Jared put his box marked EXPLOSIVES on the fancy dining room table and pulled a switchblade from his waist. "My time, my agenda. And your mamsy-pansy baloney concerns come later."

For the first time, Nicola was glad for Jared's interruptions. She had no interest in hearing the whos and whys and hows of Sugar and Cash. Even if Cash hadn't known that Nicola was alive, he could at least have the decency to knock boots with someone a little less vamp-on-display. Though her belt buckle was kinda awesome. *I wonder where she found that thing.* Whatever. Sugar and her glammed-up face, super fun shirt, and awesome belt buckle could go somewhere else.

Jared pulled out the brick of ammo and put it on the delicate lace tablecloth. He took out another box. What the—?

"Jared. Stop. Right now." She moved fast, almost dropping her coffee mug and pushing the man over.

"Princess, what the hell?"

Nicola picked up the box, examined it, then unpacked each small box from the larger one.

Jared tried to take the one in her hands. "Get off my—"

"Jared, shut up." If this hadn't been a big what-the-hell moment, she might've looked up to see how Twinkle Toes reacted to such an order. But nope. She was dizzy with questions.

She popped open the box top and rolled out the large round. Blue tipped with a fleck of red. Incendiary and armor piercing, just as requested. Matching the mark on the boxes, there were the micro-engraved letters 'AS' on the bottom of the round.

That egocentric jerk.

"Where did—" Nicola smirked "—*Sugar* get this?"

Jared made a move for the ammo again. "I don't ask questions. I didn't even call her."

Cash spoke up. "Winters called her."

She pointed to the base of the round, ignored Cash, and handed the bullet to Jared. "AS. Antilla Smooth. This is his product. He likes to use his initials for his watermark. Your girl buys from a nasty, illegal arms dealer."

"She's legit." Cash stepped forward to defend that woman.

Freakin' awesome. "Yeah, she totally looks it."

Jared nudged Cash back. "I'm not going to separate you two, and you're still working together. So deal. Now."

They both murmured about nothing to get over. *The tension in this room would choke a horse.*

Jared gathered the small boxes and dumped them into the bigger one. "I have to roll out. What's here is here. I suggest the two of you find some way to work together with your clothes on, and move forward on the butler. Do your jobs."

He grabbed his EXPLOSIVES box and stormed out. Jared didn't really walk into or out of a room. He didn't amble or dawdle. The man stormed and marched, always with gray clouds in his eyes.

Cash stared at her. "Nic—"

"I don't want to hear it. I'm here to do a job." She picked up her coffee mug, needing something for her hands.

"That's it. A job? You see one thing from my past and you're don—"

She blew out a breath. "Excuse me. I have to make a call."

"To who?"

"Not your problem."

"Cut the attitude. We're partnering on this, so it is."

"I'm calling my handler. She needs to know Smooth hardware is popping up in Virginia."

"Mind focusing on one job a time?"

She held up a finger. "One phone call. One minute."

"Suit yourself."

Nicola walked to a window, and Cash stepped out of the dining room. Breathing got easier the farther he was away from her. Dialing a secure number, Nicola waited until Beth answered.

"How goes the sleepover?" Beth's curiosity made Nic's stomach turn.

"It went, and it was a mistake. And, nope, I don't want to talk about it."

"You did bring something lacy!"

"Seriously, Beth. He's got a girl. Kinda. I think. And I met her." She shook away the image of Sugar wrapping her body around Cash. "And that's why I'm calling."

"No, babe. We're not putting out a hit on the girl. Girlfriend or not. Sorry."

Wouldn't that be nice? "I just saw ammo from our favorite deceased gun dealer. Did you have any idea he had networks in this area? Sellers?"

"Nope."

She sipped her lukewarm coffee, thinking out the next move. "We need to meet."

"You're working with Titan. I'm hands off until further notice."

"What if I promise to kiss and tell?"

"Would you?" There was a pause, and she could feel Beth weighing the pros and cons of the dirty details. "Then yes. I'm there."

"Meet me for lunch in Tyson's Corner in an hour."

"Done."

She clicked off the phone and went to find Cash. How did she end up at the Titan retreat without a ride? One mistake after another.

Clearing her throat, she grabbed his attention. "Cash, I need to borrow your truck."

He laughed. "Try again."

She turned toward Roman. His brow furrowed. "Don't even think about asking. I'm not getting into it with either of you."

Shit. It's not like a taxi was going to pick her up in where-ever-the-hell-Virginia. "Damn it, Cash."

He smiled, knowing he was her only option, and she hated it. "I'll drive ya. Where we going, Nic?"

If he would hand over the damn keys, everything would go easier. Maybe she could find them in his room. "*We* aren't going anywhere."

"Yeah, guess that's true. I stay. You stay. We all get to stay." He flopped on the couch next to Rocco, who was watching the latest installment of their drama. "If you change your mind, I'll be here." He turned to Roman. "Hey, man. Throw me another biscuit."

Roman chucked the biscuit across the room, and out of nowhere, Winters's dog nabbed it mid-flight. Roman tried again, successfully.

How did anyone put up with these men? Her foot tapped, and her mind ran the gamut of getaway vehicles, but she turned up nothing. Damn Cash.

"All right. Let's go."

"While I drive, I'll explain Sugar, and you'll listen." He didn't look at her. His voice was even and bored. Rocco, on the other hand, wasn't bored, and Cash didn't look at the man's head slinging back and forth between them. "Those are my terms. Take it or leave it. But I don't think you'll find someone willing to risk their life and give you a ride."

Risk their life? Come on, Cash!

She dropped her head back and huffed. Mark today down as the most unprofessional day of her life. "Fine."

"Fine."

Rocco laughed. "You two are great. When are you coming back?"

"Shut it, Roc." Roman didn't like the theatrics at all. Nic didn't either. Maybe it was a family thing.

Trapped again in his truck with Nicola proved to be much different from the night before. There wasn't that would-they-wouldn't-they vibe.

Nope.

Now it was nothing but hold-your-breath-and-hang-on kind of tension, and it still made him want to beat his head against the steering wheel.

"Where to, Nic?"

"Tyson's Corner."

"Got it." He rolled out of Winters's driveway. "Sugar. Let's just get that over with."

"I don't care." She shrugged and tugged at her hair.

"Pretty sure you do." A pissed-off Nicola was cute. The madder, the cuter. Bet she'd get furious if he told her as much. "There's nothing to be jealous—"

"Are you kidding me? Jealous? Hardly." She scooted farther away and leaned against her door. "That's ridiculous. You're ridiculous. Sugar, for that matter, is ten shades past ridiculous."

Silence except for the click-cl-click, click-cl-click of the blinker when he changed lanes. Everyone was ridiculous? She might as well have a banner proclaiming the same thing about herself.

"The lady doth protest too much."

Nicola smirked. "She's quite the girl, that Sugar. Your type is so… slutty."

You know what? Enough with this.

He pulled over. Hard. Dirt and gravel spun cycles in the wheel wells. The truck rocked over a bump on the shoulder.

"Why are you so mad? I didn't know you were alive! Fuck." He unsnapped his seatbelt and turned, hand gestures flying. "It wasn't serious, so what's your problem?"

Nicola didn't answer. Her fingers drummed on her thigh.

"Nicola, what do you want from me?"

She didn't turn to look him in the eye. "She's re-selling from an illegal arms dealer."

He shrugged. "We don't know what's going on there. And that's not your problem, is it?"

Now she pinned him with a glare. "She's a slut."

"She's a cool chick and not a girlfriend. Not relationship material. Not that I wanted a relationship with anyone. She's a flirt. And I am—was—whatever—by myself. She didn't want anything other than to shoot guns and... it worked out."

"Sure seemed into a relationship with you this morning."

"I didn't say Sugar wasn't competitive."

Nicola snorted. "Ha. Competitive."

He grabbed the gearshift but didn't take it out of park. They should hit the road. Sitting here wasn't doing either of them a lick of good. "I'm sure you've been the poster child for abstinence over the last decade."

She rolled her eyes, but stayed quiet.

"I didn't take you for a quitter, sweet girl."

Her face screwed up tightly. "I'm not a quitter."

"But you can walk away from us again?"

"There is no you and me, Cash. It was an old habit."

"Bull-fuckin'-shit."

"You're—"

His lips covered hers. How he crossed the space, he had no recollection. The only thing he knew was she smelled sweet, tasted sweeter, and kissing her was the only thing he'd wanted to do since Sugar walked into the room.

Her smartass remark morphed into a kiss. It melted against him, then roared to life. The air sizzled and popped. Her hands wrapped into his shirt. Yeah, there was no easy walking away. There was a spark. Hell, more than a spark. It was a smoldering ember that had blazed unattended and ignored. With a gust of wind, a sweet kiss, a hot night in bed—whoosh—they had wildfire. And he wanted to chase it down to see how hot it could be.

Her tongue teased his. Firecrackers spun and sparkled, rocketing his body to life. His fingers threaded into her hair, and he lost focus. He wanted to growl the goddamn truth to

Nic. Until they weren't, they were together. He wanted to—a car flew by too flipping close to his truck, honking a horn.

Whoa. He had to calm this down. They were on the side of the road, for chrissake.

Her lips slowed to brush his. "Maybe I was a little jealous."

Cash chuckled. "I want to take out any man who's ever thought of you naked, much less seen you, if that helps."

He inched back to his seat, studying her warm eyes and the way her flushed cheeks screamed that she wanted more than their roadside make-out. Both of his hands were needed on the steering wheel, or they'd never make it back onto the road. He took a deep breath. Her breath mirrored his from the passenger seat. Their matching cadence slowed to normal. He didn't know about Nic, but he was always catching his breath when she was around.

"Sugar shouldn't have that ammo." Nicola rearranged her seatbelt.

Nope, she was always thinking about the job around him. *That's just marvelous.* Someone out there would commend her. He'd rather she stayed hot and bothered and thinking of him, but that'd make the meeting with her handler a-w-k-w-a-r-d.

"She shouldn't. I know. But she's on the up and up, so there's something more to it." Cash sighed, sitting up and shifting into drive. "Looks like you and Sugar are headed for a sit down. I'll referee."

"Let's bring Rocco too. At this point, I think he'd be upset if he couldn't watch."

CHAPTER SIXTEEN

The sun was blinding bright. Nicola shuffled through her purse for her sunglasses. They were in a little Coach case that matched her little Coach purse. Maybe camouflaged was a better word than matched because she couldn't find the flippin' thing.

Cash walked through the parking lot with her. She wasn't sure what he was going to do. He didn't seem like the wander-around-the-mall type, but he'd insisted on driving, so he was stuck there. His activities for the next hour or so weren't her problem. Where were her sunglasses?

"Looking for these?"

"Yes!" She reached for them, and he held them high overhead. She jumped but still couldn't reach them. "Please. Give them to me."

"Are you still worked up about everything?"

"No." She jumped again. "Damn it, Cash. Give them to me already."

"I don't believe you." But he lowered the case to a snagging height. Jumping up again, she was almost nose to nose with him. His peppery scent flooded her senses, reviving memories of him in bed. Everything paused, and then her hand felt the fabric case, and life sped back up again.

"Why do you have my stuff?" This wasn't at all what she was worked up over.

"It just fell out of that black hole draped over your shoulder."

Why was she so nervous and twitchy? Oh yeah, because unless Cash found somewhere to wander off to, she was going to have to make introductions. There was no telling what would come out of Beth's mouth, especially after Nicola'd mentioned on the phone that Cash *maybe* had a girlfriend. And how Nicola had *maybe* shown off the little lacy number.

Beth waved at her from the patio at P.F. Chang's. Nicola's fingers tapped along with the nervous drumbeat in her head. Fifty yards and closing in on Question-Mageddon. Instead of a world-ending battle, Nicola expected an interrogation worthy of drop-dead-embarrassment. Or defensiveness. Hell, probably both.

Waving back to Beth, Nic turned to Cash and gave him a thanks-for-the-ride-see-you-later smile. He cheesed it back and stuck with her.

Twenty-five yards out.

She could ditch him. She had to. Beth had a cocktail in her hand. Cash had to go elsewhere, pronto. There was no telling if this was Beth's first or third, and after their thirsty throw down at her apartment, it didn't matter if it was only the first drink. The woman was primed to pry. Maybe she'd just push Cash and run.

"Cash, we're going to talk about girl stuff." He kept the slow pace, not moving from her side, and looking totally aware she wanted him gone like last week's garbage. "Like tampons and Spanx. You want nothing—"

"Girl, if you were into getting spanked, all you had to do was—"

"Spanx. *Spay-nhxx*. With an X. They're undergarments. Tummy suckers. Fat smoothers."

"None of which you have. That'll be a quick convo. Besides, I met Beth for a second at the Farm. She seemed like fun."

Fun? Try ready to incite a social disaster. "We have important personal stuff to talk about, and you're not invited."

"You're going to talk bedrooms and the Bullet? Or is that the Rabbit? I can never keep up with you girls and your toys."

"Cash," she hissed, abandoning the slow crawl and daring him to keep pace with her Olympic-speed race walk.

His long legs ate asphalt, easily keeping up with a casual amble. Ten yards out, and she hadn't scared Cash away yet.

Shit.

With an abrupt stop, Nicola turned to him. Maybe boring him away would work. "And recipes for gluten-free quiche. We're going to swap cooking tips. I recently learned how to poach an egg."

"I'm hanging out so you can't poison her opinion of me." Cash grabbed Nic's hand and swiped it to his mouth for a quick kiss. Oh, he was making a point, and knew damn well she wanted to dish on the Sugar incident. The guy should go into politics if he ever stepped away from the bam-bam-you're-dead business. He had a knack for putting on a show.

"Oh, you think you are so cute."

"That I do, sweet girl. That I do."

Ground zero. They were here. Beth stood, smiling, definitely on her second Sichuan Mary, Bloody Mary's pepper and spice cousin. Cash leaned over and kissed Nic's cheek. Damn him, he did that on purpose. Beth all but squeed.

Eh, maybe Nic did an inner squee too. When a man who caught everyone's attention passed out kisses, those kisses generally earned tummy flips. When those tummy-flipping kisses were accompanied by a grasp around the waist like he was doing now, they were bound to create moments of flash-bang paralysis.

A light breeze caught Cash's blond hair, ruffling it with an airy kiss and teasing her with the lavender smell of her shampoo. *Hmm. Showering with Cash.* It almost made her forget where they were and what they were doing.

The sound of a metal chair scraping on the patio brought her back to reality. Beth was all lip gloss and giggles. Great. That had to be her second drink.

"Beth, this is—"

"We've met." Cash leaned in to give Beth a hug.

Beth definitely squeed this time. *Fabulous.*

"I'm going to need a cocktail." Nicola looked for the nearest waitress and the specialty drink menu. "Something with a little kick—"

"I already ordered you a Twisted Whiskey Sour." Beth looked at her, then at Cash, and back to the drink menu she clutched. Concentrating, she studied it then glanced back at the towering man. "I'll order you a Warrior Smash. Sounds like it'd work for you."

"Cash was just leav—"

Beth protested, her mouth forming a big O, and Cash said, "Nope. I'd love to join you."

Nicola growled at him. Yes, she needed to hash out the Smooth ammo, but she *really* wanted Beth alone to hash out the Cash issue. Her and Cash. Sugar and Cash. Working and Cash. Everything. She needed Beth, by herself, and she didn't want to share.

Cash kicked back in a chair. He was all long legs and broad chest. The sun shone down on him, and he positively glowed. Such a gorgeous son of a bitch.

"Fine." Nicola huffed and sat down, still mentally willing Cash to get up and go inside the mall. He didn't move. Her Jedi-mind powers were a big, fat fail. "Let's talk Smooth ammo."

Her handler and best friend leaned forward, eyebrows bumping up a notch. "Let's talk about you two, since I have you both here."

"Very professional, Beth."

"Whatever. I'm pulling the best friend card right now." She feigned innocence. "Besides, technically, you two work together. I have paperwork and questions. Very important questions. Promise." She crossed her heart. The waiter arrived. Beth ordered for Cash. This was looking less and less like a working lunch and more like they were going to slurp lunch from tiki-umbrella-garnished glasses.

Batting those blond lashes, Cash played along with Beth. *Damn them both.*

"Question one. Go." His voice sounded husky and low. It made her want that Whiskey whatever-it-was-called. Right. Now.

"Question one: How's our girl look after ten years?"

A hot blush shot up Nicola's cheeks so fast that she thought steam would shoot out of her ears. "Beth!"

Cash laughed, leaned forward, and pinched a very serious face. "Better than she did the last time I saw her. And the last time I saw her, she was very cute and very naked."

Nicola tried to gasp, but couldn't. Stomach, meet throat. Throat, meet stomach. No need to breathe right now. Her insides were switching places.

Their drinks arrived, and if Nic could've talked, she'd have asked the waiter to bring her refill already. Or a pitcher.

Beth looked thrilled, positively couldn't-smile-bigger thrilled. How was that little gem about Nicola being cute and naked going to spell out in her CIA paperwork? It wasn't because this was a free-for-all fishing expedition. Nic should've promised to give every hot and bothered detail, and then maybe this wouldn't be happening. Plus, Rocco was missing this, and he'd just about die to see this installment.

Nicola took a big sip and a big breath. "Can we pul-leaze talk about the Smooth ammo?"

"Nah," Cash drawled. "This is way more fun. My turn. I know I'm a far distant second to the job, but when she called you, what came first? Me or the ammo?"

"You." Beth told the truth. She'd pay in some fashion.

"I knew it." He winked at Nicola, and she made a valiant effort to suck down her entire drink.

"Look, you two." Nicola needed to change the subject. "I'll play Truth or Dare, I'll get out the freakin' Ouija Board, but I want to get Smooth out of the way."

"All work and no play—" Cash started.

And Beth finished, "Makes Nicola Garrison a very boring girl."

Cash smiled. Big.

Oh no.

Cash smiled from her to Beth and back again. She knew what was coming. "Did I mention I was Cash Garrison?"

Sichuan Mary shot out of Beth's nose in a laugh and a cough and a choke. Her hands wrapped around her face, and the drink dribbled down her chin. She jumped—one would think to mop up the spillage—but nope. As soon as Beth looked able to ignore the peppery-vodka sting in her nose, she pointed at Nic, mouth hanging open. "Oh. My. God." Then she pointed at Cash, then her again. "Garrison? Garrison. Garrison?"

Patrons at the tables around them watched, amused, and having no idea what the deal was. Rocco would've got it. Man, he was missing another great episode of My Fucked-up Life.

Cash handed Beth a pile of napkins. How gentlemanly of him. Nic would've rather he choked on his Warrior Whatever because now Beth would have way more questions than when they'd started. She'd put all the blame for that in Cash's lap. It was easier to get mad and blame him than feel embarrassed about it.

Right...?

"Scandalous." Beth slapped her Sichuan-Mary-covered napkins down, and a tipsy giggle bubbled up. "Tell me more. There's got to be way more."

"I'll go tit-for-tat again." Cash loved this. She'd get him later too.

Beth wiped her hands on a clean napkin and tried, failing, for a serious stare. "Now, this may be the Absolut talking, but I think you two are cute together. Cute. Very—"

"Got it, Beth." Damn that vodka. P.F. Chang's needed rolls or breadsticks. Nic needed to shove a pile of carbs down Beth's throat to soak up some of the booze and maybe stifle her BFF's brilliant analysis.

"Cute," Beth continued, nodding her head up and down, on repeat. Where was a breadbasket when Nicola needed it?

"Did you know Nic has a very cute snore?" Cash asked.

Beth perched on the edge of her seat, clearly ready to get the juicy details. "Ten years ago or ten hours ago?"

Cash half-cocked a grin that flashed a dimple. "How much should we tell our good friend, Beth, Nicola?"

This was too much fun for both of them, and she wasn't touching that conversation topic to save her ever-loving breath. "So about the ammo—"

Beth ignored her. "Are all you guys at Titan super-flippin' hot? Cash. Roman. Jared." She ticked names off on her fingers. "We've got nothing right now. No one interesting. Well, David's interesting, but that's another story."

Man alive, the Sichuan Mary was courage in a glass. Nicola should have stolen Cash's keys when he wasn't looking and come alone.

Cash raised an eyebrow, laughing. "No comment."

Beth and Nicola reached the bottom of their drinks with a slurp. As if the waiter had been watching, he arrived with fresh drinks the second they came up for air.

"You'd better not hold out on me." Beth made a big show of switching her straw from one glass to the next, even though the new one already had a straw. "You're running around with all those Hottie McHottersons, and I want some of that."

Cash shrugged. "That could be arranged, I'm sure."

"Yes." Beth beamed, a third-drink-on-an-empty-stomach smile plastered on her face. "Thank you. Cash, I think I love you. You're the man."

Beth was throwing L-bombs and boosting his ego. Nic needed to catch the buzz train fast, or she was going to have to run to the bathroom and cry or scream or send a return-your-BFF-card-here text message.

The waiter was suddenly there again. Maybe her second whiskey had packed more of a wallop than she'd realized. "Would you like to order?" He stood there as if expecting... something. "Food?" he prompted.

Beth studied the drink menu for a second. "Noodles." She leaned over to Cash, her new best friend, and yell-whispered, "Do you want noodles?"

He gave her a wink. "I want whatever Nic wants."

Beth sighed loudly enough to turn the table behind her. Nic waved her glass to them, then looked at the waiter. "Can we have a sampler or something with lots of carbs?"

He nodded, clearly trying to figure out if they were good for their bill.

Cash spoke up. "Make that two samplers. And lots of noodles."

The big guy needed his food. Nicola finished off the rest of her drink and admired the way his shirt clung to his pecs.

Cash leaned over. "See something you want?" A flush flashed from her cheeks to her chest. "On the menu?"

Nicola pushed her shoulders back and smoothed a napkin over her lap until it started shredding. "I'd like to talk about David the Butler now. That is, if you two can handle it."

Beth's buzzy nod said so much about what she could and couldn't handle now or remember later.

"We already have our plan for the butler," Cash said to Beth. The grand plan must have been discussed when she wasn't listening to Jared yammer on because she had no idea. Cash continued, "And we're going to talk to Sugar—"

"That's her name? Sugar?"

Thank you, Beth. It was about time you pulled your BFF weight.

Cash laughed. "Her, huh?"

"Of course she told me about her." Beth was going to get a headache from all of her nodding. Well, and from all the vodka too.

"Nic's reading into something."

"I am not."

He shrugged one shoulder.

"So what's your get-the-butler plan?" Beth asked. Good thing Cash was there to explain it to both of them. And here he thought she was being über professional. In reality, she'd been lost in the Cash-clouds.

He cracked his knuckles and got serious with a swig of his Warrior Smash. "Simple. Nic and the butler have to partner, per the CIA's request to work it out, so as they do that. Nic slips in a few tracers and bugs. They do some bogus assignment together. Titan harvests the intel to bring the fucker down. Nic plays it all nice and sweet." Cash stared at her a hard second. "That is, if she can manage to keep her left hook in check. She's got a quick temper."

Oh, for God's sake. She didn't have a temper. Maybe a short fuse, but that was a byproduct of her ex-boyfriend run-in. Now that Cash clued her in to the plan, it sounded reasonable and simple enough. This plan, for that matter, sounded too safe. It sounded like Cash and Jared were keeping her at arm's length while they did the fun work, or was her Whiskey Whatchamacallit making her paranoid?

She took a sip and added, "But if I see an opportunity to take him down and have cause, I'll do it." It wasn't a question. It was a statement of fact.

"Not according to the plan," Cash countered with a hint of a growl.

"Plans are meant to be adapted."

"Not this one." He sounded smug and sure and steadfast.

I'm going to wring his neck.

"This is about me being in the field again, isn't it?"

"What?" He shrugged, looking guiltier than sin. "No."

Yes. "I cannot believe you and Jared. You two can't handle it."

"Actually, not Jared. He thinks you're fine to do whatever you please. Roman and I have reservations. We don't want you running around when we can take care of it."

"Not your call, Cash."

"It's better that—"

"Stop. Just stop." She tried for a deep breath, but fury and frustration built in her lungs. "You said we were okay. That we'd work together, that you understand I'm good. Shit, I'm better than good."

Beth nodded. This nod was a serious one, trying to reinforce the truth. "She is."

Cash swallowed the rest of his drink. "We are working together. Just let me do the heavy lifting."

"I might if you talk to me about it first! That's how partnerships work. You can't—"

He pushed out of his chair and stood to his impressive height, then leaned over her chair, imprisoning her in his protective arms. "Why not? It's safer—"

She jutted her chin up to meet his sapphire stare. "To quote the great Cash Garrison, *bullshit*. You can take a bullet between the eyes as easily as me, so don't tell me it's safer for you."

She pushed a hand against the expansive plane of his chest and stood, matching him. Cash versus Nicola. Losing ground on this would be detrimental to her professionally.

They didn't say anything. No one around them did either. Every person on the patio stopped and stared. The waitstaff watched. Someone, somewhere clanged a knife on a plate.

"Check please," Beth whispered.

CHAPTER SEVENTEEN

Being stuck bitch in a Cash-and-Beth-sandwich on the front seat of the truck proved annoying. Beth was passed out and propped up against the door. Cash had an arm draped over the wheel, humming along with the radio like he wasn't a macho jerk.

Everything he'd said in their spar hadn't meant a thing. She thought she had a grip on her and Cash, but she was wronger than wrong. She felt plain stupid for assuming that he'd be different than any other man, not seeing what she wanted and instead playing big dog. His delivery, acting all cocky and beating his chest like Tarzan, hadn't helped. So he wanted to protect her. Too freakin' bad. It wasn't his call. Shit, she wanted to protect him. Bet that'd make him shrivel up.

"I'm not sorry." There he went, running his mouth.

"Couldn't care less."

"Well, I'm not thrilled you're mad at me."

"Still don't care."

Beth smacked her lips as she slept. Her occasional snore broke the hum of the road as Nic directed Cash to Beth's condo.

"I'm good enough to be out in the field, Cash. I'm strong and I'm smart and—"

"I get that," he said on a breath. "But I'd rather just take care of it. It's a man thing. A protective thing."

"You don't know me at all. I don't want to be protected. I like protecting. I'm a sleuthing badass. I like what I do, and you stepping in isn't, isn't—"

"Isn't what, Nic? Not my call? 'Cause I'm making it my call."

"It's not fair." She pointed for him to make a left turn onto a tree-lined road. "It's not fucking fair."

"Babe, life's not fair. You of all people should know that."

"But I can choose who I work with, and that means I don't have to work with you."

"You do through this assignment."

"Well, screw that. You and my big brother don't call the shots."

"Yes—"

"I'll go out alone. You and Roman can sit around like old biddies and bitch about that. I don't care." She took a breath and pointed. "Pull in right there. That turnabout."

He slowed into the horseshoe driveway of the high rise building, then turned to her, his eyes almost pleading. "You wouldn't."

"Obviously you don't know me as well as I thought you did. I was out there by myself before you two came along. The only reason Titan's involved is because the CIA wants this one off the books. I'll go off the books for both Titan and the CIA. I want this fucker. If I get the chance to take him out, bring him down, or just entrap him, he's mine."

He shut his eyes. Worry creased their corners. "Nic…"

"Blah, blah. I'm sick of it."

Beth stirred. Cash parked his truck and got out, leaving Nic alone with Beth, who had gone back to snoring. Very slowly, Cash opened the passenger door. Beth was still very much passed out.

"Grab her stuff. Get her keys out."

Nic stared at him. "What are you doing?"

The whiskey in her blood slowed, as she understood his plan. Click. He undid the seatbelt and extracted her snoring best friend. Beth nuzzled against his chest. Cash was a protector. He did it without thinking. Without being asked. He did it because he probably expected no less of himself. Damn him, all well-rounded and caring.

Nicola pinched her eyes tightly. Cash wanted their heavy lifting because of who he was. Nic in the field threw that balance off. Too bad. He needed to find a new center of gravity.

With Beth draped over him, Cash started toward the front doors. The doorman opened without a sideways glance. Nicola could do nothing more than watch Cash.

"You coming?" he asked over his shoulder.

The keys jangled in her hand, kick-starting her butt into gear. She led the way to Beth's apartment.

Nicola had taken Beth's shoes off and left her a glass of water and two Tylenol on the bed stand before they left.

"Thanks. For helping Beth."

He chuckled. "She's a lightweight."

"Trust me, she's not. I'd chalk that up to an empty stomach and too much excitement."

Cash shrugged, and they walked down the corridor. "Let's get out of here."

"Look, I didn't mean to get so upset. I've worked hard to prove myself and… I know it's in your nature. I just… I don't know."

They stopped in front of the elevator, and he pushed the down button and popped an Altoid. "We're finding our equilibrium. New partners and preconceived notions." His voice was quiet, but he still didn't sound willing to budge on David the Butler.

"Maybe." She watched him in the oversized wall mirror instead of pacing the length of the waiting area. Since he'd called her fidgeting habit, it was on her mind. *Don't squirm. Don't fiddle.* Don't, for the love of God, give Cash a reason to get in her head.

"Let's work the ammo angle. We'll go see Sugar, get that over with, and then we'll be working together. Just like you want."

"Why?" Sugar? He wanted more drama?

"Why not?"

"Because we're fighting, and Sugar isn't going to help."

"Nah, this is more like a disagreement. A work-related disagreement. I don't think it has anything to do with you and me."

"It has everything to do with us."

"Us at work."

"Us in general." She shook her head.

"Nope." He paused and looked her over from blonde bun to butt-kicking boots. "We're disagreeing, and it's bothering you because you care. Don't know if you realize that, but it's true. And I'm apparently the problem, and it's because, I guess, I care."

The elevator dinged open. *Hurray! Get me out of here.* He walked in and held the door, waiting for her to join him. *Hmm. Confined space.* Maybe she should've hoofed it down the stairs. Nic moved to the corner opposite. His truck, the shower, and now the elevator. Too many closed in spaces.

He leaned back against the wall, surveying. "Whatcha doing way over there?"

She fidgeted with her purse, repositioning it from one shoulder to the other. "The more space, the better."

"Are two little things like Sugar and the butler gonna keep you a rifle's distance away from me?"

"I don't really know you, Cash. I don't know what you want. What I know is that you want to mess with my job."

"Screw that. Here's the truth. I lost you once." He pointed at her, then back at him. "I like this. I like us. And I liked last night. A lot. You're more than a fun fuck, and I don't want to lose you again, so there you go, sweet girl. Maybe I'm all lost in nostalgic malarkey, but not only do I want you in bed, I want you out of bed. Which, as you've been clued in to, isn't my MO. So shit's different with you. You can lie and say you don't feel it too. That's cool, but know that I know."

He knows? He knows nothing. He had no clue about the confused ramblings bouncing in her brain, no clue that she had to double check his reaction to make sure she didn't cry out the words, "I love you."

Over the elevator door, the numbers counted their downward drag toward the ground floor. Why hadn't they bottomed out yet? She needed out of the elevator, but it barely slid from floor to floor. At this pace, they wouldn't hit G until tomorrow.

Tomorrow would be too late.

Prolonged exposure to Cash caused blips of lust-soaked anxiety. Her heartbeat picked up its tempo—bump, bump, bump—and she wanted to climb the walls.

Since when was she claustrophobic?

Oh, who was she kidding?

Cash stretched high overhead. Just another day, making women swoon. That damn shirt hugged his muscles, and her mouth went dry. She tried to swallow around the knot in her throat. Tried to ignore the knots re-tying in her stomach. Even his belt had a look-at-me quality, wrapped around his toned waist. Flashes of his rippled stomach burned through her memory. *Whoa, God.* This elevator was teeny-tiny. He lorded over it in his corner, watching her watch him, and she needed the emergency escape hatch.

A slow smile flickered across his face. "Nothing to say, sweet girl?"

She shook her head. Nothing to say. Nothing to do except hide in her corner. Maybe dig in her purse a little more or check her phone or... Cash stepped to her. One step. Two steps. She looked at the ceiling, then at the elevator display. Button after button, unlit. Nineteen more floors to go, and Nicola couldn't move, frozen and frying in his gaze.

He had her. Sliding a finger down the curve of her neck, his finger flicked the purse strap, and with that grazing touch, it dropped.

Loud thud. Intense moment. Pounding want.

Nic's tank-top-clad back pressed against the cold wall. Her bare shoulders were aware of the barrier. A heat ignited, and anticipation tingled from the perk of her breasts to the tips of her fingers.

Inches.

He was inches away and closing the distance. Cash palmed the elevator wall on both sides of her head. "I'm throwing lines about in bed, out of bed, and you're standing, stoic like this is a cold shoulder challenge, and you want to win a trip to the freakin' Arctic Circle." He kissed behind her ear. Whimpers escaped her lips, then he whispered again. "After last night, I thought it was game on between us."

Close enough for him to feel the rise and fall of her chest, close enough for her to smell the mint he'd long-since devoured, Cash nudged at the wall of buttons. Click. The lights dimmed. The elevator stopped between floors.

No alarms.

No sirens.

Just them, stuck in an elevator with the emergency lights on, and now she really couldn't breathe.

"There are cameras in here. I'm sure there are cameras." The words came out breathy and wispy and screaming, "Please kiss me again."

"What is it you think I'm going to do?" He crushed against her. His smooth cheek grazed hers, and his lips brushed against her ear. "What is it that you want me to do?"

Her libido did jumping jacks and her mind, somersaults. All she could see was the deep blue of his eyes. His weight pressed her in place. His palms cupped her face, igniting a fire wherever he touched. Never had a torturing burn felt so damn right.

"I want…"

Cash dipped his head. Soft hair teased over her cheek, and soft kisses turned her stomach. It was a cacophony of cravings. Heat pooled inside her. The very core of her body moaned for his contact.

He repeated what she'd started. "You want…"

"You."

She felt his smile on her skin. His full lips thinned into a grin, and his tongue sliced across the side of her collar bone, sweeping the strength out of her legs. Nicola hooked her thumbs into his belt loops. One of her legs snaked up his thigh. Trying to breathe was a wasted effort, and—

Ring. Rrr-ring. Ring.

What was it with the interruptions?

Cash pulled back to stare at the elevator's phone box, slid his hands down her body, letting one rest on her hip, and opened a small door with the other, grabbing the phone. "Hello." Amused, he dragged the syllables before he made it to a long oh. A few uh-huhs later, he winked at her, flicked the elevator RUN button back to ON, and said into the handset, "Must have bumped into it. Sorry."

With the elevator phone back in its box and their ride creeping toward the ground level, they locked in a gaze. Nothing saying. Nothing doing. Just waiting.

The doors opened, and a pudgy security guard waited for them to exit, hands on hips. "You two okay?"

Yup, definitely cameras in the elevator. Just like the CIA: someone's always watching.

Cash took her hand in his. "Couldn't be better."

This may have been a mistake. As mistakes go, it may have been a jumping-off-a-bridge bad idea. The GUNS sign was dead ahead on the right, and Cash braked, turning off the road and into a parking lot with a rusted, charging bison mascot snarling at every truck that dared cross into Sugar's parking lot. The thing had to be the size of an army tank.

"We're here." *And so is she.* Sugar's '69 Mustang Boss 429, the same color as the lipstick she wore, sat in her parking spot. The twist in his gut and a flash glance at Nic said this moment was leaning toward colossal catastrophe.

No time to backpedal. Jumping out of his truck, Cash saw the security camera track him. Sugar knew they were there. Nic got out and slammed her door. At least she was down for their Q and A session. A second later, his girl was on his six, and they walked toward the gated-up, locked-down door.

His girl.

She was definitely his girl walking into Sugar's lair. He'd iron out the semantics later.

Moving from the focus of one security camera to the next, he waved hello at the lens over the door, and a series of locks disengaged mechanically after someone approved their entry.

They walked into the waiting area lined with wall-mounted guns and knives. Glass cases housed a few more beauties.

Sugar's heels clacked down the hall before they could see her. It was Sugar. Only she could make footsteps sound like the sway of her hips. Her perfume drifted in before she did, and her entrance was nothing short of a sultry explosion.

"Cash, baby." She ignored Nicola, lasering onto him with lethal accuracy, and wrapped an arm around his back to kiss him hello. "I knew you'd be back soon."

This was about what he'd pictured. To Nic's credit, her boot didn't bounce-bounce-bounce. This was work-Nic. The professional Nicola. Cool and calculating. Nic didn't flinch at whatever else Sugar babbled about. Probably several variations of, "let's get into bed. Or drop to the floor."

Sugar turned to Nicola and shook her head, faux confused. "And what was your name again? Sarah? Julie?"

"It's Nicola," Nic said with a touch of bring-it-bitch. "I understand if it's hard to remember names that aren't tangible."

Annnd, the ladies were off and running.

This was everything Rocco probably dreamed of watching in real time. If the ladies were still standing at the end of this visit, he'd give Roc a serious recap.

He stepped a boot between them. "Can we go to your office, Sugar? We have—"

"Baby, you're the king of the castle for all I'm concerned. Lead the way."

Cash fought the urge to roll his eyes. Instead, he studied the guns lining the walls. Sugar could build the hell out of a specialty request. The display paid homage to that talent.

If he could focus the ladies on guns and ammo, this convo could stay on the up and up. "Why don't you lead the way?"

"Not sure that I want Julie, eh, Sally, whoever, running around back there though." She turned to Nicola. "I can have someone bring you a chair, and we'll make you comfy right here."

Cash gave a chuckle, impressed that Nic appeared unfazed, and said, "Not gonna happen like that. The three of us have business."

"I don't trust her," Sugar replied.

No bounce-bounce-bounce shoe taps, but he saw it in Nic's face. The charge had been set. No telling when she would strike. He needed to diffuse this blowup and get down to the warlord arms dealer business.

One bounce. He heard Nic's shoe bounce once. Then a bounce, bounce.

"Sug—"

Nic started in. "You're selling illegal ammo, and you don't trust me? Screw this, Cash. I'm calling ATF. They can deal with her." She rifled through the black hole bag. The cell would eventually be found, and Nic didn't look like this was a bluff.

Sugar looked ready to pounce. "Excuse me? What the—"

"Ladies, backroom. Now. Nic, put your cell away."

Without a word, Sugar turned and stormed down the hall. Nic gave a smirk and shrug, following after her. Their two sets of feminine ass-kickin' boots were readying to loft him a good one where the sun didn't shine if he didn't rein this situation in on the quick.

Their threesome stopped in Sugar's office. He'd only been in there a couple of times and hadn't been intent on checking out the décor. Now, his objective was to keep them civil and productive.

He looked at the bright fuchsia wall and over-the-top furniture. Sugar's office was the Home Depot version of her, something he should have noticed before. *Bet lots of interesting things go down in this room.*

"Speak," Sugar ordered Nicola. "Fast."

Nic smiled as if ice ripped through her veins. "Where'd Jared's ammo come from?"

"None of your nosey-girl business."

"You know who Antilla Smooth is?"

Sugar cocked an eyebrow and looked at Cash. He was content to let them work through this. For now.

Sugar pivoted a gaze back to his girl. "BFF to Mahmoud Ahmadinejad, big fan of the Hussein brothers. What does that have to do with me?"

"Ever move his product?" Nic asked.

"Never seen his product. Never been overseas to do business. Cash?" Sugar turned to him, a flash of concern coloring her glance. "What does this have to do with me?"

He zipped his lips. Not his interrogation.

She turned back to Nic. "I run a legit shop. I buy, sell, and trade. I design and build. I don't play with third- or first-world arms dealers. No one in Europe, the Middle East, or South America. I don't use Swiss bank accounts. Cold, hard good ole US of A cash exchanges. Fess up, Garrison girl. What's up with ATF threats and name dropping the likes of the Bin Laden clan?"

"The ammo you sold Titan is Smooth's."

"Not a chance."

"Ever seen anything of Antilla Smooth's?"

"Why would I?"

"He marks his product with—"

"Oh, fuck." For a split second, shock shut Sugar silent. "With an A and an S." Pure surprise dripped off Sugar's painted-on face. The woman didn't know. Nic had to see that too. Sugar was as caught off guard as he'd been when she rolled heels first into Winters's living room.

"Who'd you buy it from?" Nic followed up on that revelation.

"A legit source." Sugar started to straighten a pile of papers that were already squared off.

"You're not naming names?"

"I'm not giving up my seller to some—"

"Sugar." Cash nailed her with a watch-your-ass look.

She pursed painted lips and started again. "I'd rather keep my rifle rolodex to myself, thank you."

Nic pushed her. "Your guy has connections you don't need."

"I'll be the judge of that."

"Smooth arrived in the U.S. three months ago. We've been mapping out his network."

"I'm not part of his network."

"Didn't say you were, but I'd like to know who you know. We didn't think he'd sell to legit sources." Nic used air quotes around legit. *Wasn't that nice of her?* "And we didn't think it'd infiltrate this far south or this fast to consumers."

"And who is we?"

Nicola paused. There's no way she'd say CIA. "Titan."

He didn't expect that either. According to the look on Sugar's face, neither did she. Nic wasn't exactly Titan. She was contract help. But better that lie than no response. They should have worked out a little back story before they went in, questions ready to fire.

Sugar tapped pink nails on her desk, quick taps, one right after the other. "Cash, you two go out back. Take your pick from my private gun stash. I have a couple calls to make."

"All right. Let's give her a minute. Come on, Nic."

Nicola dropped the huge black hole bag. Everything spilled out. Why'd the woman need all that stuff?

"Sorry. Sorry." She scooped it without looking, shoving it all back in from where it came. "Sorry."

He didn't take Nic for the bumbling type, especially after the ladies had gone back and forth like that. A lip gloss-lipstick thing rolled under Sugar's desk. "Oh, you—"

"I'm ready."

"But—"

"Jesus, Cash. I got all my stuff. Let's go."

Oh no, she didn't. The glimmer in her eye said oh yes, she did. Titan had their toys. The CIA had theirs. Nicola had a listening device that looked like a tube of fancy-dancy lip gloss.

Listening devices weren't necessarily legal. Then again, when did he, Titan, or the CIA play by the national security rule book?

His gut re-twisted. This was Sugar though. He trusted her. *Right?*

Nic led the way out, and they shuffled to the outdoor course after grabbing a couple long rifles from Sugar's stash-o-guns. He waved to a couple folks he knew and took every opportunity to catch Nic's eye. She wasn't having it, and he wasn't talking about it. Who knew who else was listening?

They headed to the outdoor course. Manmade hills, swaying tall grass, and creative-assed obstacles that Cash knew exploded in colored smoke were dead ahead. Flags showed a mild, five mile per hour breeze. The sun had started to sink, but they had hours more of summer daylight.

He took position, loaded up a .45 that was eons away from as much fun as Miss Betty and fired. Blue smoke burst and billowed.

"Nice shot," Nic said.

"Easy shot." Her approval was completely unneeded, yet it tugged on his cheeks. Maybe now he could push her on the lipstick move. "Nice move."

She squinted. "I haven't gone to the line yet, crazy."

"Yet you've already crossed it."

Nic mouthed a dramatic oh. "'Cause she's your friend?"

"Because I said she could be trusted."

"I don't trust anyone. Hazard of the job. I tried earlier today with you, and it bit me on the ass. I'm playing by my rules now."

He ignored the jab and chambered another round. Aim. Shoot. Blue smoke.

He emptied the spent round and turned to her. "We need to do something normal."

"Fine—"

"I gotta go home. I owe my mom a visit. Since you're alive, you should see your folks."

"I called them. Gave them the whole spiel, told them what Witness Protection told me to pass along since I'm out and about and want to keep mobster crosshairs off 'em."

"You don't want to go home?" he asked.

She pulled down her sunglasses, stepped to the line, and fired off her weapon. Different target hit. Green smoke. She didn't turn around, just stayed, staring down range.

"Nic?" He took a step forward and spoke lower. "Nicola?"

Nicola cleared her weapon and turned. "Look, I can't handle seeing their faces. Okay? I talked to them. They know it all. They had the same reactions you and Roman did. I'm devil daughter. I get it. I don't need to see it."

"Don't you miss—"

"Of course I do. I've missed them every day. Just like I missed you and Roman."

She turned back toward the last of the wafting colored smoke. He placed his hands on her shoulders. "Let's go see them."

"I can't."

"Yeah—"

Spinning fast, she stabbed him with a glare. "I'm not strong enough. You happy? Is that what you want to hear?"

"I don't believe you."

Nicola glared at him. "They deserve better than me."

"I know your folks—"

"No you—"

"How about this? I'm going to go see them. You're welcome to join me. Then we'll go do something boring and normal, like catch a movie or something. You need to chill, and I'm gonna help."

"I don't know." She looked terrified.

"We'll go after this. You can sit in the truck while I do the parental drive-bys if you want to hide. Then we'll go make s'mores or something. Something nice and normal and boring." They both heard Sugar's heels before she announced herself. Cash smiled. "Or you can always stay here with Sugar."

Sugar held Nic's lip gloss listening piece high overhead. She looked... not pissed. What the deuce?

"All right, Nicole Whatever-Your-Name-Is." Almost her name. Sugar was in the same ballpark as Nicola. It was progress. Sugar continued, "Cute. Very funny. I respect the effort. Cash, scram. She and I have business."

Maybe not progress.

Nicola looked at him. "See ya. Have fun at Mom and Dad's."

CHAPTER EIGHTEEN

Cash took his sweet time leaving, dragging one boot in front of the other. Nicola and Sugar watched. Maybe he hoped they'd call him back. Maybe he was concerned about pitting two lady bulls against one another with no one to enforce ground rules.

Sugar cracked a piece of gum between her teeth. "So, you and Cash?"

"Or is it you and Cash?" Nic pushed back. This was why Cash wanted to be here. Chick fight and dirt digging.

The plastic smile on Sugar's face softened a flicker, then went back to its tough girl routine. "You're still going to call ATF, aren't you?"

"I might."

Sugar cracked her gum again. "Why wouldn't you?"

"I'm not sure if it's in my best interest yet."

Sugar didn't look convinced. "Well, it's definitely not in mine."

Nicola eyed Sugar, for the moment, restraining the urge to slap the lipstick off her face. "So we've got something in common."

"You mean besides banging Cash?"

And, back to her casino-worthy poker face. She would've smacked Sugar if there was anything to be gained by it. Nic felt Sugar analyze her reaction for a lightning strike of jealousy and knew she'd given nothing up. *Thank you, CIA.*

"What's the deal with you two anyway? Last name's Garrison. You were married? He doesn't seem like the type."

"No, he doesn't."

"Not going to explain anything?" Sugar asked.

"We're old news." Nicola shrugged through her lie.

"Not according to that I'm-dreaming-of-lights-out look he gave you. Anyway. You left this in my office." Sugar held out the listening device. Odd that she could pick it out. It looked like any other tube of Clinique gloss. It was also more than noteworthy that she transitioned from Cash without batting a false eyelash.

"You don't care about Cash and me?" Nic asked.

"Not really. Cash and I were just fun. Nothing special. But I did like trying to make you squirm."

"You certainly made him."

"Fun, right? I like fucking with him. Keeps his boots on the ground. He's a cool dude. I didn't pick him for a one-gal kinda man, but what do I know?" Sugar cracked her gum again. Annoying habit. "Back to your super not-so-secret bug. Spill it, and I might give you something on the ammo."

"It was the best I could do when you stonewalled me. I hadn't planned to be here anyway."

"And?" Sugar raised a perfectly plucked eyebrow.

"And?" Well, shit. She had to give Sugar something, or this was pointless. "And I'm tracking Antilla Smooth. Cash isn't necessarily thrilled that I'm on the hunt. He'd rather handle it for me." Word hadn't hit the street yet that Smooth was six feet under with a clean shot above his nose.

"Macho prick." Sugar smiled.

Nicola laughed. "Indeed."

"Good in bed though."

No, she didn't. "And back to Cash. You sure it's all, 'I'm cool, he's cool, we were just having fun'?"

Sugar studied her. "You play by some kind of rule book? Don't kiss and tell? Don't leave home without a bug?"

As a matter of fact, nope. She was flying by the seat of her Seven jeans. "Maybe it's more a matter of decorum."

"Well, decorum this: that man is good with his hands. And his—"

"Sugar!"

Sugar shrugged, laughing. She extended the lip gloss tube. "You're cool, Nicola Garrison. This shit's expensive. You can have it back. I like the ballsy move, and I hate getting messed with. If I sold Smooth ammo, and it sounds like I might've, let's just say, I believe in retribution."

Retribution, Nic could work with. Maybe even Sugar she could work with. Cash wouldn't like this, and Sugar wouldn't follow any kind of plan. Nic could tell. This was one of those the-higher-the-risk-the-greater-the-reward moments.

Nicola pocketed her Clinique bug. "What would you say if we smoked the bastard out together?"

Sugar blew a bubble and chewed in silence, bright red lips pursed in thought. In the background, someone fired through a magazine. Nic pushed her sunglasses into her hair and stared back at Sugar.

Finally, Sugar smirked. "I could do that and stomach you."

"Marvelous, Sugar. So glad to hear it." Just when Sugar's bitch level dropped below intolerable, she pumped it back up. "I have to work an assignment out of the country, but I'll get a hold of you. And as a matter of good faith, I won't listen to whatever you said in front of this." She held up the lip gloss.

"Doesn't matter. I have a jammer. You didn't get crap." She jutted a hip, planted a hand on it, and grinned like she saw Nic coming straight from Langley.

Sugar had a jammer in her office? What else did that woman sell? Nicola looked at Sugar's outfit, thought of Cash, and decided she didn't want to know. "I'm going to regret this."

David had no time or patience for the hand-holding required to secure his financial future through the *new and improved* Smooth Enterprises, sans Antilla Smooth. They still moved illegal weapons. They still supplied the ammunition to half the world's terrorists. Nothing but the leadership was new. But his client required it, just like he required code names. Maybe *Mister Mars* was afraid to jinx their project. Whatever the reason, David still had to answer when called Mister Nero, and he still had to kiss ass until the final exchanges were complete.

He surveyed his notes, smiling at his anticipated profit. David's decision to pad his pockets while Smooth Enterprises experienced a turbulent changeover was risky but had a huge payout. He studied the stacked boxes of products piled in his home office. Ammunition and automatic rifles were the easiest to sell. No one had noticed that he'd removed the high-powered inventory. How uncomplicated had it been to steal? After all, most everyone within the organization had thought he was a butler. Butlers organized. They cleaned. They directed. They did trivial tasks, and no one paid attention to them, especially as he had box after box loaded onto a truck and driven to his home.

Every cent he made selling Smooth product was one hundred percent profit. Those gun show rednecks had bought everything he'd tried to sell on his first venture into the local market. They couldn't pass his prices. He needed to troll the local papers and see where the next meet up would be. All he had to do was forget to shave in the morning, slap on some POW paraphernalia, and he was legit. *Morons. Every last one of them.*

But the biggest bunch of morons? Titan Group and their ridiculous reputation. Big money. Big guns. Big balls. *Just a big load of bullshit.* David would kill the fucker who'd punched his face. The blond-headed asswipe. That man would get his due.

David clicked through the address book in his cell. Nicola. She'd get hers too. That bitch. He hit okay, and the line rang.

Voicemail. A generic message given by a robot operator.

He cleared his throat. "This is David. I'm excited to work with you and clear the past between us. Misunderstandings happen. We'll move on. Turkey is fabulous, and this will be an easy in-and-out. Our flight leaves tomorrow morning. But I'm sure your handler has filled you in. Looking forward to this job. Good-bye."

Their assignment was basic. Transport a document, and while in Istanbul, arrange for a run-in with an undercover needing a back story confirmation. That would be simple. A quick, "howdy, how are the kids?" The undercover would have another layer of history. The undercover's contacts would think the run-in happened by chance, and David would have a way to find out what the CIA knew about Smooth Enterprises.

Damn if this wasn't getting easier. There were so many opportunities to diversify his portfolio, with a much better return than a 401(k). How smart the Farm boys thought they were. They didn't have a clue.

CHAPTER NINETEEN

When Nic bounced back into Cash's ride, she wasn't the woman he'd left with Sugar. She had a glimmer in her eyes that warned of trouble. She pushed past her seat, grabbed him by the shirt, and nailed him with a kiss that might've peeled the leather off his boots. If he hadn't been positive there was a security camera aimed at his truck, he would have undressed her and gotten down to business in less than twenty seconds. Hell, less than ten.

Making a dumbass excuse to himself for not fucking her in the parking lot, Cash hit the road. With Nicola tucked under his draped arm, he needed to focus on anything but the swell of her breasts. She hadn't moved far when he'd said they had places to go. Even now, her hand traced invisible patterns on his thigh.

She smelled of burnt gunpowder mixed with the flowery scent of her shampoo. Who didn't like a woman who could hit a shot three hundred yards away with an unfamiliar long gun and still remind him of the shower where he'd made her moan his name?

"Was that your peace offering?" He had to know what brought about the smoking kiss that still burned on his lips.

She paused her finger on his thigh, and Cash wished he hadn't opened his mouth. "I thought we weren't fighting. Peace offerings aren't needed for work disagreements."

Her laugh made him want to pull her closer. "I don't care what you call it. As long as you do that after every I'm-right-you're-wrong moment."

Nic laughed again. She went back to connecting imaginary lines and dots on his leg, and he sent up a prayer of thanks. With her under the crook of his arm, the radio playing some summertime tune, and the open road reaching away from the outskirts toward the mountains, Cash was sure this was what people wanted in life.

Life was a long-assed time. Since Nic had tumbled into his line of sight, his clusterfuck of broads and blowjobs seemed pathetic. *What's done is done.* This was one of those fuck it and drive on moments. He had to let go of that lost time and embrace life with the safety always off.

He'd given up the idea of a woman to kick it with lifelong when she'd died, when he had that ring and no one to give it to. Was it even possible for him to think long-term, or rather, think about someone other than himself long-term?

Maybe.

Maybe not.

He'd boxed up that part of his brain ten years ago and shipped it off to some unknown address.

Whatever. Nicola wasn't going anywhere. She also needed to chill out, completely forget about work, and he'd make sure that happened. Downtime was a Cash Garrison specialty. He intended to make sure she knew the full reach of his getting down skills.

The sun sank into the Virginia hills. His truck powered and growled around another bend. The straight-to-the-skies incline disappeared into a green canopy of trees. Truth: he loved this truck almost as much as he loved his new digs. Not that his last place was bad, but the new one was badass.

He flicked a glance down at Nicola. A pang of pride exploded in his chest. When he'd bought the place, he had no idea she'd ever see it—her being dead and all—but now she was about to and that was... unexpected. It was pretty damn cool.

They hit the driveway. Gravel spun in the wheel well. She'd been sniper quiet, her finger tracing stopped, exhausted into a simple hold. Her gaze fell absentmindedly out the windshield. That private Sugar convo must've been a heavy one. *Or a bitchy one. Nothing telling either way.*

Finally, they arrived. A world away from Winters's madhouse, Tyson's Corner, and Sugar's House of Guns.

"This isn't your folks' place." She looked out the window. Her eyes were wide, her tongue flicking over the bottom of her lip.

"Nope. It's not."

His house hid tight in the thick, green woods. The area looked untouched, but he'd had Titan 'n Boys hotwire the thing NSA-style. Breaching this place would be like burrowing through the impenetrable layers of the Pentagon with a pencil sharpener. Here, if a deer so much as sneezed, Cash could check a readout and know what time and why.

They were alone. This wasn't just a man cave, it was his man castle. Him and her, and nothing to do... but relax. *Relax.* That was the point of this trip. Nothing to do with that teasing tongue and lips that made him want to jump out of his hide. Nothing to do with that drop-and-get-me-naked kiss in the parking lot that made his blood surge even now. Cash took a breath, trying to resuscitate his voice of reason.

He stopped at the gate, entered a code, and pressed his finger on a scanner. The high-and-wide swung open.

Shifting under his arm, Nicola took another sweeping glance from driver to passenger side. Her hand brushed dangerously close to his cock. "This isn't where Titan bunkers down?"

"Nope. Guess again." He had a sense that she knew where they were when her hand caressed him. *That her innocent act is anything but.* Yeah, they'd end up in bed together. He had no doubt. But seriously, he had to show a little something besides an interest in banging her. *Right? A little restraint.*

They weren't strangers. They were far too familiar. Yet here he was, hoping she liked his digs, wondering how much was too much. All things he knew nothing about. Things that meant he was totally feeling her.

They crunched over a few rocks. The front side of his house came into view. It was a log cabin on steroids. All timber façade and picture windows. As broad as it was tall. He'd had no idea what he was supposed to do with all that space. For now, Miss Betty had a room to spread out in, and the living room rocked a billiards table and fully stocked wet bar.

Oh, and the hot tub on the back deck. Maybe he'd convince Nic to take a dip. *Her hair might be piled on top of her head. Her cheeks might be flushed.* And alone in the woods, hot water bubbling around them, there wouldn't be a hint of clothes. Her full breasts bobbing on the water line, her toned arms wrapping around him. Thoughts of her in there with him, the sway of the trees, the sun going down behind her, made Cash shift in his seat. His cock wanted out of his jeans, hardening with mental images of Nic in his arms.

Not yet.

He hit an overhead button. The middle garage door rose.

"This is your place?" Her voice had a twinge of holy shit, and his chest swelled with an old fashioned, "hell yes."

But instead, all he offered was a nod. "Yup."

The garage door shut behind them as he turned the ignition off. Florescent lights flicked on. *Nothing but space to fill. A whole lot of potential.* If they didn't make it into the house, if he had her up against the hood of his truck, their voices would echo around them. Their names. Their breath. The sounds would bounce empty wall to empty wall, screaming their satisfaction back to them. He realized his fingers were trailing up her sun-kissed bicep and the slope of her neck.

Nic met his gaze, now not looking at all like they had the same thoughts. She eyed him, a splash of confusion on her face. "Between this place and Winters's... did you guys win the lotto or something?"

He laughed, definitely not thinking about the hood of the truck. "Private sector always pays better, babe."

"Oh." Her hands smoothed across the top of her long legs. "Your house is gorgeous."

He took a stabilizing breath and tried shake the lust from his voice. "I promised you normal stuff, and I intend to pay up. You should see my DVR. I've got great taste in TV." He got out of the truck, hating the cold sensation when he left her side, and she followed him through the garage.

Maybe he should've parked in the front and got out under the wall of pine trees. The needled-scented breeze always made this feel like home. *Maybe next time.*

They walked into the living room. He slid his keys onto the table and unholstered the concealed .38 from his waist. "There was a *Die Hard* marathon last week. I have to squeeze in my yippy-kay-yay motherfucker fix. Probably a few episodes of—"

"Cash?" She glided around the kitchen, one finger trailing over the granite island that separated the kitchen and living areas. Huge leather couches wrapped around the great room. Her eyes bounced from corner to corner, while his snaked from her melt-his-heart gaze to the legs he'd die to have wrapped around him.

"Yeah?" The urge to christen his kitchen pulsed under his skin. He moved behind the couch, keeping his erection to himself. Normal stuff, he chanted silently. Movies and reruns. Popcorn and frozen pizza.

"What do you think of our two projects converging in Maine? Your team? My team?"

Work. *She wants to talk shop.* He cleared his throat and tried to ignore thoughts of what she'd look like naked in his bed and how damn close they were to his king sized mattress. His *new* king sized mattress, that'd only slept him, alone.

"I think no good decision ever came from bureau chiefs creating plays from their swivel chairs while drinking no-foam lattes." He was rambling. That was a lot of words to say the bureaucrats fucked shit up, and it didn't make him think any less about his empty bed.

"Not what I meant." She locked eyes on him. "Do you believe in…" Her gaze, so intense, so goddamn gorgeous, almost brought him to his knees. "Point me to your bathroom."

Believe in what? He sucked a breath and focused on powering down. "Down the hall, to your right."

He believed in the power of bourbon. He needed a drink to quick-cool his fired up impulses. Jumping her in the kitchen wasn't the right move. Just like it hadn't been in the parking lot this afternoon.

Wining and dining. Fancy party dresses and cocktail hours. She might've been a spy, but working the Smooth angle had been all high society and hobnobbing. The tuxed-out men making moves on her had buffed fingernails and chauffeurs. He was nothing but a man with a reputation that'd make a sorority girl blush and a hard-on that all but had Nic's name tattooed on it.

Maybe he'd nix the *Die Hard* marathon and find something more like *Sleepless in... Cincinnati*? No, that wasn't right. *NYC*? *Los Angeles*? No, that was some lawyer-cop show. Maybe he'd find that 'had me at hello' movie about sports agents. Didn't Tom Cruise rappel out of a skyscraper in that? That'd be cool and wouldn't have him begging for a kiss.

Shit, he shouldn't have thrown away that Netflix advertisement.

Cash poured the shot of Jim Beam and swallowed it. Assessing his boots, jeans, and t-shirt, he decided to hate Nicola in the field even more. All those Gucci-clad GQ fuckers could kiss his trigger finger. He went into the field, covered in camo and caressing Miss Betty. Nic worked an entirely different angle. He thought of her in the gold dress, hanging on Antilla Smooth, and his stomach turned.

Another shot poured. Another shot down the hatch. He slammed the shot glass on the bar, more than a little jealous that some—

"Hey, I've got a better idea, Cash." His cowboy hat hung on her head. Too big. Tilted to the side. She wore a too large, barely buttoned shirt. His shirt. And that was all he could see. The tease dancing across her face made the room spin sideways.

Goddamn, if she didn't have him at hey. Screw Tom Cruise and *Sleepless in South Carolina*.

She was freakin' gorgeous. All tan and legs and flashes of red lace lingerie. He nodded like she'd asked a question and tried to swallow, but his throat ignored the request. Like the rest of him, it froze in place. His pulse quickened, and somehow the heat in the room flew up a couple degrees.

Her voice was a little quieter, pulling him to her. "I found this button down in the bathroom. I didn't even know you wore dress shirts."

He'd wear them every single day if she'd walk into a room, giving out half-naked surprises like a Mardi Gras queen. Her sultry smile issued him marching orders. *She's all mine.* The words bit through his thoughts and hung on his tongue. Huge steps later, he was on her, around her, and pinning her against the wall, rough and tumble, so damn hungry for her and not at all sure how he'd pull himself away to find a bed.

An oh twisted from her lips, but it wasn't a complaint. Hell no. It was a bring-it-on breath. She latched one leg around his thigh and took his weight like a champ. Instinct took over. Cash cupped her rounded ass cheeks and squeezed the soft flesh, lifting her into his embrace. Her hips rolled in perfect reply.

"Forget *Die Hard*," was all he managed, sounding ragged and hoarse.

Her quick tongue and lips worked their way under his earlobe. Every muscle fiber in his shoulders and neck tightened and tensed. The rest of his body replicated the sensation, a tidal wave of arousal pounding through his flesh.

"My idea is better," she purred against his neck.

"Fuck yes."

Nicola locked eyes with him. Intoxicating chocolate eyes. With that hat cocked on her head, like some sexy country pinup girl, he'd walk across hot coal barefoot and sell Miss Betty to make Nic happy.

Her other leg snaked up his body and locked around his hip. Her arms wrapped around his neck. She felt weightless, like he held nothing and everything at the same time. Cash mentally ordered himself not to drop his pants and slam into her.

Her lips crashed against his, sucking and biting and erasing, kiss by kiss, his idea to act like a gentleman. Her plan oughta be called cowboy up because this woman was ready for a ride.

The room was a sauna. She was almost too hot to hold. Almost. He fought for control, wanting desperately to give her something that she deserved.

His fingers found the brim of the hat. He needed it off. Needed his hands in her thick hair.

She stopped mid-kiss, forcing his eyes to match her laser-sighted intensity. "That's mine. Don't touch it."

"My—"

"Not playing." Nic bit his bottom lip, refusing to release his gaze, then said, "Try me, and see what happens."

Oh, she wanted to play? So did he. His brain buzzed. Her lips branded him. Everything burned stronger than the shots of liquor. Cash went for the cowboy hat. Her hand slapped his away, but he pinned it to the wall. "Not a chance, babe."

Her legs squeezed tighter around him, grinding against his throbbing erection. *Fuck, yes, sweet girl. Rub me like that.* Resolved for another round of smack and grab, he went for the hat again. She slapped with the other hand, and he pinned that delicate wrist. Both hands were restrained high above her head, leaving her immobile and defenseless. He needed her now. More than the moment he first saw her, the moments before in bed. He needed hot and hard this goddamn second.

The cowboy hat stayed in place, and it looked too good to fuck off. But it'd be fun to try. Not a regular rodeo. A white hot, soul stealing ride.

"It's going to be like that, Nic?" he graveled, and she arched against his mouth.

"I want the hat on."

"What else you want, girl?" He switched to the other side of her neck, raking his teeth across her slender neck. "Tell me. I want to hear it."

Nicola murmured, her body playing with his.

"What was that?" The harder he kissed her soft skin, the more he nipped against her throat, the louder her response. Each moan made his dick throb. Each time she twisted against his hold, his throat constricted a little tighter. His breath came faster, and he was closer to losing his mind.

"I need you."

The words sparked a line of fire that ripped through his veins. Cash looked down and admired her gyrating, vibrating body. Breasts overflowed their lacy cups. The supple mountains were taut and demanding his attention. He'd die to bury his face in their valley, to hold and pinch until she cried for more, ravishing them until she came from that alone.

The vee of space between their chests was his private viewing gallery. The single button still fastened on his shirt didn't hide her flat stomach or red lace thong. She turned him on in ways he couldn't have dreamt of, and his imagination wasn't boring. He lusted for her. Ached for this. His teeth grabbed skin, and his tongue soothed away the sting. She jerked toward him, pushing him for more. More might never be enough.

"The hat stays on," she moaned, head dropping back and eyelids fluttering to stay open. A flush painted her cheeks as her hips flexed and rolled. He wanted part of that rhythm in the most ungentlemanly of ways. Craved didn't describe it. Addiction might. "Do what you want to me, Cash, and it better be hard and fast. But the hat is mine."

Heaven help me. He was far from easy right now, but she didn't want easy. Not at all. One hand grabbed her two wrists, kept them overhead. Her legs flexed apart, wicked heat radiating from between them. Cash worked his belt buckle and zipper one-handed. His cock sprang free and rubbed against her lace-covered mound.

She bit her lip, groaning at his touch. "Don't be easy with me."

That wouldn't be a problem. He feathered his fingers over the lace thong. One heavy gasp, then another poured over her full lips. His fingers slid over her sweet pussy, then retreated, reminding him that she may very well be his only damn weakness.

"You sure?" he asked, scared he'd read this big fucking blast of obvious all wrong. Nah, she wanted him like he needed her. Her body made it more than evident in what her end goal was. Him. In her.

"Fast and furious. Now." Her chest heaved. Her voice fed his need, stroking and fueling him. As if he could get any harder. Her stomach, her sex rubbed against him. He bit her neck, right above her collarbone, and she tasted like sweet perfection. "Cash," she urged him again.

He tugged his jeans and boxers down, the belt buckle clinked against itself, and he let them fall. Cash reached between them, slipped her thong to the side of her slick folds, removing the barrier between her hot flesh and his. His palm met smooth, hot, wet arousal. Thumbing over her wasn't enough. Not now. Not like this. And it didn't matter. Her pussy reached for him. His cock ached to bury itself in her silky tightness.

"Now. Cash." She struggled against his palm, flexing into his hold. The heat pouring from her body made him sweat. "Fuck me."

If this was what Nic wanted, it was dream-come-true material. Nothing right now should be all sweet and soft. They'd had that before in a bed. They'd have it again later. Right now, this was energy and anxiety. This was fuck-against-the-wall sex. All anger and forgiveness. Loss and lust.

The head of his cock surged and pressed against her tight entrance. Her breaths were rabid, her head nodding into his shoulder. She begged against his skin, her tongue skimming, teeth biting. He pushed into a lava wave of heaven and thrust. From the base of his cock, to the depths of his soul, he felt Nicola Garrison.

It was one strong glide with little tease, no prep. She screamed his name and clung tightly. Nothing had ever been so sexy. His eyes slammed shut. His jaw dropped to his chest. Their cheeks touched.

His entire length was gripped by her core. Nic was on fire. Inside and out. He couldn't move. Her tense muscles grew accustomed to his intrusion. Cash placed his free hand under her ass, then tortured her with a slow withdrawal.

They gasped together. He plunged into her again, fucking her deep with hard strokes. She moaned long and sweetly for him. When he could take no more, he dropped her wrists, and she encircled his neck. Fingernails clawed his back. Her hands pulled in his hair, and the sting was paradise. He couldn't possibly get enough of her. He might never let her go.

Everything felt violently sensitive. Shudders ripped through his muscles. His mind raced to stay in the moment and not come as she called for more and more. He fucked harder, deeper, and she pushed for her release with each roll of his hips.

Against the wall, in his hat, hadn't been the plan.

"More, Cash."

But he hadn't known this Nicola before tonight. And in between her heavy breaths, Cash knew sex with this woman was it for him. *Absolutely it.* He was ruined for all others. There was no slinking away, no hiding from her or the fireworks that exploded when they tumbled together.

Her ass lifted off the wall. Their flesh slapped together. Her juices coated him, running between them. Her pleas drove him into her, flagging him toward the climactic goal line.

The thick air dripped with desire. He tried for deep breaths that didn't exist. He couldn't catch his breath and didn't want to slow enough to try. The heavy beat of her breathing powered him on. She fought against the wall, slammed herself against him, and thrashed her head from side to side. Her long hair whipped his face, lavender scented, sticking to the sweat on his temples.

Nic's latched legs ratcheted up another level of corkscrew tight, and she wailed for more and more, biting down on his shoulder. The hat stayed on, God only knew how. The thunder of her muscles began to pulse around his cock. He was starving to feel her come and drove with all his strength, meeting her at every angle.

Nicola cried out. Her body went taut, then exploded around him, the climax more than strong enough to trigger his release. But, hell no. Once wasn't enough. He wanted to give her more. Anything to provide for her. To know he could drive her past the burning edge of satisfaction.

As she came off her high, Cash pulled her to him, spun for the couch, and after a long jeans-tangled step, fell back onto the leather cushions. Beneath her touch, her aftershocks still throbbing, he could stay like this forever. Silky hair hung over her shoulders as she straddled him with a smile. That buttoned-down shirt, hanging on for dear life, had to go. He tore it from her shoulders, and the lone button popped off. Another quick rip, and her thong and bra were lacy goners.

Cash palmed her stomach, and his hands locked to her hips. Nic rocked, the rhythm swaying her breasts. He loved fucking her, filling her, and he loved those beautiful tits. Cash honed in on the peaked nipples reaching for him. He took the swollen weight of her breasts and clutched his fingers into natural plumpness. She groaned, leaning into his palms. His fingers tightened and massaged. Every time his thumbs swiped her pink pebbled tips, her bottom lip shook, and her jaw hung until he stopped.

Sweet girl, hot damn. He wanted this woman for himself. Heart pangs rippled through his chest. No one else should've ever had the chance to see this view. When her head tilted back, the cowboy hat finally fell off. She didn't even notice, completely in the midst of losing control. The best thing he'd ever seen.

She rose up on her knees, dropping onto him. The tickle of her fingertips dusted over his sweat dampened chest. Burning breaths pushed in and out of his lungs. His body more than reacted for her. It dive-bombed into Lake Ecstasy.

There were no words right now. If he had to say something, he'd ruin it all. Rough and coarse as the wall-to-couch screw-fest was, something surreal was happening, something more than he understood. His insides glittered like sparks against a black night sky, his mind shattering in rapture. The only thing he knew was their release was mission critical. It had to happen. She deserved it. He'd die without it.

Nicola sucked her bottom lip. Cash's body jackknifed in a blissed-out frenzy. Liquid fire coated his cock. Perfect pouty lips swelled from his kisses. And she rode him. Hard.

He gripped her hips tighter, sliding her faster. She came again, forceful and blazing, and locked chocolate eyes on him. They stole his breath. Hell, it didn't matter. She'd stolen his heart. Whatever the fuck had happened years ago, it wasn't important. Whatever fucking excuse she had for disappearing, he couldn't remember.

She was his.

And she fucked like she knew it.

Again, Nicola's climax started. He could feel it grow around him, surrounding his shaft, and her face was painted in what almost looked like pain. Her reddened lips opened, short gasps escaping as they clawed toward their zenith.

"Cash!" Nicola's head rolled back. His name bounced off the walls, echoing around them. Her pussy ground into him as a convulsion blew through her and began the unstoppable quake in him. He grabbed her waist, all his muscles corded. Everything sizzled. Hot streams of his release flowed into her. Silky muscles gripped and relaxed again and again.

His mind stilled, and all he could do was feel the sparks moving from pecs to glutes. From his boots on his feet to his fingers digging into her sides.

This was a Nicola supernova. Her brilliant burst of energy, the beautiful illumination of her face, would stay branded in his memory. A deep mouthful of air later, Nic collapsed onto his chest. Her pink-flushed cheek pressed against him. The air smelled like lavender and sex. Of satisfied woman.

Cash wrapped his arm her, holding her in place, never letting her go. His chest still heaved, but fuck it, he didn't care. The roar of her gasps slowed. Nicola caught her breath quietly against his lips.

Seconds. Minutes. Who the hell knew how much time passed? Their bodies needed to be held. Their minds needed rest.

Late afternoon light had shifted deeper though the windows since they'd walked inside. She shifted under his arms. Her finger traced a path on his bicep.

He whispered, "Sweet girl?"

"Hmm?"

"You're in charge of all normal activities from here on out." Cash stroked her hair, trailing his hand through it, then caressing her shoulder.

She laughed softly against his chest, and it felt damn good. "No kidding. You were going to make me watch *Pawn Stars* or something. Don't lie."

Maybe. "Stay here tonight."

"I can't."

"Wrong answer."

"I have to prep before I meet the butler tomorrow afternoon. We fly out to Turkey for a simple drop and dash."

Cash propped up on an elbow. "What? When'd that come through?"

"Check your messages. I found out on my way out of Sugar's."

"You're not going anywhere with that asshole until Roman and I suit up and—"

"Shut your face, Cash. You're ruining my post-orgasmic glow."

Shut my face? Most women clamored for the right thing to say to make him stick around after a quickie. Not Nic. And this wasn't a quickie. He tucked her back against him.

He could handle this. He could. And he could do it without killing people for no reason other than to protect her.

CHAPTER TWENTY

There were a lot of ways to wake up in the morning. Nicola turned in the rumpled sheets to snuggle against Cash's naked chest. Her legs entwined with powerful thighs and calves. One of his arms was pinned beneath her. The other arm drew her closer even though he never seemed to wake. A sleepy sigh blew into her hair, stubble brushed her skin, and her lips tugged into a grin. Yeah, lots of ways to wake up, but this was the best ever.

"Going somewhere?" his sleep soaked voice asked as he pulled her tighter then kissed the side of her head.

"Good morning," she whispered, not wanting to disturb the morning quiet. A warm rush of tingles ran through her.

"Yup, it is, but go back to sleep. You kept me up entirely too late last night."

She laughed, recalling the night. They'd lain on the couch forever before he'd baked a frozen pizza. Cash really needed something besides frozen food in his kitchen, but those were the breaks of the job: never knowing when he'd be home. Pizza was the most benign problem he could have in the housing department.

Nic shook her head, not wanting to think about the sacrifices and decisions their jobs drove them to. Instead, she remembered Cash rocking her world in bed. And in the whirlpool bath. No wonder he was still out. Blissfully numb, Nicola smiled at the ceiling, ready to sink back to dreamland.

"I don't want to deal with today yet, Nic. Go back to sleep," he murmured.

Today, she'd have to deal with David the Butler and milk enough intel to warrant an on-the-books espionage investigation. At least Istanbul was one of her favorite cities, and she had the opportunity to wear another designer dress, paid for with the CIA's credit card. Beth would pick out another beauty, arrange for all necessary documents and back story, and have it delivered to her apartment by the time she arrived home. Too bad Cash wouldn't be able to see her dress. Maybe this one would survive the job, and she could wear it out sometime. Or at least try it on so he could take it off.

Nic closed her eyes, drifting to sleep, and hoping to dream of him.

Cash eased up on the gas. They were closing in on Nic's apartment, and he wasn't ready to let her go. Nor was he ready for her to fly halfway around the world with the freakin' butler.

"This sucks." Cash blew out another annoyed breath.

"Get over it, Cash. You can't throw tantrums every time I have to work. You knew partnering with me meant that I had to go on assignment with David first." Nic pointed to the front of her apartment, a first floor balcony setup.

She really shouldn't live on the first floor. Too easy for an asshole to slip in, even if the apartment was wired, and she slept with a gun under the pillow.

"Yeah, yeah. I know." He could bitch all he wanted. Nic heading into the field with that dickhead David wasn't doing much for his mental state. Anxiety burned off his good mood and made his hands itch to palm a .45 and follow her around. Just in case.

"Don't worry about me. I'll be back in a couple of days. I'll send you intel as I can. You'll hear from me a thousand times before my feet hit U.S. soil again, then we'll hook up and take the fucker down."

He grumbled, staring at the too-high bushes near her windows. Those should really be trimmed back. He could do that for her while she was gone, make the place a little more safe.

How had he given in on this partner shit anyway? Oh yeah. She gave him no choice. Plus, she could handle herself. All things he knew well, but they didn't do shit for his nerves. A man-gene somewhere in his brain lit up like a neon sign, screaming for him to put an end to this operation, or at least put an end to her hopping on a Learjet with a double agent and doing a Farm job.

She didn't direct him to a parking space, which was just as well. Nic leaned over and gave him a kiss.

"It's going to be fine, Cash."

"I'm not worried."

She laughed. "You look ready to rip the steering wheel off its column."

Cash shrugged. "Not going to rehash it again. If you change your mind, call me. There's always a plan B."

Nicola kissed him again. "The reason you love—like me is I don't need a plan B."

"True." He pinched the bridge of his nose. She was going to say love. People say love all the time. He loved pizza. He loved working for Titan. They didn't cut back and say like. Casually, the words were interchangeable. Unless they weren't. Holy fuck. Or was he over-thinking this? Cash cleared his throat. "Bye, sweet girl."

Waving over her shoulder, Nicola bee-lined without looking back and opened a door. One set of keys for one lock. Easy deadbolt action. She needed more security than that. He revved the engine, toying with the idea of telling her that now. It'd only take a second. But, shit. She wouldn't see it like that, would she? Nope. It'd be all, "I can take care of myself."

He put the truck in drive. Maybe he'd go track down Sugar and see what she had to say about her one-on-one with Nic. Maybe not. He wasn't trying to piss Nicola off, just get some details.

Pulling out of the apartment complex, he reached for his phone to call Rocco. Calling Roman would be a mistake. Rocco knew enough about him and about the situation to provide some kind of sounding board, even if he only did it to have a live role in their drama.

Two rings and Rocco was ready for his role as Dr. Drew. Good, because Cash was throwing him a big one.

Cash merged into traffic and let the convo rip. "Roc, man. You think love can be all just add water and resuscitate?"

Rocco choked on something and coughed for the next thirty seconds. Someone in the background asked him if he was dying. After a pop and fizz, Roc gulped into the phone, then hacked out, "Come again?"

Yeah, that was about what he should've expected. Cash bobbed and weaved through traffic, wanting like hell to get back home. "Like if you felt all happy ever after about someone once, but it didn't end up like that. Do you think if the chance came up again, it'd happen fast?"

"Fuck me. Are you serious?"

Maybe calling Rocco was as good an idea as leaving Nic and Sugar alone. "I'm having freakin' issues, man. I need some kind of advice to move me from the Hugh Hefner side of the game to… like… see, I don't even know an example. Someone who doesn't have a cell phone full of names like Blondie-Bartender and Purple-Car-Pink-Thong."

With a full mouth, Rocco garbled, "There should be more stable men with families on television than Bruce Jenner. He shouldn't be the poster child. Nothing about that Kardashian clan should be the gold standard."

"Spare me the social commentary, Roc."

"So what do you want from me? Could you love her? Well, shit. From what I've seen—"

"I didn't say a thing about being in love." Cash blew out a breath. "Christ, man."

"Listen, asshole. You said happy ever after. Like Disney fairy tale bullshit. That means the L-bomb. All those Tinkerbells and mermaids end up in a castle with a prince. It's the same fucking thing. Right?"

Nic's still in love with me. Cash's stomach was on the spin cycle. He checked his rear view mirror and saw that he was smiling. He didn't want to, but a huge grin was plastered across his goddamn face. *Oh, hell.* He hit the gas and passed a couple of cars over a double yellow line.

"Roc, if you breathe a word about this to Roman, I'll—"

A cell phone rang. He checked his. Nope. Rocco was still on the line. Another ring. Cash looked toward the noise. Down on the floorboard, Nicola's cell lay face down. He tried to grab it and watch the road.

"Gotta go," Cash said.

"You're welcome, dick."

Click. End call. He pulled hard into a parking lot and clipped the corner curb. The cell continued to ring. He grabbed it and looked at the caller ID. Unknown Number. Of course. She needed this before leaving with the butler. She'd probably get a burner phone for the trip, but she probably needed this phone too. And if he brought it back to her, he could mention the whole one deadbolt didn't do shit thing.

Drumming his fingers on the steering wheel, he decided to return the phone. Cash squealed tires and gunned it back to Nic's apartment. It wasn't like he could call her to say, "hey, I found your phone." He wanted to look into her eyes and try to see into her brain. Check out that whole love-like conundrum.

What would it even mean if she did love him? His stomach flipped into his throat. His mouth felt dry and watery all at the same time, and that fucking smile tugging at his cheeks was enough to give him a headache. His head pounded like a freight train burning coal.

Like. Love. He felt like a lunatic.

What if he went down that road? It was all good and fine to grab her and say mine. And he'd loved her once.

Could he...

Or rather was he...

In a blink, Cash was in front of her apartment and uninterested in finding a parking spot. He parked in the fire lane, holding her phone in his hand like it was the only damn reason he'd flown back to her place. His lungs pumped in his chest, and his blood raced. Such a familiar feeling. Like high school, driving to her place before Homecoming or before their pool party for two.

He rapped on the door, his gut full of butterflies on crack, whirling in a tornado. Why? What was he even going to—?

A man in a towel opened the door. Wet hair. Damp chest. About to die.

"Who the fuck are you?" The bellowed question came from the bottom of his boots and burst from his mouth, as Cash stepped through the door. He heard a shower running.

"Hey! What the hell?"

Cash clearly had the advantage. Dude looked GQ, even in his towel. He'd kill the bastard. "Where's Nic?"

"The goddamn shower. Who the fuck are—"

Bam. Cash cold-clocked the fucker and sent him flying across the living room and into a side table. It crashed over. A lamp and picture frames shattered on the tile floor.

Nicola rounded the corner in a towel, soap suds dripping from her hair and a gun in her wet hand. He marched toward the .357 pistol, daring her to put that dual action recoil to good use.

"Goddamn it, Cash!"

"Goddamn me? Goddamn me!"

Nicola slid back the cover plate, ejecting the loaded round. "You have to go." The man was still out, and she stepped to him. "Get out!"

Everywhere he looked, Cash saw red. No. Actually, he saw exactly how he pictured Nic decorating her place. Muted colors. Things all matchy-matchy. It made him sick. The knocked out asswipe on the floor made him sicker. "Explain him. Now."

"To the raving lunatic knocking out people in their own home?"

It was his home?

But it was her home.

This was *their* home.

The bile in his stomach churned. A spot behind his eye throbbed. Both reactions were much better than grabbing the dude in the towel and draining the life out of his limp-assed body.

"You forgot your phone." Cash threw it against the wall. It shattered. Stepping over the man, he slammed the door on the way out. Screw her.

CHAPTER TWENTY-ONE

Nicola grabbed a napkin and mopped the soap from her eyes. *His Garnier Fructis shampoo might actually have a splash of citrus.* Her right eye stung like it was drenched in fresh-squeezed lemon, and she blinked rapidly. *What the hell just happened?* This was a nightmare situation, Jackson wearing a towel, just out of the shower. Her in the same getup. This was beyond bad, in a lose Cash kind of way.

Her roommate was still out cold. Shit. She shook his shoulder. Nothing. Grabbing the throw off the couch, she draped it over his damp, cold skin.

"Wake up!" A trickle of blood ran down his cheek. Nicola shook him again. "Come on, Jackson. Wake up. Now!"

First aid kit.

She ran to the kitchen and trashed the cabinet under the sink. Nothing. Where would it be stashed? It'd help if she was here more often. Nic slammed through all the cabinets. Nothing again, and the whap, whap of the doors opening and closing didn't cause Jackson to stir.

Linen closet. Nic ran around the corner and threw the door open. Towels hit the floor. A storm of wash cloths followed.

First aid kit! She found the blue box with the red cross and ripped it open. Band-Aids flew everywhere. The CIA would be very disappointed in her chaotic response right now.

Yes! Smelling salts.

She booked it back to Jackson, grabbed a pillow to stuff under his head, and cracked open the tube under his nose. His nose twitched. Once. Twice. Eyes flew open. His head tossed to the side, and he groaned, repulsed. His eyes were all kinds of confused.

"Jackson? Jacks? Are you okay?"

His hands went to his temples and then his mouth. The blood was still fresh. His memory seemed to kick start as his eyes went wide. Oh, his metrosexual side would be pissed when he saw the bruise.

Fumbling for words, he sputtered something about her being okay. Damn men. He was knocked out one second, then asking if she was okay the second he regained consciousness. *Hello, I'm the deadly one who lives here.*

He tried to sit up too fast and caught himself. Cash would be a dead man when she got her hands around his neck. Dead. She continued to pet Jackson like it would soothe away her guilt. "Jacks, I'm fine. I'm sorry."

It took him a second to focus. Jackson sat up, taking in the towel and blanket, then rolled his eyes. "Sexy, right? I'm the man of your dreams."

"Are you okay?"

"I'll be all right." He brushed her hand from his hair, righting himself against the couch. "I'm good. I'm pissed. But, yes, I'm all right." Jackson eyed her. "You have soap bubbles drying on your forehead."

"And we have to buy a new lamp."

He looked at the glass shards and busted accessories. "Fuck me."

"No kidding, right? I'm going to kill him."

"That's Cash?"

She nodded.

"Think you could've mentioned me?" Jackson asked.

"It seemed complicated at the time."

"A sucker punch to the dome uncomplicates shit fast. He's going to be tough to partner with if you don't. Or maybe that was your angle all along." He laughed. "Or maybe, subconsciously, you just don't want to let go of me."

"No. I just... didn't find the right moment." And she barely lived there. Why bring up her ex as a roommate?

Jackson rubbed his forehead. "Yeah, I bet."

"You seriously okay? 'Cause I need to get back into the shower."

"Call your boy." Her phone was in pieces on the floor, and he caught sight of it when he cracked his neck. "Temper, temper. You love the macho type, don't you?"

"Are you jealous, Jacks?"

"Want me to be?" A sad smile flashed across his face. If she didn't know better, she'd feel bad.

"Nope." Jacks was such a good guy. Maybe unsure of his platonic place in their friendly relationship, but he epitomized a comfortable closeness.

"Too bad for me then." He took a deep breath. "Then, no, I'm not jealous."

Nicola leaned over and kissed his forehead. "You're a catch, Jacks."

"Yeah, yeah. Catch and release."

"That was jealousy. I heard it." She tried to fuss over him. Maybe he needed an ice pack.

"Nope. Sorry, babe. That's the chemicals in your shampoo making you hallucinate."

Nic walked to the kitchen, stepping over all the Tupperware and napkins she'd thrown in her search-and-find mission. She fashioned an ice pack and brought it back to Jacks, who sprawled on the couch, leaning his head back. The view would be enough to make some women swoon.

She handed him the ice pack, apologized again, and jumped back into the shower. Jackson was a male model lookalike with a pretty boy smile that made all the girls at the FBI giggle, blush, and forget about the agent badges clipped to their hips. They were all skip-down-the-hall happy if he threw them a smile. They also got all knock-a-bitch-out when she visited him at work.

Drama, drama. Nicola hated drama but felt like she was drowning in overprotective men. She re-washed her hair and considered how the conversation with Cash would go. If she could get a hold of him. Nothing pleasant would come of that discussion.

Toweling off, Nic found her burner phone and buzzed Beth. She needed to clear her head before going wheels up with the butler.

"Yes?" Beth answered after a short ring. Her voice was hesitant. Of course she'd be concerned the call wasn't from Nic's personal cell.

"Cash and Jacks just met."

"Oh, bet that was fun."

"What do I do?"

"Well, how bad did it go?"

"Um, I forgot to mention Jackson to Cash. I'm pretty sure Cash thought Jacks and I were, um, showering together."

"What I wouldn't do to shower with that man. I bet he's totally hung. Is he hung? He's totally—"

"Focus, Beth."

"Fine. Focused."

"Cash knocked him out."

"Oh my God! Well, you know Jacks wouldn't put up a fight with those precious bomb tech hands. It's like he's a freaking brain surgeon or something."

"Yeah, I'm thinking it went something like, "hi," punch."

"You have to talk to Cash. Explain everything."

"I don't know."

"What?"

"I could walk away and survive without him."

"What!" Beth yelled into the phone.

"I did it once, though it about killed me." And now, could she do it again? No. She couldn't...

"Why the hell would you do that?"

"I'm better alone. Bad things happen when I'm involved with others."

"Nic, you can't blame Cash. He shouldn't have knocked Jacks out, but shit. You didn't tell him. He had no idea. Guys like that, they go all ape shit whenever they think some man checks out their girls. Jackson's lucky to be alive."

"First, I'm not *his* girl. I'm *a* girl he has an attachment to, and the sex happens to be... volcanic. He feels protective and possessive. Give it a few weeks, and I'd bet he wants to get back to his bangin' ways. Until then, there's carnage. First, Roman was hurt. Now, Jackson."

"You need to call him."

"That's what Jackson said too."

"But you called me instead."

"Yup." Nic nodded into the phone. *Such a bad habit.*

"Call him and say, 'Cash Garrison, this is Nicola Garrison, and I love you.'"

"What! I don't love him." She scoffed and scowled. "What are you talking about?"

Beth laughed into her ear. "Yeah. And I'm not on a Mojave dry spell right now, wondering if your ex is hung."

"You can have him."

"Eh, you know who I wouldn't mind? Roman. I met him when you and Cash brought in David. Nothing to complain about in the looks department."

"Ew, he's my brother. Besides, he's as bad as Cash. They're all assholes."

"Someone's beeping in. Call Cash, and check in later with David and Cash updates. Bye."

Nicola finished packing and grabbed her burner phone again. Time to call Cash. *Hmm, if only I knew his phone number.* She went back to the hall and picked up the pieces of her cell to see if it would turn on enough for an address book search.

Nope.

She sent Beth a text, asking her to track down Cash's number. Beth was good. The best damn handler she could've wanted. Until the number appeared in her phone, she was content to sit on the bed and watch for it.

Cash banged on the door. The wrought-iron security door rattled. It was after hours, but that '69 Mustang Boss 429 sat in its spot. The hood was still warm, so whereever she'd gone, she was back.

"Open up," he yelled at the security camera.

Click. The door unlocked, and he pulled at it before the last deadbolt disengaged. Finally, he was in the dark room and heading down the hall. Sugar's steps came from her office.

"What the hell, Cash?"

He stormed toward the indoor range and didn't wait for her to catch up. "Load me up. Now. High powered anything."

"Cash—"

He slammed to a stop and spun around. "I've never asked for anything, but I am now. Right now. I want a gun and ammo."

She stared at him for a second and turned around. He continued toward his destination, picked a firing stall in the middle, and propped his elbows on the wall. *Fuck me, my head hurts.* He tucked his head into the nook of one elbow and pinched his eyes shut, hiding his face from the whole damn world.

He heard Sugar's heels before she spoke. "What crawled up your ass?"

Where to fucking begin? And why would he confide in Sugar? "Nothing."

He peeked at the weapon. That he could deal with. She placed the Colt Competition rifle and high capacity magazines in front of him. Cash straightened from his woe-is-me position. Making quick work of it, he loaded the lightweight long gun but didn't move to the wall. Neither of them donned their ear guards. He just stood there, big-assed gun in hand and big-assed problems on his mind.

Sugar spoke softly. "She seems like a good woman. Certainly has a set."

"Seems. Perfect description. She seems like a decent person."

"Well, I'll be damned. Are your feelings hurt over a chick?"

"Back off, Sugar. Not in the mood to talk about it."

"Well, shoot or talk. One or the other, buddy. Otherwise, you're going to accidently lose it and punch someone just because. I'd like it to not be me."

"Too late, and no accident about it."

Minutes ticked by in the dark. The illuminated target provided the only light. Taking the line, Cash threw on his ear guards, clicked the safety to rock 'n' roll, and let it fly. The kickback felt good. The power and fury released by the trigger press helped. Some. Not a lot, but no other solutions popped into his head. He released the empty magazine and backed out, pulling off his ear guards and placing the rifle on a nearby stand.

"There's someone else." It was all he could say, all he would admit. Sugar laughed. *Screw her. Screw them all.* "What's so damn funny? You think this is karma or something?"

"Hell, no. But I think you're wrong."

"Trust me. I'm not."

"She told you that?" Sugar shook her head. "I don't believe it."

"I saw it with my own eyes. Twenty-twenty, perfect freakin' vision."

Sugar laughed again. "You only know what you think you saw. Just like what she saw with me and you."

"That's different."

"Why? Because we've screwed?"

He shrugged. "Well, yeah."

"Big fucking deal, Cash. So the woman's had sex. Unless you walked in and—"

"I can't believe I'm talking to you about this shit."

"Bang out another mag. You'll feel better."

He slammed in the fresh magazine and turned down range. Before the safety flip, he called to Sugar as her heels clacked away.

She popped her head back into his stall. "Yeah?"

"Why don't you ever have someone serious? You and me. You and whoever. It's never serious and steady."

"Cause it's more fun that way."

"Truth. Why not?"

"Cause it'd take some asshole with big boots and a big cock to tie me down." She winked at him. "You're lacking the attitude problem, as is every other man out there. So, I do my thing and don't lose a wink of sleep at night. It was fun, Cash, and I suspect we won't happen ever again. At least I'm hoping not, cause I kinda like that Garrison girl."

His gut twisted. *I kinda liked her too.*

CHAPTER TWENTY-TWO

The hangar and private jet looked the big money part. Nicola shifted in her Ferragamo heels, ready to get this trip over and into the done column.

The catering company loaded the last cart broadside, and Nicola figured the trip had another upside. Playing the part of a well-to-do socialite also meant an onboard chef ready to make some five-star dinner as they flew overseas. Lobster. This trip called for some serious lobster and something with truffles in it.

After the Town Car dropped her off, Nicola had breezed through the private check-in for charter flights out of Dulles International. The TSA woman had been far more intrigued with Nic's new Tom Ford sunglasses than her almost-the-real-deal credentials. She'd have to thank Beth for airbrushing the headshot. Her skin looked flawless, and there was no way someone would call her passport and license fake. They were as genuine as you could get, considering they were made by the U.S. government.

Her cover name for the trip was Sarah Beth Pennington. Pretty, with an old money flair. Not too memorable, but specific enough to provide support for another CIA undercover team who needed an additional layer of back story. Plus, she could keep this round of designer duds. That included this very cute, very out of her price range, Jil Sander shirt dress that she now rocked. It fitted and flared in all the right spots. Cash would've liked it. Too bad.

It didn't go unnoticed that a few items in her Louis Vuitton luggage didn't fit and weren't intended to. Beth hadn't purchased Nicola's long legs petite-sized pants for nothing. Nope. Beth was the petite one, and that was all right with Nic. She eyed her carry-on. The luggage was a loaner. It'd have to be returned. Eventually.

"Gabriella," David the Butler said from behind her. Her back shivered and shuddered as if a thousand spiders skittered across her skin. "Oh, pardon. Nicola. Either way, a beautiful name."

Nicola rolled her eyes. His way of speaking wasn't just for his butler gig with the Smooth family. Every time she'd seen him since the Smooth showdown, he'd had the same mannerisms, inflection, and cadence. Slimy bastard. No doubt, the ass was a double agent. "Hello, David."

"Oh, you sound so cold. We're only here because you don't trust me, and the powers that be want us to play nice. I'm willing if you are." He looked at a paper in his hand. "Sarah Beth, is it? Lovely."

She eyed his plaid sports coat and D & G pleated trousers. Yeah, he looked the part of Mister Pennington. His handler did good work. Together, they'd look the part, even if sleazy and slight of build wasn't what did it for her.

Cash did it for her. Her mind flashed back to him. Tan muscles flexed and rippled when he moved. Blond hair, the occasional blond scruff, and soul-piercing, sapphire eyes haunted her memory. Her stomach slung sideways, thinking about his chiseled jaw and full lips. How he trailed kisses down her stomach and—

"Nicola, eyes are on us. Or Sarah Beth, rather. So many names, you'd think I'd be used to it in this job. I believe the Captain is ready and waiting."

Buzz kill. "Dav—"

"Michael. Michael Pennington."

"Whoever you are, the Captain won't think anything of a married couple bickering. You've been put on notice. We're bickering, and I'm not talking to you right now."

David flashed a smile. The bile in her stomach sloshed.

"You don't mean that, dear." He extended his elbow.

No time like the present. She had work to do. "Fine."
Nicola pulled out her powder compact to pat her nose and removed the first, microscopic listening bug she was to plant on David. Slipping it onto her finger, she closed her compact with a tight smile and locked arms with him, dropping the clear plastic listener onto his sleeve.

They boarded and went through the whole routine. The Captain had the face of an old-school Pan Am pilot with a present day uniform. It wouldn't surprise her if he was a model hired for the part of charter Captain, and the real captain was in his late fifties with a gut and balding hairline.

The stewardesses made their appearance next, but the chef was who Nic was really interested in. Finally, he said his hellos, talked about his best friends Mario Batalli and Wolfgang Puck, and made his way back somewhere. *Hopefully to find me a lobster.*

Nic's phone rang. It was Beth. Nicola stepped aside from David, who made use of the leather seats and flat screen television. Closing the door to the lavatory, she activated the small jammer which would allow her phone to work but block out listening devices. "Hello?"

"Did you call Cash?"

"Tried, no answer." Nicola picked at her fresh, light pink manicure. It had to last the weekend and wouldn't if she kept that up.

"I could find him on satellite if you want."

She couldn't ask for a better best friend. Or one with more resources. "I don't want to know where he is. I could guess, but what's the point."

"I want to know. Where is he?"

"Probably with Sugar."

"Ass! You want thermal images? You want to know where she is? Consider it done."

"Let me re-phrase. Cash is probably fucking Sugar just to prove a point."

"Oh." Beth paused. "That sucks. Nothing we'd want to see on thermals. I could just track down his truck. See where it is—"

"Not worth it. He'll have to pick up the phone when I call in a few hours. I left him the details about when I was to meet up with David. He should be able to lock into the transmitting data from the listening devices. Cash, if nothing else, is a professional. The job's the job. He'll work it and move on. I'll give him my details like I should."

"Sorry, girl."

"At least it was fun."

Twenty-two hundred hours. Right on time. Cash held his phone in front of him and glared at it as he walked out of the Granville Bar and Grill, an extra-large meat lover's pizza balanced on his palm, burning his skin off. No frozen DiGiorno deep dish tonight. If he didn't have to wait for Nic's intel dump, there'd be major bar action going down, shot-glass first, to accompany the omnivore overload he had planned.

The phone continued to ring. This was the first time he'd ever hesitated to jump into the action, even if the action was only to receive and document intelligence. Nic had called before she left stateside, and he knew that had nothing to do with hopping on a plane with that dickhead. Nope, it was all about towel boy, but this call was scheduled. It was work. It had to be answered.

He answered her like he would Jared. "Yeah."

"Hi." The sweet quietness of her voice made his heart hurt. *Damn it. And damn her.*

"Do you have an update?" Cash knew his voice was harsh, worse than when he spoke to the guys in the field. There was a definite hint of fuck you.

He balanced the phone against his shoulder, pressed to his ear, and put the pizza on the roof as he unlocked his rig. Click, click. The doors unlocked, and he grabbed the pizza and got in. Two mosquitoes floated in and out of his cab. Maybe he should've rolled the windows up before he went inside. Maybe he'd think about anything and everything but how he felt when it came to the angelic voice on the phone.

"Anything to report?" he asked.

"Cash, I—"

"Anything on the job to report?" He put the key in the ignition and turned. *Ping.* It *cha-cha-cha*-ed, but didn't turn over. God, he didn't have time for this—

Oh, damn.

Nic blabbered something. He didn't hear it. He wasn't listening. Cash closed out all the outside noises and replayed the last thirty seconds of his conversation. Blah, blah, blah. Ping.

He put his hands on the steering wheel and ratcheted down his breaths the way only a good sniper could. Very slowly, very calmly, he began to say her name.

"What? Are you even listening to me?"

"Nicola. I'm at the Granville bar in Fauquier County." He spoke as evenly as possible, trying not to move his mouth, his lungs. "I just activated a detonation trigger tied to my ignition. Most likely there's a failsafe under my seat. I need you to call Jared. Now. The Granville in—"

"What?"

"His number is—"

"I have his number. Don't move."

He didn't respond. *Slow breath in. Slow breath out. Slow my pulse. Slow my heart rate.*

"I only have one phone. I could ask Dav—"

"No. Hang up. Call Jared."

This place was deserted enough. He'd parked away from other cars and the building. He would wait with his thoughts, until Jared and God knows what army showed up to get him out of this hot seat.

"Wait. Nic?" *What the fuck? Don't stop the savior brigade.* What did he even want to say anyway? Maybe he needed more oxygen to his brain. The line was dead anyway. She'd disconnected. "I'll miss you, sweet girl." Except she wasn't there to hear it.

Jared's blacked-out, chromed-up Expedition screamed into the parking lot a long-assed thirty-five minute wait later followed by two similar looking vehicles. No lights and sirens. Thank God Nic'd listened and let Titan take care of this situation in-house. No police, no freakin' FBI profilers nosing into the who and why in search of a motive.

For a Saturday night, the Granville was empty. Maybe that's why'd he stopped in for a brewski and pizza. As company went, Cash was of the worst variety. He was pissed off, angry at the world, and more than he wanted to admit it, hurt. Here in the Podunk bar, he'd had no worries about the ladies. They'd all shown up on the back of their men's Fat Boys and certainly weren't looking for a piece of action like him.

The Expedition door opened, and out stepped a grizzly of a man. After surveying the parking lot, Jared marched toward Cash's truck, seemingly unfazed that Cash likely had C-4 strapped to his ass.

"Don't move," Jared said through the half-open window.

He didn't move his head. "No shit. Thanks for the survival tip."

"Ass. I was neck deep in two broads until this shit popped up. We'll put this in the you-owe-me-huge column."

Cash would've laughed if he could. If his life weren't on the line and all, it'd be funny shit to pull his boss out of a three way. Knowing Jared, he probably took Nic's call mid-fuck, then pulled up dick and walked out. No way he had the ladies at his place. No way he said, "thanks, see ya later."

Out of the corner of his eye, Cash saw Jared duck down out of view. Time ticked by. There was definitely something attached to the undercarriage if it took that long to inspect. Finally, Jared stood, turned around, and waved toward the two unfamiliar vehicles.

"You're not going to like this. I'd guess the secondary's set on a pressure switch, so you can move your head. But don't move from your torso down. I mean it."

"Yeah—"

"I suggest you at least turn your head and compartmentalize your shit before you accidently blow up. And it's not like I have another sniper on standby, so do me that favor. I've got you booked for a while."

Cash turned his head a fraction and caught a glimpse of a man. *Are you fuckin' kidding me?* "No—"

"Shut up, Garrison."

Towel boy? There was no mistaking that pretty boy face and shiner beating feet toward his truck. From the neck down, the man was in bomb tech gear, helmet in hand. Cash wanted to rage, but he forced his muscles to obey. "What the—"

"You had Nic call. She said she knew a guy, then gave me a rundown of your day. I'm concerned that you're stupid enough to move. Don't. Rocco and Brock are out on a job tonight, so I didn't have a choice. Plus, from the sound of it, he's one of the best in the world. Your lucky night." Jared shrugged, not looking concerned enough to back away from the truck. "I'll hold both your hats if you want to go to blows after this shit is over."

Towel boy arrived next to his door and stood three feet away. The urge to kill was a live wire. *Live through this and it's game on.* Kill or be killed, although towel boy might be slightly harder to take down if he expected an attack.

Jared gestured to the man. "Jackson, here you go. Don't kill my boy, or I'll kill you. Slowly." With that, his boss stepped aside, and Jackson, AKA towel boy, stepped up to the window.

"Don't worry. I don't want to be here either, asshole," Jackson said. "Don't move."

Christ, would people stop telling him that? The bulky, bombproof hat went on, and Jackson disappeared down the side of the truck. *This guy might kill me on purpose. I'd think about it if I was him.*

Dude popped back up and spoke through the plastic vent near his mouth. "Not an amateur."

"Nice update," Cash snarled. It could be good or bad. Good, meaning no fucked up wiring mistakes would blow after it was disengaged. Bad, meaning that disengaging wasn't going to be easy-peasy. His pizza would def be cold when he got home. One disappointment after another today, all of varying importance. Large to small.

"You're an ass," Jackson replied, studying his wheelbase.

"What are you going to do about it, Jackson?" Maybe he should tone down the I-might-punch-you-again voice. It'd probably increase his chance of living to the next fist fight.

"An 'I'm sorry, I'm a dick' would go a long way."

Cash moved his glance another slight turn. "I may kill you when this is over, so maybe you want to walk away."

"And disappoint Nic? Not after she asked so sweetly that I save your sorry ass."

Anger swelled in his fists. It took a significant amount of energy to compartmentalize. Cash took a short breath in through his nose and let it slide out his lips.

Jackson continued. "I'm going to open your door and see what we're dealing with in here. Stay as still as possible."

Cash rolled his eyes toward the ceiling. *Got it. Jesus Christ. I won't move.* The last thing he wanted was towel boy between his legs. *Worst day ever.* He had to will his knee to stay in place and away from Jackson's pie hole. Nothing good would happen from knocking him out again.

Maybe later.

The door opened, and Jackson poked around under his legs. Wasn't this a little uncomfortable? Dude's fucking bubble hat kept touching his calf. Half a minute later, the guy stood next to him.

"Don't—"

Cash smirked. "Move. Got it."

"The pressure detonator is the problem. The ignition detonator malfunctioned and isn't an issue," Jackson grumbled. "I'd rather get you out than try to diffuse it."

"Meaning?"

"Your truck's gonna blow."

"Prick." Cash swore a line of curses. "You're doing this on purpose. Aren't you?" If Jared wasn't actively ignoring him, he'd offer his willingness to wait for Brock or Rocco.

"It's a truck."

"Are you even a man?" Cash asked, annoyed on so many levels.

Jackson looked ready to walk away. He turned, caught sight of Jared, and turned back to Cash. "Look. We do this, and we both go home with less of a headache than we already have."

"It's just under my seat?"

"Huh?"

"The pressure plate. It's only triggered by a shift in my weight?"

"Yes. Look, man. You're tempting fate for both of us as long as we both sit here and dick around."

"Grab my rifle and pizza."

"Excuse me?"

"Get the goddamn rifle and the pizza, and I will do whatever you want."

Jackson stood silent, eyes narrowing. "Nic owes me. Man, does she owe me." He walked around, carefully opened the door, grabbed the rifle case, then the pizza. He put the case down, and chucked the pizza into a nearby parking space. *Asshole.*

At least the gun survived. That gun signified his whole world.

After speaking into a mic, Jackson came back to Cash's door. Two men got out of the third vehicle, both in their bombproof moon suits.

"Now what?"

Jackson pointed at the men. "Now, they pull your ass out while I hold down the sensor and try to disengage it without hurting your precious vehicle."

All right. At least the asshole had a plan. Jared took one large step back. *Okay, then. The plan must not be one hundred percent foolproof.*

One man held what looked like a lead blanket, the other grasped his arm. Jackson knelt by his knee. They gave signals, someone gave a countdown. "Three, two—" and a noise. A beep. A roar. Blast!

CHAPTER TWENTY-THREE

David drummed his fingers inside the pocket of his Armani tuxedo pants. The impeccable tailoring was only one of the many reasons he looked ready to waltz Nicola into this gala, if she'd ever show up. She was late by at least twenty-five minutes. He waited in his chauffeured Rolls for her to grace him with her unrefined presence.

But he was refined. Refined manners. Refined looks. His high cheek bones and sculpted nose were perfect, all healed from his scuffle with the exception of fading bruises covered by makeup. He had aristocratic bone structure, bless his mother for that, and his father's conniving skills allowed him to float in and out of this world, dripping in diamonds and silk, without so much as a hiccup.

He'd absolutely been born into the wrong class of people, and as luck would have it, he was corruptible. Moral flexibility was a wonderful characteristic to have, once he'd learned how profitable it could be. David hadn't even known that about himself when he'd started at the CIA. They didn't see it in his profile. *Surprise, surprise.*

Maybe Nicola was late because everything on the home front was going according to plan. Mister Nero would be thrilled, and David would love to see the look on her face once she learned her parents had been blown sky high.

He'd tacked the blond cowboy on as an added bonus. Had that fool cracked his jawbone in their scuffle, David might've considered letting the Gianori mob take their time with his demise. Regardless, the guy had to die, and a bomb would do the trick. David was too powerful, had too many connections to let some wild-West blowhard get away with hitting him.

Funny, he thought, how he now bartered and traded outside of currency. The better things in life couldn't be paid for out of Cayman Island bank accounts.

After David found out the how and why of Nicola's background—that the Gianori Mob wanted her head—his plan fell into place. He knew Mister Nero wanted Nicola for infiltrating Smooth Enterprises as a CIA operative, even if she was ineffective. Mister Nero had preached the power of retaliation and could not wait to take her parents. *An eye for an eye. Bloodshed for bloodshed.*

The Gianori mob wanted Nicola because the mob never forgets. He promised her to the mob only if they could complete two tasks. The first was Mister Nero's: blow up the parents. The second was his: take out the cowboy.

There'd be no way to connect the parents' demise to him, and the mob would never be able to find him once he handed Nicola to Mister Nero. The Gianori clan would be shit out of luck, but it wasn't his problem. The CIA had trained him well. David could disappear into a crowd of one, and they'd never find him.

This was a new way of doing business and, thus far, it worked out beautifully. David chuckled at his ingenuity.

A flurry of black silk and chiffon caught his eye, and he stared out the window. Nicola was a beautiful woman. She looked rushed. Worried. A pleased smile dripped across his face. The explosions must've been a success. Parents and cowboy, check.

The worry washed away when she slipped in through the chauffeur-opened door. It wasn't his imagination. It had been there.

"Michael," she crooned in front of the chauffer before he shut the door. Nicola leaned over and kissed his cheek. It was a very appropriate response for an untimely wife. "I apologize for my tardiness."

The chauffer slid into the driver's seat, and the Rolls began to glide toward their destination a block away. "But of course, Sarah Beth. You look stunning, as always."

She did present a nice picture. Gorgeous woman, really. When Mister Nero finished with her, if she was still alive and relatively unmarked, he might keep her for himself.

Nicola swirled the Dom Perignon in the crystal champagne flute. Slimy David had had his hand at the small of her back all night long, and it was pure training that kept her from removing it from his body and handing it to a waiter to take out with the caviar-covered trash.

"Is something wrong, sweetheart? You look tense."

Yeah. You keep touching me, and I want to vomit. "Of course not, Michael." To be this man's wife would be torture. His fingers were both cold and sweaty. How was that possible? If he dragged them over her Pucci gown one more time, she was sending him the dry cleaning bill. That was, before he was taken to a federal pen for espionage.

"Perhaps a massage is in order when we arrive at the hotel."

Do not gag. She repeated it several times. A massage wasn't what she wanted. She wanted, no hell, she needed information.

It was too early in the night to step out of this party. She wanted to excuse herself and hit redial again and again until someone answered. She'd tried to call Cash a hundred times before this godforsaken gala. Each time, she got voicemail. She'd called Jackson and Jared. No one answered.

In the background, the orchestra struck up another slow number, and she glared off David's invitation for a waltz.

Thinking about the unanswered calls made her pulse race. Something must have happened to Cash. What if Jackson didn't get there in time? Or if the blast took them both out? And where the hell was Jared?

Since their arrival in Istanbul, Nicola had slipped several more listening devices onto David and his belongings. If he'd found any of them, the bastard hadn't given it away. Maybe Cash was at home, listening to all their conversations, listening for dirt when she wasn't in the room with David.

That had to be it.

Cash wasn't going to die in a car bomb. He wasn't. He played life too fast and furious to be taken out sitting on his ass outside some bar.

Life's not fair. You should know that better than anyone.

His voice replayed in her head a thousand times, and her head spun. She threw down the rest of her bubbly, impatiently waiting for their assets to show up. Soon as this gig was done, she was pulling David out and flagging down the nearest Learjet back to the States.

"Sarah Beth, darling." David's voice had a serious ick factor. "I believe we're on."

The target couple stood dead ahead, living replicas of the pictures in Nicola's briefing book. *Wonderful timing.* The assets greeted their marks, two men who looked up-to-their-mustaches in selling stolen third-world secrets. Everyone was in place. *Showtime.*

Nicola raised a bejeweled hand and called over in her haughtiest voice. "Frederick? Elizabeth? Is that you?" She walked gracefully toward the foursome with David in tow. He too murmured their cover names. "It is them. How delightful."

Frederick and Elizabeth smiled. The woman waved hello. Emeralds glittered from her bouffant to her pedicure. "Oh, it's the Penningtons. From New York."

The man turned to their companions and started introductions. Something about how the Penningtons made their supposed loot in the chemical market. Something vague enough to be untraceable.

Elizabeth kissed her cheek. "Sarah Beth, I didn't expect you!"

"We made an unanticipated stop. Mallory had a European qualifier in her show jumping competition, and since the jet was fueled and we were so close..." Nicola shrugged a silk-covered shoulder as elegantly as she could. That was the extent of her lines. Time for David to shine.

Nic glanced at him. He was on a roll. This was his type of work, hobnobbing and schmoozing. How boring, especially when real life waited for her thousands of miles away. At least she hoped it was life waiting and not a soul-wrenching obituary.

CHAPTER TWENTY-FOUR

Their minor assignment was a success. Nicola and David were back at the hotel, and her room was packed. Nothing left in her closet, designer or otherwise. The Louis Vuitton bags rested by the door, awaiting a bellhop. Having a jet on standby was convenient, but they both had to agree to leave. The bag brigade was nothing more than an effort to convince David they were leaving tonight, but he wasn't budging.

At least she'd kicked him out of the bedroom to one of the smaller adjoining rooms. Nic swept the room for bugs, set up her signal jammer as a just-in-case backup, and thought about getting the hell out of Istanbul so that someone could give her some intel. All she needed to know was that everyone was alive and kicking. *That Cash didn't blow up in his truck.*

Ring. She lunged across the room, catapulting across the king size bed to grab the phone. She didn't look at the screen, only accepted the call and prayed for good news.

"Nic." The sound of Cash's voice hugged her tightly, making her believe in the power of desperate prayers.

"Thank you!" she cried, realizing that tears streamed down her face. "Cash, you're okay. Oh God. You're okay."

Her breaths surfaced, rapid fire. All of the pent up emotions boiled into a fierce mess of wet tears, running down her cheeks. She sniffled and rambled without the slightest clue what she said.

"Slow down." He paused. "I'm okay."

The words didn't work. Tears raced down her cheeks, blurring her vision. Her mind sped, swirling into an anxious frenzy. "I thought this is how we were going to end," she whispered. "That you wouldn't be there when I came home. That I left and lost you once. That you died tonight, and I lost you—"

"Who's Jackson?" The sharp-tipped question sobered her from the nightmare of possible bomb blast causes and effects.

"What?" She shook her head, wiping the tears away with the back of her hand. *Jackson?* This morning seemed years ago. Had that really happened?

"Tell me a lie, and I swear to God, sweet girl. You will lose me. No explosive charge needed."

It had really happened. Cash was alive and... angry. His voice scratched through the phone. The not knowing. The bomb scare. Everything else was trivial. Everything was trivial except him. Her throat tightened. She couldn't imagine the words to make it better.

"Nic!"

"He's a bomb specialist for the FBI—"

"I've learned that much on my own. Who is he to you?"

"We dated."

"You live together."

"Technically—"

He coughed a harsh laugh in her ear. "You've got to be kidding me. This is karma. This is for all the nice girls who I should've called and all the bad ones I should've left alone."

Are you serious? Nicola smirked into her handset. "Like Sugar?"

"Yeah. Like Sugar. Hell, woman. You've got everyone fooled, including Sugar. You know, she tried to take up for you tonight. Like—"

"I knew it. I knew you'd go see her, you ass. Fuck whatever walks, Cash. Fuck me. Fuck her. Fuck every goddamn woman you see. That's you. I get it, but you certainly don't know me if you think I'd sleep with you and then go home to someone else."

Silence.

She checked the phone. The line was still connected. Nic was content to wait until he had something to say.

Silence.

He had the same plan.

She took a deep breath, then continued. "I dated Jackson. Past tense. I broke it off more than a year ago, amicably. We're good friends. There was no pop and sizzle. When I took the Smooth assignment, I got rid of my apartment because I'd only be home once every few months."

"Go on," he said, not nearly as sharply. Hesitation still hung in his voice.

"I crash at Jackson's. He has the master bedroom. I have my own bedroom. I've stayed there three times, and you have shitty timing because I jumped in the shower after he jumped out. So there's the truth, and I wouldn't dare lie to you."

Silence.

"Goddamn it, Cash—"

"Tell me another truth." Again, his voice wasn't as angry. It still grated, and the intensity was still there, but it didn't rasp in rage.

"Another truth... I'm hurt you ran off to Sugar."

"I ran off to the closest place I could unload an automatic weapon."

Somewhat believable. "So you didn't...?" She closed her eyes, hoping and listening for his response.

"Nope. It wasn't even a passing thought."

"What was then?"

He laughed quietly. "What was on my mind? Simple. The urge to kill."

All right. She could handle that. "I'm glad you didn't. Jacks is a good guy. Plus, he was useful tonight. Right?"

"My truck's a goner. I'm pretty sure he did it on purpose."

Oh, he loved that truck. Insurance would cover that, wouldn't it? "He didn't blow your truck up on purpose. Anyway... your turn. Tell me a truth."

She waited patiently, wondering if it was going to be another complaint about her being in the field working a job.

"The phone was an excuse." Cash spoke deliberately. A long pause expired. "It wasn't the reason I drove back to your apartment."

Banging on the door drew her attention. "Hold on a sec." She lumbered off the bed and cracked the door to see David's weaselly face. "What do you need, David?"

"We have to head home. Something's gone wrong with one of my back burner projects. I'm needed in the States. You've been trying to go home. Let's go."

A mischievous glint in his eye made her stomach tense. Instinct was a precious tool, and hers was precision honed. Something wasn't right. Her gut screamed for her to backtrack and bed down. "I'm exhausted. We can leave in the morning."

"You're already packed."

"I've been packed for two hours. Now I'm ready for bed. Leave without me, if it's so important. I'll hop on a commercial flight."

David studied her, and her muscles tensed, the hair on her forearms standing at attention. There was an edge to his voice and an off-kilter air about him that made her skin shiver.

"Fine. I'll have the jet prepared for a seven AM departure," he said.

Nic shut the door without responding. Her skin continued to crawl. She fished the phone from her robe pocket and pushed it back against her ear. "Cash? You there."

"Yup."

"Sorry. What were you saying?"

"Nothing much. Just that this bed is lonely without you."

"Truth?" She missed him deep in her heart. It was just the two of them, eating through the burner phone's minutes.

"Truth."

The word made her smile. "It's no fun to make up with you when there's an ocean between us."

He laughed, and the sound felt like an embrace. She remembered the warmth of his body and how he could flash a look that made her nerves spark to life. They'd have to time their disagreements better.

"Get in bed, and let me tell you a good-night story. Before you know it, you'll be home with me."

Falling asleep to his voice, now that was a plan. She double checked the door lock and chain, shed her robe, threw back the comforter, and tucked herself into the mess of a cotton nirvana. "All right. Tucked in. Tell me a story."

"It's an interactive story."

"Hm-okay." Whatever. As long as he kept talking, he could call it whatever he wanted. His voice always sounded sinfully delicious. He could read her the classifieds. A thesis on temperature variables affecting long range fire power. Hell, he could recite the telephone book from A to Z. There was something so tangible in his voice that just did it for her.

This was never going to put her to sleep, but she'd give it a try. She closed her eyes and blocked out everything but his voice.

He started, slow and deep. "So, there was this guy and this gorgeous girl. Amazon-like, mythical-proportions-kind-of-gorgeous. They were lovers."

Nic's eyes flew open. "Lovers?"

"Lovers," he repeated. She heard the smile in his voice and felt her cheeks flush. "What do you think their names were?"

Oh my God. "Describe the guy to me, and I might be able to tell you."

"Oh, that's easy. Tall, tan, and terrible with self-descriptions."

She shifted the phone from one ear to the other. "I think we should call him Cash."

"That sounds about right. We can call her Nic. Cash and Nic."

Nic giggled and nodded.

"You're nodding, aren't you?"

She smiled against the soft pillow. "Maybe."

Cash laughed quietly. "Back to Cash and Nic. They'd had a disagreement. The latest after a couple of 'em. Nothing insurmountable, but—"

"Does Cash say he's sorry? You know, in the story?"

Long pause. "Yeah. He's sorry. But that's back story, and that chapter is boring. Just know he's sorry for conclusion-jumping and friend-punching."

"Good to know."

"Anyway." He cleared his throat. "You know, this'd be a lot easier if you played Nic. You could do a little improv."

"So you're Cash?"

He laughed quietly again. "That works."

"Now what?" she asked, a little nervous and excited.

"Now you should make damn sure your phone is charged and you have a transmission blocker turned on," he growled. The order raked over her body like he was there, in the flesh, and purring into her ear.

"Why?" she pushed, hoping for that feeling again. The whispered tension double-knotted her stomach.

"Because you're about to find out how bad I want you in this bed, next to me."

Her chest constricted. Her lungs went on strike. "Tell me."

"Close your eyes, Nic."

Tummy flip. Eyes closed.

He kept to the low murmur. "Remember in the shower. The water and the steam and the need. Did your heart beat faster? Did you want me to kiss you?"

She nodded in the dark. "Yes."

"And did you want more? When my hands ran up and down your wet skin, do you remember how ready you were for me?"

"Uh-huh." It was all she could manage. His voice rocketed sensations down her spine.

"Touch your lips for me, Nicola."

She complied. The rich texture of his words coated her in heat. Her fingers brushed softly over her bottom lip while her ears begged him for more.

Cash continued. "The harder I kissed you, the harder I got, sweet girl. When your little tongue moved over mine…" He took a long, slow breath, blowing into the phone. "I wanted to feel it everywhere, but not before I tasted you."

"Oh." Blood thumped in her neck, racing through her veins.

"And I kissed your neck," he whispered. Nic moved her fingers to the slope of her neck and felt her pulse. "It took all my strength not to move too fast. Not to touch and kiss where I was dying to end up."

"Where was that?" Her insides melted, overcome by the memories of him nudging her knees apart. Him creating such intense pleasure, she thought she'd drown in him, awash in undeniable bliss.

"Your sweet pussy. But I'm getting there tonight. I don't care how far away from me you are."

Oh. They were only words, not a sinful touch or a kiss that made her knees weak. But the way he said it made agonized need ricochet from her hips to her core. She was alone in a dark room with eyes shut and could've sworn he whispered into her ear, tickling her skin with his promise.

"Are you in bed, Cash?"

"Yeah, and I'm naked, missing you." His voice was an electric jolt. There was nothing hesitant, nothing held back. Everything about Cash was strong and direct. A live wire.

"Are you…?" She trailed off, wanting for the right words, wanting to be as bold as he was.

"Hard and in my hand," he answered for her. The revelation jump-started her imagination.

Her heart was in her throat, pounding and punching for attention. "You're stroking?"

"Good girl." She heard his approving smile. "Yeah, I'm stroking. Thinking of how good you feel. Where's that beautiful touch of yours?"

"My neck."

"Is that where you want it?"

She shook her head silently against the pillow.

Cash urged her on. "Just relax with me, sweet girl. Tell me what you want, how you love it. Let yourself go for me."

This was too revealing. Embarrassingly scary. She didn't know what to say or do. Being this vulnerable with him so confident made it all the more erotic. More intimate. "Cash—"

"You can do this if you want. You don't have to. But you could."

"I want," she promised.

"Then trust me. Listen to me, and know there's nothing in the world I wouldn't do to make you come for me tonight."

"I'm listening." Heat bloomed between her legs. If he kept saying things like that, she'd beg for release soon.

"Tell me a truth, Nicola. Touch your gorgeous body, and trust me with another truth."

Her hands grazed her nightgown. Her breasts anticipated, her breaths shortened, and quick flashes of electricity fired beneath the surface of her flesh. *A truth.* Nicola pressed her lips together, summoned another round of courage and said, "I've been dying to taste you too."

His breath hitched. "Christ."

She swallowed away a sigh. Her confidence blazed at his reaction. He was just as needy as she felt. This was erotic power. Seduction.

Nicola confided, "I'd kneel between your naked legs. Your powerful thighs. And then I'd kiss you." Cash groaned quietly into her ear, daring her to continue. "Your hands twist in my hair, and you're rock hard, scary large, but the silkiest, smoothest thing I've ever touched."

"Lick," he growled, low and deep.

She nodded, her fingers knotting in the silk nightgown. "And suck."

"Goddamn, woman. You're not shy. Tell me more."

That was all she needed. He fortified her, pushing her past steamy to audacious and adventurous. "And hum. My lips vibrate around you. My tongue caresses you. You feel it?"

"Hell, yes, I do. What I wouldn't give to flip you around, with your mouth still tight on me, and love that sweetness of yours." The breath fled from her lungs as he painted a carnal picture. "I'd hold your hips in place, press you to my mouth, and drive you crazy."

Nic's fingers toyed with the top of her underwear, sliding back and forth over the elastic band. Damp heat teased between her legs. From a thousand miles away, Cash aroused her. She needed him to continue, needed him to voice every amorous thought. "Tell me more. Tell me everything."

"About how I'd make you scream my name?"

She nodded, and her fingers slipped under the fabric. "Uh-huh."

"Are you touching yourself, Nic?"

She nodded, moaning her answer.

"Good, sweet girl. You're wet for me. Aching."

"Hm-hmm."

"I'd hold you close, hold you open. Suck your perfect clit until I felt you tremble. Shudder and shake. Then one finger. Two fingers. In and out."

She could feel him. Her hands. His words. Their actions. Turned on and bolder by the second, Nicola continued. "My hands would wrap around you, sliding in time with my mouth."

He groaned. "Fuck yes. Tell me how good we are together."

"The best."

"Tell me what you need."

"God, Cash. You. I need you."

"Come with me, sweet girl."

She moaned into the phone. Her fingers worked magic like they were his. Her core throbbed. Her defenses were gone. The build unraveled in a powerful riptide. She could hear him, feel him. The strength and the arousal. Their desire. Her body craving his, sensations exploding.

Cash whispered her name into the phone. Ripples of satisfaction slammed through her. They were in concert. Climaxing, wrapped together as one, thousands of miles apart. She loved what he did to her with words, with trust. She loved him more than she could ever explain.

Their breaths pounded and started their sated descent, entwined through a cell phone signal. Knowing Cash held the phone to his ear felt like a lullaby, soothing her into sweet dreams.

"Nicola?"

"Hmm?"

"You're still awake? Thought I lost you."

"You're never going to lose me."

"I have to tell you something." Cash sighed. She waited. "I… I need you with me. Here with me. Come home to me."

She nodded, sleep and contentment dragging her. "I will."

In the room adjoining hers, the door opened and closed, jolting her back to real life. The job. David the Butler. "Cash?"

"Yeah, babe."

"Got a second for work?"

"Guess so."

"Get anything good off the listening devices on the butler?"

"I think so. You want to know now or when we debrief tomorrow after you return?"

"Now is fine. He just slammed a door, and I'm awake again."

"All right." Cash cleared his throat, shuffling what sounded like his covers. "Two things of interest. First, he's conversed with someone named Nero. He calls himself Mars."

Her stomach bottomed out, shooting her straight up in her lonely, rumpled bed. "What? What'd they say?"

"You know Nero?"

"What'd they say?"

"Package logistics. Nothing I can make heads or tails of, though I haven't tried that hard yet. Why? Who's Nero?"

"Antilla Smooth was obsessed with Roman history. One of the reasons why my cover worked so well... he could—"

"Get to the point, Nic."

"Nero and Mars. Roman gods of war. Mars may have been subservient to Nero, and if you translated some texts, even his wife. But mostly—"

"Smooth's dead. I blew his brains out. Clean shot."

Nic nodded. "I saw him, but the hierarchy didn't fall apart completely. Maybe they picked up where Antilla left off."

Cash whistled. "This is what we need. Tip of the iceberg, this will prove the butler is a double."

"You're right. So this godforsaken trip is worth it." She paused, letting it sink in and squelching the urge to confront David in the next room. "What's the other interesting item?"

"He's logged phone time with someone named Gianori. He's connected to Smooth somehow, and I haven't looked him up yet, but—"

Nicola reached to the nightstand and palmed her chromed out .38 Special. "They're not connected."

"Sure sounded like it."

"That's wrong. They're not."

"How would you know that?"

She was a Gianori encyclopedia, that's how. "Salvatore Gianori. Mafioso boss for the Gianori clan. His sons, Basilio, Durante, and Emilio, are all named Italian versions of 'I'm king motherfucker.' They deal in gun smuggling, bid rigging, and loan sharking. But Salvatore, his specialty is violence."

Her insides shook, recalling everything she knew about the mobsters who were never nailed for anything, ever.

"Nic, why do you know that?" Concern edged his voice. Not panic, which he surely heard in hers, but ice cold concern. "Tell me you just know your mobster history, that this David asshole doesn't know about…"

She double checked the .38. Locked and loaded. Nic propped up on a pillow, facing the only door. "He must. He knows. It was the Gianori mob. Very few people know that, and he's not on the short list. He sure as fuck shouldn't be talking to them."

"Grab your piece."

"Done."

"And don't move 'til I get there." Cash's voice vibrated through the phone.

"Istanbul? We'd be wheels up before you got here. Our plan isn't changing. Not because of this."

"Why would you get on the plane with him, knowing that he—"

"Because it's the operation. The job. I'm not blowing my cover because of an added layer of danger. The fucker is a traitor, and we're taking him down."

"Nic—"

"We move forward as planned."

He huffed. "Give me your tail numbers, your flight plan. I'll have a jet escort you in. And I'll be on the tarmac—"

"Cash."

"Waiting for you, ready to—"

"Cash!"

"What?"

"Ready to protect me? That's not the point of any of this. He'll know that we know. I'm not your girl right now, I'm your partner."

"Damn it, Nicola. You're being so hardheaded right now, trying to go all Lone Ranger." She waited, hoping something decent would come out of his trap that wouldn't ruin their night. He sucked a breath. "No matter what you're doing or where you are, nothing's going to change my need to protect you. I'm that asshole, okay. It's in my blood, in my brain. I'm fucking hardwired to step in front of you. To cover and protect you. So, Christ almighty, know that I'm trying."

"Make me understand that you know the difference between partnership and possessiveness."

Cash sounded clear and cutthroat. "You're sitting with a flimsy-assed hotel door between you and someone who might hurt what's mine. I'm an assassin. A contract killer. It might be for the good guys, but still, that's me. Let's not play and pretend that it hasn't been ingrained into me to seek blood or to watch your ass. Trust me, Nic. Know that I've got your back. Few people in the world truly understand a phrase that gets tossed around as easy as that one does. Few people understand the responsibility that comes with that vow. I've got your back. I trust you to make the right move. But if something happens, I'm there, itchy trigger finger and all. You're mine to protect and possess."

"I'm yours?"

"Was there some confusion about that?"

"Well, no. It's just we haven't really talked about anything. We've just sort of... slept together."

"God, Nic. This isn't college. I don't have time to write notes during English one-oh-one. Let me be clear. I don't want you with anyone else. I'd think knocking your roomie out made that clear."

"But see, you didn't say, 'I don't want to be with anyone else.' You've been king of the players for a long time. A month stuck with me, and you'll be raring for something new and improved."

"Hardly. And you've leapfrogged from us to the job to us. Like I said, I need you, sweet girl. I'll be ready for you stateside. Don't fall asleep. When you see him in the AM, be polite, be courteous, and have a plan to kill everyone in the room."

"Advice like that makes all the girls swoon."

"Only you, Nic. The only girl I want is you. Keep the safety off, and I'll get eyes on you soon as I can. Put the phone on speaker. I'm with you all night long."

CHAPTER TWENTY-FIVE

Only an hour had passed since they'd left Istanbul's modern airport. The trip had been more than productive. Nicola now knew that she shared a private charter—complete with a culinary genius and a stewardess who must've gone to the Emily Post School of Etiquette—with a double-crossing traitor. Seeing David strung up by her brethren at the CIA would be so damn satisfying.

She knew some talented men who worked every day on their information-eliciting techniques. She hoped to God that David would hold out on his explanations so those men could have a go at him. That was if Cash didn't kill him first. There was always that chance. David would be dead before he took a second step out of the jet and before anyone heard the gunshot. Cash's .50 calibers were good like that. The bullet always beat the sound barrier.

Eyeing the bastard, Nic worked to act as normal as possible. It was a chore considering that he was involved with the Gianori clan, but she kept her casual disdain alive. Without that, David would sense a problem. She didn't watch him too closely. She didn't nose about his personal items. She was simply ready for whatever came her way.

Her phone vibrated. It'd been about an hour since she'd last checked in with Cash, and she wasn't due to talk to Beth until after they landed. Pulling the phone free of her bag, she looked at the Caller ID. No numbers were programmed in, but she knew this one.

"Hey, Jacks."

David looked up from his book, eyebrows high as if he hoped to see her receive bad news. *Well, fuck you very much.*

"Nicola." Jackson sounded agitated. "When are you coming home?"

"I told you I had to work."

"I just thought you mentioned you were coming home last night. When I woke up, you weren't home. I worried."

Honestly, if she'd landed last night, she wouldn't have been home anyway. She would've been with Cash, preferably in bed, but that wasn't worth discussing with Jackson in front of David.

David smiled sickly, interrupting her daydream of Cash. "Everything all right?"

Nic nodded and wished he didn't look so damn excited all of a sudden. It made her stomach queasy. "Fine, David."

"Michael," he hissed. "The stewardess might hear you."

"Fine, Michael."

"Nicola, are you there?" Jackson asked. "Who's with you?"

"Who's that?" asked David.

Too many men needed her attention. One was dangerous, the other annoying. Both needed to shut up.

"David, it's my roommate," she said, ignoring his annoyance that she didn't stick to the married-to-Michael act. "Jacks, I really have to go. We just left Istanbul, and it'll be a while before we land. But don't expect me home tonight."

Really, don't expect me home ever. That's not your concern as my roommate.

"Why not?" Jackson pushed.

God, he was getting on her nerves. *Time for a subject change.* "I wanted to thank you for that project you worked on. Really good job."

Jackson needed a bone thrown his way, she could tell. Not wanting to go into any details in front of David, that was all she'd say. A good job and a thanks.

"I only did it because you asked me to, Nicola. You honestly have to know that."

Christ. Jackson wouldn't let anyone blow to pieces. It wasn't his nature, but he was obviously still raw about the

Cash-punch thing. David scowled at her, rummaging through his carry-on bag.

She sighed. "Whatever the reason, thanks. I really have to go."

"We should talk when you get home. I need to make sure you're okay. I don't know that I like you working with Titan Group."

Was there something in the water? What else would cause perfectly normal men to lose perspective and act this damn overprotective?

"Got it." Her phone went dead. No white noise. Nothing. She looked at it and saw a full charge and great reception. "Jackson? Jacks?"

David smiled, showing far too many teeth. "Must've lost your connection."

Bullshit.

He'd found a listening device, or maybe he just wised up. Whatever the reason, David had turned on a cell frequency blocker, and she had no way to communicate with anyone outside the jet.

Welcome to the game, David. I've been playing since you boarded the flight to Istanbul.

"Nic'll be wheels down in—" Cash checked his watch "—thirty-three minutes. You think you fucks could hurry the hell up?"

Watching Jared and Roman dillydally punched at his patience. They were a five minute drive from their rendezvous point, another five minutes to get into position and watch Nicola deplane with that piece of shit, double-dealing butler. The rest of that time made him vibrate with impatience.

Cash was armed to the teeth. More than armed. He could outfit a third-world tribe with enough brass to create a serious change in the balance of power, and that was only what he had strapped to him. The Hummer's trunk told a whole other story.

Jared looked him over, boots to collar, and grumbled. "You plan on redefining the word overkill? We're backup. We're not storming an Iranian missile silo."

Can never be too prepared, or some Boy Scout shit like that. He'd been to the site twice today, walked the perimeter, memorized every outbuilding, every hangar, nook, and cranny. If someone was there who shouldn't be, if something moved that wasn't supposed to, Cash might shoot first and ask questions later. He'd let Jared deal with the nuclear-fallout-sized headache and handle the question-and-answer portion of their day. That's why boss man made the really big dollars: to fix whatever wrongs Cash was very ready to do.

"Get your asses in the rig. Let's go." Cash ran through his mental checklist and jumped in. Rolling the window down, he circled his hand. "Now."

Shit. Giving orders to Jared was as smart as licking an electrical socket during a hurricane. Not the cleverest idea he'd had all day. No worries, though. He had some brilliant beauties ready to make up for it. First, his dead-dropped listening devices were stashed in either of the private hangars Nic's jet could pull into. Second, he had a remote and a recorder running already. He'd hear everything in his earpiece, as would Jared and Roman, and it'd all be transmitted to Titan HQ, where Parker, their techie genius, would save it to hard drives or computers or whatever.

Jared and Roman re-checked the last of their gear and joined him. *Finally.*

They sped down the back road to the private airport where her plane was expected. It was easy to have the flight rerouted away from the public airport, even if it had a chartered section. *Nothing like Jared's rolodex of people who owe him favors.* They were able to amend flight plans mid-journey. Their vehicle moved through security, passing without a single curious glance. They simply rolled up, and the gates rolled open. The officers manning the station even made it a point to look the other direction.

With the stealthy efficiency of men trained in the art of camouflage, the three moved to their designated spot inside a hangar. Small windows allowed a view of the runway, the secondary hangar, and their position could survey all exits. A solid location, if there was one, to set up for a game of wait-and-watch.

Cash's trigger finger curled, relaxed, then repeated. *Too bad waiting blows.* The beat of his fingers kept pace with his nerves. Drumming wasn't helping him, but he kept at it. *Shit.* He was a sniper. His bread and butter came from lying in wait. The only difference was that he waited for Nicola instead of a moving target. He thought of David. Well, not a target he could take out right now.

"Calm your shit," Jared growled at him. He'd been growling all day. "Roman's holding his shit together. You can too."

Roman rolled his angry eyes. Cash knew his spotter better than anyone in the world. Roman was on the edge, a nasty word away from cutting everyone's throat open with a butter knife.

Ping. Ping. Ping.

Jared lifted his chin. "What's doing?"

Cash studied the alarm reading. "Perimeter's broken in Hangar B."

Roman spoke up and put his ear bud in. "I cleared it this morning with Cash. No personnel expected in for the day. Nothing's scheduled."

Cash and Jared copied Roman, sliding their earpieces into place. Heavy footfalls clunked, echoing in their ears.

Cash mouthed to the men across from him, "that's a man's step." They nodded their agreement. A cell phone rang into their earpieces. A man's voice. "Hello."

The tick, tick, tick of time passed as Cash counted seconds in his head. Who was in there?

"No," the baritone in their ear pieces continued. "No. You tell him that Emilio Gianori gave that order. My name will make him piss himself. And if he dares slink away from a direct order from me, you tell him to kiss his wife and children goodbye."

If they laid a finger on Nic, Cash would use them for target practice, working his way from the outside in. *Feet and hands, knee caps and elbows. Balls to breastbone.*

Nicola needed to know what she was walking into. He'd been out of communication for an hour. Her burner phone wasn't connecting no matter how many times he tried to call.

Using hand signals, Jared told them both to sit tight, keep listening.

Cash raised an inch, readying to... to do something. Jared pointed at him and slashed at his throat. It wouldn't be a stretch for someone else to also bug this private airport. And considering they had Titan Group, the CIA, and the Gianori mob all in play right now, it was a reasonable assumption.

Emilio Gianori's cell phone rang again. Another hello. Another round of threats. *The prick must suffer from a Napoleon complex and have an inch long dick for all the bitching and whining about his super-duper special outlaw powers.*

The mobster continued. "I don't have time for this. I've wasted my day chasing after a fool, one airport to the next. Think before you speak. What do you mean the truck blew up without the man inside it?"

Oh, fuck you! That prick stuffed C-4 into the undercarriage and hot seated his ride? He'd pay for that shit and for the freakin' headache Cash got explaining— or rather not explaining— how his truck blew sky high and didn't have a corresponding police report. Not even a blurb on the local news. All the patrons at the Granville had been more than happy to take some cold hard Benjamins to forget they saw anything. *Amazing how much moolah Jared carries.*

Jared's eyes steeled. A direct non-verbal order: don't move. *Well, don't forget who's armed to the eyebrows and itching to brawl.*

Gianori couldn't keep his mouth shut. *Good for him.* "What about the second package?"

Cash's mind spun. *Second package?* Did he hear that correctly? He bounced a questioning look to Roman, then Jared. They heard it too.

Second package? What had they overlooked?

"I confirmed the parents' address. The address was correct. I was told it would be delivered by your lieutenant. What do I need? A fucking Fed Ex tracking number?"

Parents?

Goddamn.

The world stilled. Roman paled. Anger vibrated at the cleft of his chin and worked its way to his eyes. Fury and wrath boiled in a clear, ready-for-blood stare. It had to be training that kept him in place, alert, and waiting for orders. *That and an attitude problem trained deep into his soul.* Cash wondered if Roman has the ability to feel fear when vengeance was such an easy emotion to replace it with.

Cash's mouth baked dry. His lips stung. The metallic taste of blood skimmed over his tongue. He realized he'd bitten his lip to keep from hollering a war cry. The cold tingle of apprehension shivered across his chest. Nic's story about what sent her on the run and into witness protection, of the Gianori clan murdering the family members of one of their own, filtered through his brain.

A bomb ticked right now, waiting to blow. His stomach roiled. The pattering beat of his heart quick-stepped, needing to protect the parents he was as close to as his own. *But Roman.* Roman looked deadly. Just when Nic was almost back, a threat over his parents was primed to… explode. *Damn.*

"Go," Jared ordered, pointing toward the other hangar. Roman moved on toward the closest exit, as silent as he was speedy.

Cash followed on his six. If there was ever a time to squeeze intelligence out of a criminal, this was it. Reaching the hangar door, they slipped out and into the open outdoors between the two buildings.

They looked around. Nothing suspicious. Out of the reach of potential listening devices, Roman pulled out his cell, hit a button, and pressed it to his ear.

The waiting game, part two. No answer. Roman cursed, then slowly said, "Dad. Stop what you're doing. Call me now. Do not get in your car. Do not check the mail. Don't touch anything. Just call."

Immediacy and dread tinged his voice. Roman dialed again— no answer—and left the same message for his mother. His face pinched. His eyes shut, the creases in the corner aging him in a way Cash had never seen.

"They're fine," Cash said, not sure what the hell else to offer.

Roman gulped a swallow, opened his eyes, and focused on Cash. Agony speared Cash's gut. His best friend squeezed his eyes shut for one more long second. "Let's go."

"We need him alive, man. We need to know what he knows."

"You think I don't fucking know that?" Roman spat back.

"So question first, kill later."

Roman flashed a look that said something along the lines of, "maybe, we'll see."

Cash fell into quick step behind him. They were lifelong partners. They knew all the moves. Roman moved one way, Cash another. They circled down and tightened in until Cash could see Roman opposite him, inside the hangar, readying for an attack.

One man.

Only one mobbed-up jerkoff, paced in the empty hangar. No body men. No armed protection. Gianori dialed into his voicemail, putting it on speakerphone, and picked at his fingernail. *Freakin' manicured piece of crap.*

Cash did another check and held up one finger. Roman did the same and nodded. They had a single target.

Roman moved closer, going for the grab. Gianori listened to voicemails, not hearing Roman creep closer. Not that he could've if he'd listened. Roman crept as silently as a drift of deadly smoke.

Ten yards. Five yards. Still, the mobster was oblivious, ignoring his surroundings. Not a great habit to have in the mob business.

Ten feet. Five feet. Four, three, two.

Roman paused. *Oh, shit. He wouldn't kill the bastard yet. Right?*

One.

A tornado strike of muscle and fury. Roman clawed his hand over Gianori's face and had him planted onto the tarmac floor before Gianori had time to yell.

The barrel of Roman's pistol pressed into the mobster's temple. *Don't pull the trigger. Yet.* Cash moved in fast, ready to pull his man off if need be. Alive. They needed Gianori alive.

Pure white hot hatred spilled off Roman when he reared back. The pistol-whipping crack knocked Gianori out cold, landing him face-first on the concrete.

"That'll work," Cash said. The whirring noise of a plane coming in for a landing pricked his ears. "Let's roll."

Roman nabbed Gianori, throwing him over his shoulder, and hustled back to Hangar A. Blood marred the light gray floor. Cash pulled the army green bandana from his neck, mopped up the mess with his boot, and kicked the ruined rag behind a mechanic's station. *One more thing ruined by these guys. Screw them.*

Catching up with Roman, Cash watched the Learjet complete its landing on the far airstrip. They pushed into Hangar A, eyeballed Jared, and shoved Gianori into a closet after gagging and immobilizing him just in case the fucker decided to rouse. Roman and Cash spread to their corners to watch outside at the airstrip and maintain a tactical advantage if the jet moved into the hangar.

The Learjet turned from the end of the airstrip and made its way toward them. Flight plans had them parking in Hangar A, but who knew where the hell they might deplane their passengers? A black Town Car pulled into a waiting area, apparently also unsure where the passengers were disembarking.

They stopped, and Cash waited, drumming his fingers. The door hatch popped. Stairs unfolded from the opening. No Nic. No David. No one got the hell off the plane. He grabbed his binoculars, needing to see inside the oval windows.

The sun glared high overhead. The Town Car moved into place as Cash heard the pilot cut the engines. A creepy quiet returned. Too quiet. Too much was in play that he didn't understand, and Nicola was in the thick of it.

A bomb targeting her parents floated out there, unaccounted for. Nicola had no idea and was stuck with Benedict Arnold. The Town Car waited for its passengers. Finally, the good CIA agent and the bad one made their way down the stairs. Nic flashed Cash a subtle sign, a quick flick of her wrist, knowing that he had eyes on her. It wasn't much reassurance for him, considering he was only back-up, but a mobster in the closet was a good consolation prize.

Jared whispered into his mic, "Roman, circle up, grab help, and find that bomb."

Roman was in the Hummer without throwing back a visual confirmation. Shit, if it were Cash's parents, he'd be rolling out the second he could. Surely, one of the guys would go with him. Rocco or Brock or Winters could defuse a bomb. Brock would do it the quickest. Winters might opt to let it blow somewhere with the least damage. Who knew how Roc would handle it?

Blinking into the glare, Cash refocused his binoculars. This was the second time he'd seen Nicola through a high-def, military spec optical piece. The Antilla Smooth snipefest felt like years ago, but it was so vivid and intense, seared into his frontal lobe.

The driver opened the door of the Town Car and loaded their baggage into the trunk. Nic and David took to the backseat. Damn, how Cash wanted to kill that man.

Moments later, the driver had them moving down the airstrip. *Wait, no.* They stopped. A second later, the Town Car zoomed toward Hangar B. *Guess what, you fucking turncoat? Your mobster isn't there.*

At the front of Hangar B, David exited the car alone. Cash's earpiece provided audio, but gave him nothing more than footsteps. What he would do to see David standing there, stood up like a blind date. Ten minutes later, clear and crisp in Cash's binoculars, a pissed off, red faced David the Butler exited the hangar door with a slam and made a phone call, out of the range of any listening devices inside the hangar.

Cash's cell phone buzzed.

"Better be important," Jared growled over his shoulder.

The screen showed Sugar's GUNS bison emblem. He hit ignore. Sugar redialed. Twice.

"What?" Cash answered.

"Nic told me to call you, dick, if I couldn't get a hold of her. About this Smooth ammo."

"Now's not the best time."

"I'm supposed to meet my point of contact at some dinky airport in some one-horse town. He just made contact. Pissed off about something. I'm five minutes out, but not headed in. Doesn't feel right."

Wait, what? "What's the guy's name?"

"David—"

"Are you fucking kidding me?" Man, their problems were getting a little incestuous, in an arms-dealing, illegal network kinda way.

Jared looked over. "What's going on?"

"Who's that?" Sugar asked.

"Jared."

She mumbled something that he could've sworn translated to, "tell him I say hi."

He rubbed his temples. "We're at that dinky airport and need a set of wheels. Can you get over here?"

"Yeah, yeah. I'll be your taxi."

He gave her their coordinates and details, hung up, and holstered his phone.

"What'd she say?"

"She'll be here." He gave the rundown of the Sugar-Smooth ammo airport connection.

"Anything else?" Jared asked, not looking at him.

"Anything else? No." What was up with those two? He shook his head, keeping his eyes on the Town Car. "What are we doing? Playing telephone?"

Cash watched until the black Town Car was through the gates and Nic was on her own, as planned. She'd do all right. She'd be fine. They had listening devices everywhere. Parker was listening now, and Roman could tune in on the receiver in the Hummer he'd taken.

Still, Cash's stomach twisted. Jared spun in his boots, yanking his attention back to the here and now. They had a mobster to work over. Cash cracked his knuckles and watched Jared rub his hands together, seconds from opening the closet door.

CHAPTER TWENTY-SIX

Cash took a deep breath after his turn on the Gianori piece of crap. He watched Jared wrench Emilio's twisted arms high behind his head. The bastard and his mobbed-up family would pay for taking Nicola away from him a decade ago, for trying to take out Nic and Roman's parents, and for blowing up his damn truck. Whatever Jared had planned would be too nice, and Jared was a bastard's bastard, trained in ways that made sadistic fucks cry for their mommies.

Blood trickled out of Emilio's nose. The punch hadn't been enough. Pummeling his face into the asphalt wouldn't have done it either, but if the piece of shit couldn't talk, he wouldn't be much good.

Sugar rolled into the hangar in a nondescript white van with no rear windows. Maybe the woman knew what they had planned. Either way, Cash'd have to commend her on her choice of rides.

"Smart choice." Jared beat him to it, handing out compliments for maybe the first time in his life.

Tall boots capped Sugar's knees. Her short skirt barely covered her thighs. The effect made Cash double-take, if only to wonder where she hid her concealed piece.

She blew a bubble of bright pink gum that matched the color of her lips. "So what's the dealio?"

"This is Fuckface Junior." Jared shook Emilio to make a point. "He and Senior, along with their brothers Dickhead and Cock-for-Brains have done a lot of wrong recently, starting with a little incident with Nicola ten years ago and culminating with a plastics project that we're still sorting out."

"That's Emilio Gianori." Sugar looked more bored by the second.

"You watch the Mobster channel on Direct TV or something?" Jared asked, squinting in mistrust.

"Yeah, something like that." She smirked. "Beats the hell out of *COPS* reruns.

So this has to do with Nicola's witness protection history?"

Jared and Cash paused.

She continued. "And Nicola would want something to prosecute him on. Do you have something, or is this the Titan version of investigation protocol?"

Emilio spat toward his boots, and Cash's hands itched to fight. "What do you know about Nic?"

Sugar cleared her throat. "Better question, cowboy. Is someone going to arrest this fucker?"

Jared grumbled to Cash. Arresting Emilio right now wasn't in their plans. Nor was detaining him in a way any law enforcement agency would approve of.

Emilio struggled against Jared's nasty arm hold and shouted, "You want to know our plans for your girl? She'd have to watch her parents—"

"Wait," Sugar barked.

What the fuck?

Jared shook the mobster. "Ignore her. Keep talking, asshole, and we might not string you up to an electrical ass probe."

"Goddamn it, Jared. Hold the fuck on." Sugar raised her voice, and they raised eyebrows at the vamped up woman with her too-glossy lips and bubble gum habit.

"Sugar," Jared growled. "Get out of here. If you can't handle—"

Emilio started in again. "David and I—"

"Do you not see what's happening?" Sugar butted in again. Jared dragged Emilio closer to Sugar, most likely to put them both in headlocks. "He's giving up the details. You need a clean arrest. All of this will get thrown out. Someone fucking arrest him already or else some million dollar an hour mob lawyer will have him out in time for baked ziti and a nice bottle of Chianti."

"Get out, Sugar. We're not the arresting type."

"You need this to be legit. You're going to lose it all. Imagine what Nicola will lose." She looked to each of them, at their weapons, and threw up her hands. "All this testosterone and muscle, and you all got nothing? No badges?"

Jared shook Emilio, looking frustrated ten times over. The guy winced, his jacked-up arms reaching toward their breaking points. Jared growled, "You want local blue and white here, be my guest. Call nine-one-one. Try explaining this scene to—"

"Jesus H. Christ. This is why I shouldn't give a king rat's ass about the people I meet." Sugar slapped her hands on her hips, cracked a bubble, and shook her head. "ATF. Emilio Gianori, you are under arrest for whatever the fuck you've done wrong and we can prove. You have the right to remain silent.

"Anything you say, or Jared All-Brass-No-Brains Westin drags out of you, can be used against you in a court of law, where we're going to prosecute your mobbed-up ass for every single thing we can find.

"You have the right to your corrupt attorney who'll buy a private island somewhere with all the money you're going to spend on appeals. Said money-making attorney can be present, if your pansy ass requests. If you can't afford one because Papa Mobster cuts you off for being a moron, one will be provided for you. I'll make sure you get one of my personal favorites. Keep answering questions if you want. Keep providing us details. It'll all be used against you. I cross my heart.

"Do you understand these rights, as I have explained them to you, or do you need me to take a breath and repeat myself?"

Cash choked on a swallow. "Holy fuckin' shit."

Sugar smirked. "Shut it, cowboy. Jared, you have any bungee cords in that bag of yours?"

Jared looked stunned at Sugar. Cash understood how he felt. "Cash, cords are bottom of the pack."

Cash nodded numbly and went to grab them, his mind spinning. The familiar clack of Sugar's heels pounded behind him. She beat him to the bag, rifled through Jared's stuff, and snagged the ties.

Who is this woman?

Bungee ties in hand, she glared at Jared. "I assume you don't have cuffs anywhere either."

He smiled, almost as if he took her slam as a dare. "Actually, I do."

"Yeah, I bet." She stepped to Emilio and palmed his wrists, pushing them toward the ground. The man cried out. "Whoopsie, did that hurt?"

A second later, she wrapped the cord tightly around his wrists, knocked him behind the knees, and let him fall over. Sugar grabbed his ankles, repeating the wrap-and-knot procedure, then looped one last bungee cord, tying his hands and ankles together. Emilio lay on the ground fighting his bindings. Sugar put his thrashing movements to a quick halt with a boot stomp into the mobster's hip.

Jared stepped toward her. "If I was ever going to fall in love with a woman, it'd be one who could hogtie a grown man."

"You couldn't handle me, big boy. Don't worry your pretty head over it."

Cash choked back a grin. First Mia. Then Nicola. Now Sugar. Jared had a soft spot for kickass women.

"Don't smile, cowboy. I'm not thrilled with either of you for pulling me out of deep cover."

CHAPTER TWENTY-SEVEN

The hairs on Nicola's neck prickled, and she pushed as far as possible into the opposite car door. The backseat of this swanky sedan was too small, and she was suffocating in it.

David snickered to himself, finding humor in something after his near meltdown at the airport hangar he'd demanded to visit. He snickered again. Probably the transmission jammer he'd set up within the last few hours, seeing as her phone had stopped working somewhere over the Atlantic Ocean.

That also meant the listening bugs were likely not transmitting. Must've found one she'd placed in his room or on his clothes. Maybe he'd even found all of them. It had taken him two days to clue in.

Not a very good spy. *David didn't sweep his hotel room? Who doesn't do that?* Especially since he sold intelligence, his care-and-concern factor seemed dangerously low, or maybe his ego-factor was tremendously high.

"Nicola, we have one stop before we drop you off. Is that acceptable?"

Is that acceptable? No, it's not. But refusing wouldn't do much in the effort of intel gathering. "Fine. No problem."

She wondered if the jammer was on him or in the carry-on bag by his feet. For as nice as that bag was, he was sloppy, leaving the thing everywhere. Helpful for her though.

David gave the driver the new location. She knew the address. *Roughly five minutes away. Not a big deal.* Maybe something would come out of it.

Counting mile markers, Nicola passed the time by ignoring David. Nothing he did was noteworthy, but she didn't trust the backstabbing fool. Minimally armed, Nic didn't want to show that her trust quotient bordered on the negative, but she took some comfort that she could get to the subcompact at her ankle.

She picked at her manicure and smoothed the designer pants. The driver pulled off the highway and into a shopping center.

"Stop in front of the Starbucks, and unlock the doors," David directed.

A shiver sliced up her spine. *Unlock the doors?*

David pointed for the driver's benefit. A tall, well-dressed man waited on the sidewalk facing the storefronts. His shoulders were broad, his stance looked... ready. *For what?*

The sedan slowed to a crawl, stopping curbside, and the doors unlocked. The man pivoted around slowly, a sinister smile smeared across his face. *Not possible.* Her stomach lurched, and she jumped toward the door handle.

David's hand clamped down on her elbow, reigniting the distant memory of its sprain. Her exit was blocked anyway, the door shadowed by an impenetrable force. The driver ignored her, even as she yelled and shoved for David to let go.

She pinched her eyes closed, desperately wanting to wake up. When she opened them, there he stood. *Antilla Smooth.*

Alive.

Angry.

And so close she could smell her own fear.

Grinning like the grim reaper at a funeral, Antilla opened the door and squeezed into the backseat, sandwiching her between himself and David. The sedan eased forward after Antilla shut the door, then all the doors locked. The noise reverberated in her ears.

"Hello, my dear. How I have missed you." He leaned against her, his cologne overpowering the small area. One cold finger traced her cheekbone as he spoke, ignoring her batting hand.

"Stop it. Get off me." She pushed away, but David was on the other side. *Shit.*

The sick smile hadn't faded, all bright and white with perfectly lined teeth, ready for display. Her reaction made his grin more vibrant. Made it sparkle.

"Speaking of getting off, that never happened between us. Did it? I intend to fix that today. But first, let's get through introductions. I understand Gabriella isn't your true name. Nicola, is it? Lovely."

Cash had to be following. She needed to see a familiar vehicle out the window. Her stomach bottomed as she swept a look every which way. Nothing familiar. Antilla's fingers feathered over her cheek, and she lashed out.

"Get off me, goddamn it." The words ground out but did zip to make him stop.

David laughed close to her ear. She turned, kicking at him, his bag, the door. Anything she could connect with.

"Now to the warehouse," David said to the driver, then looked back at her. "Antilla and I have things to work out before our transaction is complete."

"Yes, we do." Antilla ignored her for the first time. He sounded disappointed or disapproving. She couldn't tell which he leaned toward more. "The second bomb hasn't done its job, so I'm not ready to discuss—"

"Second bomb?"

"Not that it's your business, but yes, Gabri—I mean, Nicola. Second bomb. Addressed to Janet and Rick—"

Nicola slammed her fist into his face, elbowing David as he tried to pull her back. Blood trickled out of Antilla's nose, and he took a cloth from his breast pocket to dab at it.

"You will pay for that, you little bitch."

"There isn't a second bomb," she challenged him. "Leave my parents alone."

"There isn't a second bomb, just like I'm dead, darling."

David spoke up. "We should enlighten her." He turned to her. "Nicola, I was confused at first also. This is a very interesting story, so listen, and it will all make sense."

"Leave my family alone."

They drove past a warehouse with boarded up windows and no signs of life except for the hip-high weeds littering the parking lot. Trees lined both sides of what looked like an electrified fence. Parts of it were rusted out. The building looked ready to be condemned.

"Leave your family alone? Now why would I do that?" Antilla asked. "I won't walk away from this opportunity. The CIA killed my brother. In return, I'll kill your family. David was smart enough to out himself as CIA and to try to protect the Smooth family. You remained one of the infidels, part of the organization—"

Nothing made sense. "You were shot. I saw you."

"Wrong again. Welcome to the Smooth family secret. Not even David knew the truth until after the incident, but there were two of us. My identical twin brother was named Fernando. My father, a businessman, raised us as if only one child existed. It was a strategy of sorts. We were to take on his empire, which we did successfully. My name is not Antilla. Antilla is *our* name, the joint name my late brother and I embodied in the public eye. My name is Javier. He and I were perfect replicas. We spoke the same, fucked the same. No one knew the difference. Not our business partners. Not our whores. You never knew."

"And I never fucked you. Either of you, so I wouldn't know," Nicola spat.

"Like I said, that will change tonight. Willing or not."

The driver stopped the sedan in front of an abandoned building, smaller than the first ones they'd passed. She studied it. The door had new locks and hinges that gleamed in summer's early evening light. Three car doors opened, and the men got out. David and Antilla walked a few steps away, and the driver trained a subcompact machine gun on her. This driver was a real winner.

"Give me your purse," the driver said.

Of course she'd lose the purse. It was Louis Vuitton. She always lost the good stuff.

David's bag was on the floorboard.

The driver motioned with his baby machine gun. "Now get out."

He wouldn't shoot her yet, right? "No."

She stomped her feet like a child readying for a terrible two throw down.

"Listen, lady, out."

Stomp. Kick. Stomp, stomp. "No!"

Grabbing at her, the driver pulled her from the backseat, but not before she tried to do serious damage to David's bag. The jammer had to be in there. It wouldn't have worked in the plane if had it been in their luggage. Hoping to hell she did enough damage to the sensitive piece of equipment, Nicola relented and finished exiting on her own.

"Can you just search my purse and give it back to me? I've got gum and lip gloss that I need."

David shrugged. "Christ, yes. Search her stupid bag. Take anything with a bullet or blade. Just stop whining. How are you so stupid?"

Moron, the better question is, how are you this dumb?

Nicola picked up her purse, grabbed the lip gloss listening device, and smoothed on a fresh layer of Berry Cherry shine. She powdered her nose, slipping on a geographical tracking tag that dissolved immediately on contact with her skin. "Thank you."

"Whatever." David seemed frustrated. Maybe not just at her.

"Trouble between criminals?" she asked.

"Destroy her phone," Antilla, or Javier, or whoever he was demanded.

"No problem." She handed it to the driver, knowing it was her burner phone. If she had a fighting chance of Cash hearing or locating them, it had nothing to do with her phone.

"We're not transmitting out here anyway," David offered. "I set up a portable jammer after she ineffectually planted a listening device on me."

A listening device? As in one? That was good news.

She was fifteen minutes shy of a check-in with Beth. Someone would wonder about her whereabouts, and Cash was out there somewhere, as her backup. No way he'd leave her hanging, though no doubt he was sweating their loss of communication.

She had a few minutes until they realized the jammer was out. If one of their phones rang, the jig was up. No time like the present to go after the dirt. "Antilla."

"Javier."

"Whatever. Seen one twin, seen them all. Same person, right? I had no idea you were so good with bombs. Your daddy taught you that in your gun running education?"

He laughed, harsh and sarcastic. "Nicola. I delegate. You should know that about me. You did spend months by my side, though it should have been between my knees."

She ignored that and pointed to David. "You delegated to this guy? I've learned a lot about him recently. You should really pick better team members."

"Shut up," David snapped.

"Seriously. I can tell you that one bomb didn't do shit, because I spoke to the man whose truck blew. And my parents? Trust me, if you went after my parents, someone's already on it. Two dud bombs. And to top that off, you did a piss poor job of entering the local arms market. I'm telling you, *Antilla*, I didn't expect you to pull the door-to-door salesman routine after your network was disrupted. I expected you to run off to South America or the Middle East to reassure your best clients. Virginia good ole boys seem so beneath you."

"Shut up!" David yelled.

"What are you speaking of? Of course, I'm reorganizing after this CIA disaster."

"You're not moving product?"

"No. To local Americans? Not at all."

Wait a minute. Smooth didn't sell the ammo. David's face wore a splash of dread. "It couldn't be this simple."

"Shut up!" David yelled again. "Stupid woman can't keep her mouth shut."

Antilla glanced at David but spoke to Nic. "What do you mean simple?"

"I saw Smooth ammo. Only days ago. Your emblem, .50 cal, tracer, incendiary tipped. It was purchased by some yahoos in somewheresville, Virginia. I had thought," she pointed at Antilla, then moved her finger toward David, "...but, I wouldn't put it past this smarmy dude—"

David smacked her silent. The sting roared from cheek to chest, fireworks exploding behind her eyelids. *God, that hurts.*

Nicola blinked fast, tears welling, then looked down. Her feet were planted on the weed-pocked parking lot. She was still standing. Small accomplishments were amazing at times like this. The stars faded from her watering eyes just in time to focus on Antilla. Rage boiled across his face.

"No. No. No." David lifted his hands. "It wasn't me. I told you I worked with the Gianori—"

"The Gianori mob doesn't need my ammunition or arms. I do not sell to them. They do not move my product." Antilla took a step toward David, who shrank into himself. "Tell me again about the Gianori mob."

"Sorry. S-orr-y." David's voice shook. "I meant to say that I hired them to build and plant the bombs."

"And why would they do that for you, David? Give me a logical reason why," Antilla growled. "Now."

"Because..."

"Because they also wanted Nicola. Am I correct? You mentioned she could be leverage for another project. The Gianori mob wants her? You had no intention of leaving her with me?"

"I, uh... I figured if you finished with her, they could have a go at her. Both of you wanted retribution. Offing her family would do that..." David's teeth chattered as he stammered in rhetorical circles.

"Am I stupid, David?"

"No, sir."

"But you played games with me?"

"Not games. But I thought you'd appreciate the Gianoris taking out her family. You always say bloodshed requires equal or more blood. Her parents for your brother."

"And you stole from me?"

"I didn't. It wasn't much. Throwaways. Please. Please, let me explain."

"But above all, you thought you could deceive me?" Antilla laughed loudly and evilly. He looked at the driver. "Shoot him."

David fumbled for his concealed, wetting himself and moaning more explanations. A single pop and David coughed up blood. That throat shot would take several seconds to finish him off. Nicola watched blood gurgle and sputter as his hands tried to close off the wound.

Seconds later, it was over. David's crimson-lacquered fingers remained near his neck.

"Check her for concealeds," Antilla directed the driver, who was quickly proving to be very adept at several things: chauffeuring, bleed outs, and pat downs. Her ankle-holstered .38 was removed as well as the knife tucked into the back of her pants. "And get her inside."

The driver manhandled her through the door. If Cash'd seen that subcompact at her back and the unfriendly shove, there was a solid chance the driver was going to die tonight.

Despite David's murder, Nic wasn't as nervous as before. The fear was gone. She was stone-cold ready to work. Her backup was a sniper extraordinaire, and somehow, he'd get eyes on them. Hopefully, he'd heard everything.

Antilla walked to a far corner to make a phone call and started talking. Sweet Jesus, she'd knocked out the phone jammer, and Antilla was too preoccupied to worry about it. The driver walked outside, most likely to remove David.

Nicola bent her chin as close to her collarbone as possible and whispered, "Cash, can you hear me?"

She held her breath. A noise clattered on the metal roof. *An acorn or a tree branch. Something.* Something that Cash shot long range. A smile melted across her face that she faked as a yawn, just in case.

"Hi," she whispered again and waited. "Second bomb. My parents' house."

A dull bang echoed through the empty room. *Definitely Cash.* He'd take care of her family. God, she loved him.

"Fucking squirrels," the driver murmured, pulling David into a corner. "What are we doing with her?"

"We wait. I need to handle my inventory problem. Tie her to something. I don't care. And then find me dinner. Try to have it still hot when you return. And none of that American fast food crap."

The driver snagged a rickety folding chair and pushed her into it, zip-tying her arms together around a metal piece.

All right, Smooth. Just you and me now. Let's do this.

CHAPTER TWENTY-EIGHT

Whatever Nicola had done to fix their jammer problem had worked. Their earpieces squealed, and both Cash and Jared grabbed at them. *Perfect clarity that'd make Verizon jealous. Talk about a listen and learn session.* Cash prayed to the techie gods that Parker also had access to this feedback at headquarters.

"There were twins? Smooth's still alive. Fuck me." Cash whistled, lying prone on a warehouse roof. A warm breeze swirled around them, bringing with it the gasoline and plastic smells of an abandoned factory.

He looked through Miss Betty's scope and caressed her perfectly molded trigger.

"Whiskey. Tango. Foxtrot." Jared growled slowly next to him and rolled onto his back, laying the binoculars to his side and texting into his secure phone. "Talk about a huge hole in intelligence. How did the CIA not know there were two of them?"

"Not even a rumor. You know gun runners talk. Nothing." He followed through the eye of his scope, still listening. Nicola was pushing the conversation, narrowing in on a crack between her captors.

"You hearing this?"

Jared grunted. "David's going to get himself—"

They didn't need earpieces to hear the single blast of close range fire power.

"There goes Operation The-Butler-Did-It." Jared paused. "Don't take out Smooth yet. No telling what the other man will do with that automatic at her back."

Cash nodded. Endangering Nic's life wasn't worth a clean shot now. Smooth would die shortly. How and when were still to be determined, but it might as well have been etched in stone. He'd make sure both Smooth twins were hanging with an angel of death. By his hands. And Cash would ensure David was never awarded a nameless star on the inner hallways of Langley.

Jared rolled back in place, spotting and surveying for Cash. Both men watched Nicola take a push from the butt of a gun. A growl rumbled low from Cash's chest.

"Keep it together."

He was together. Never more confident in his girl, and never more ready to pull the trigger if she needed it. Though she was in the warehouse now, he could feel her, sense her. He didn't need to see her to know she was mentally the one in control this moment. After all, she'd just played Antilla's emo-card and was now one captor less. Two was better than three, even if David had been the weakest link.

"Cash, can you hear me?" her voice whispered into his ear.

The sweet question stirred his soul. Concentrating for all he was worth, he took a moment to feel the quick fire of pride flow through his chest.

With a deep breath and intense focus on an old tree leaning over the metal-topped building, Cash aimed. The silencer did its job: a muffled shot, but nothing that would register as gunfire in the warehouse.

A small branch landed on the metal roof.

"Hi."

The word melted through him, earpiece to his toes. He smiled, loving that word. *Hi.*

She continued, "Second bomb. My parents' house."

On it already. Giving her another confirmation that he was there for her, Cash slid another round forward, cradled Miss Betty to him and *bam.* More tree debris landed on the roof.

How   about   that   shot,   baby?

The fuzzy feelings drained away as he listened to a man grunting around her, moving something metal.

Cash pulled back from Betty. "How we going to get her out of there?"

"Are you sure she wants us to get her out of there? This probably isn't her first time tied up."

"Jared, I will kill you."

"What? Calm your trigger finger. I meant in the captive sense. Not whatever your perverted mind came up with."

"Uh-huh."

Jared laughed. "We've had direct orders to kill Smooth, so we're not only in backup mode, but we have to trust our girl to either kill them or ask for help. She knows we're here. She said, "hi," not "help." We're five hundred yards away and can get there quick. If Smooth was going to kill her, he'd have done it by now."

Voices buzzed in their earpieces. Jared and Cash paused, listening.

Don't touch me. Untie me first, you prick. Smooth laughed. The sound of Nicola struggling stopped Cash's heart.

"I'm getting closer. If she wants help, she can look over her shoulder and nod." Cash was on his feet, ready to shimmy down the building. "Don't lose that gun. I have a sentimental attachment to it."

Pushing from one covered spot to the next, he was at the warehouse door lightning fast. He pulled the transmitter's earpiece out, keeping Jared in his other ear. The real deal was happening on the other side of that door. He wouldn't need the transmitter.

Cash slid through the door. It squeaked, but Antilla and Nic didn't notice as Smooth cut through her zip ties with a pocket knife. At once, she popped to her feet, striking him in the throat.

God, Cash loved a good throat punch. That one was spectacular. Still, the protector in him needed to run to their tangle, throw her to safety, and shred Antilla Smooth into flesh and bone with his bare hands.

Acting as backup fucking sucked. She held her own, which was good and bad. It didn't matter though, no clean shots at this angle anyway.

Cash crept closer. The urge to annihilate Smooth beat loudly in his ears, speeding his pulse and competing with Nicola's concern that he didn't trust her to do the job.

If this was Roman, would he step in? Christ, man, he couldn't answer that. Could he? Would he jump in now for Roman?

No... fuck, no, he wouldn't.

Not yet.

Smooth rebounded, grabbing her arm. She countered, striking. *Good girl.* Nicola moved fast. *Faster than when we sparred.* She didn't run from the son of a bitch. She speared toward him, nailing him in the groin, giving cheap shots and calculated moves equal play time. Nicola was good, but she needed to end this.

Smooth went down on his knee, her follow up could—

Damn it. A hand wrapped around her ankle. She flipped through the air. Smooth was on her. They spun, growled, and grunted. Curses and war cries echoed around the empty warehouse.

Antilla slammed her against the wall. Her head lolled to the side, but righted. Her eyes locked on Cash's. A fucking smile danced across her face, mouthing, "hi."

She's insane. I'm in love with a crazy woman.

Cash took a step forward into the open. Smooth didn't see him, but Nic did.

"No," she growled, looking bull's-eye at him.

His heart thundered behind his ribs, beating so hard they would be bruised. Nicola was good, but Antilla was larger, stronger. Cash had no choice. He ran toward their fighting bodies and hooked a forearm around Antilla's neck. Nicola fell, driven away by the men's momentum.

Watching, she stood, ready for more, but at a standstill. Antilla struggled, shifted sideways, and elbowed his gut, which only strengthened Cash's resolve. One more shot at escape with a weakening foot stomp, and Antilla was fading for the final countdown.

Nicola ran forward, screaming. "No!"

What the hell?

She couldn't possibly want him to stop. Her arms grabbed Cash. Fighting through the men's weight, and their fight, she forced partially between him and Antilla. Slivers of a second passed and, ready to end this, Cash twisted the bastard's neck. Nicola pushed under his arm, then pulled back. Smooth dropped in a dead man's pile.

Behind him, a crash and a whoosh. A different man's cry spun Cash around, grabbing for his sidearm.

He was too late.

Nicola was bent over, hands pressed on her knees, head down. Beyond her, the driver lay with a tactical knife centered in his chest.

Cash's hand flew to his waist. His knife was gone. She hadn't pushed between him and Smooth, she'd gone for his weapons, grabbing his blade. *And thrown it with perfect accuracy.*

He looked at Nicola, then at the dead man with a subcompact machine gun in hand.

Holy hell, she'd saved his life.

He'd saved hers.

"Nic, baby." He was on her in a flash, scooping her to his chest, not giving a fuck who heard. "Sweet girl. My sweet girl."

Jared grumbled in his ear. "Cut the mushy bullsh—"

Cash pulled his earpiece out. He might not be able to cut the audio transmission, but he sure as shit wouldn't have Jared as the voice of God in his head.

Nicola didn't cry. She didn't whimper or scream, just caught her breath after doing her job and watching his ass.

"There's a second bomb. At my parents'." Her words came out heavy as she recovered from her brawl with a man a hundred pounds heavier than her.

"We knew already. Roman's with them. Brock and Rocco have the device. Everything's cool."

"Oh." A huge sigh of relief washed over her face. He let go, watching her process the news. At least she didn't fight him off when he'd power-grabbed her. "How'd you know?"

"We have Gianori. We knew before you did."

Her eye went goose egg wide. "What?"

"We'll debrief. There's a lot to catch up on. You did great."

"Thanks. You too." Her breaths slowed down. Cash heard nothing over-stimulated or hypersensitive in her tone. Just another day on the job for her.

He smiled. That was... cool.

"Did you hear all that, earlier?" she asked.

And she wanted to review the play-by-play, just like he'd want to rehash after an op. "That was some shit, right?"

"Damn." She laughed. "Never saw it coming."

"I didn't mean to step in—"

"No, I needed backup. That was good. We were good." She nodded, turned, and went looking for something.

A purse. She held it up, looking pleased. Well, all right then. The big brown purse made her happy. *Good to know.*

"You were seriously good, Nic."

"Told ya." She winked at him, moving stuff around in the bag.

Were all her bags that big? How much stuff did she have, anyway? She shouldn't stay with that asshole Jackson. She should stay with him. "Let's get out of here."

"I'm going to tell the CIA I want to work with you on projects sometimes. That was awesome. That whole you-twist-I-throw thing was out of this world."

Well, he'd never mention that he wasn't one hundred percent sure what she was doing. Nor would he mention he didn't hear the other man come in.

Everything in Cash's head buzzed. Loudly. His fingertips tingled and the thump, thump in his chest overwhelmed him. She was perfect—impressive—and he'd handled her in the field semi-okay. Always room for improvement, but this moment, he wanted nothing to change. That adrenaline rush pinking her cheeks was something he wanted to see every day.

"Look, Nicola. Now's the wrong time, I get that. But goddamn, woman, I'm the luckiest bastard alive. Getting to fall in love with you twice." He couldn't have stopped speaking if he tried. "Hell, I've never not loved you."

Frozen and eyes wide open. Not the look he was hoping for. Nicola didn't move. She might not have been breathing.

"Sorry to lay it out there like this. But there it is. Deal with it. Ignore it—"

Nicola lunged into his arms, smashing her palms on either side of his cheeks. "I've loved you every day. Since as far back as I can remember, Cash, I've loved you."

Tears glistened in her eyes. The tough operative from a moment ago transformed into the woman he daydreamed about. His forehead, his cheek, hell, his soul, touched hers. Her silent tear tickled his skin. "I wasn't trying to make you sad."

"God, Cash. Sad isn't what I am." Her lips brushed his bottom one as she sighed into a kiss.

Soft and supple. Her mouth was designed for him. He knew it to the bottom of his soul. The caress of her tongue brought him far away from the operation. The faint smell of lavender and flowers whisked over his senses, reminding him of every kiss they'd ever shared.

His fingers tunneled through her silky hair as he consumed her kiss. The need to breathe was secondary. The reasons he had to live and fight and survive realigned themselves. It had hit him fast and furious with such conspicuous accuracy that her exclamation of love was deafening. Life changing.

Drawing back from her, Cash memorized her beautiful chocolate brown eyes and upturned lips. Some days, moments, would be remembered for the rest of his days. This was one of them.

He laced his fingers with hers, still pressed on his face. "Let's call for a cleanup team and go home."

She signed and leaned into him, allowing him to easily envelop her in his arms. "I'd like to see my parents. I…" He waited to see what else she had to say. "Will you go with me?"

He'd been to Janet and Rick's place a thousand times, from when he and Roman raced bikes in the driveway to Sunday night pot roasts while Nic was gone. Her parents might've well been his to a certain extent. Why her hesitation?

Remembering her anxiety and guilt at the gun range, he said, "Of course I will. It'll be fine. I promise."

CHAPTER TWENTY-NINE

Nicola's small hometown remained untouched, and passing the high school, memories flooded her from every direction.

The house she'd grown up in hadn't changed either. *Stone fenced. Two-level Colonial. White clapboard. Black shutters. Red door.* Why she'd thought it would look different was beyond her. She could've driven through this neighborhood a thousand times over the last ten years. But she hadn't. And that had nothing to do with the life-altering agreements she'd made with the CIA and witness protection that allowed her to live and work so close to where she had family and contacts.

No, her avoidance had everything to do with the nauseous feeling that was making her dizzy in the driveway. She hadn't set foot outside the car, so this wasn't going well.

"Nic, you look like you're gonna puke."

She grimaced at Cash. "You have no idea."

"Put your head between your knees. Take a breath, and it'll be okay."

Easier said than done. Still, Nicola followed his directions, flipping her head down and pressing it between her kneecaps. Maybe she could squeeze away the headache that had tortured her for the past few days.

Deep breath in. Deep breath out. Sort of.

"Okay, I'm good," she lied.

He threw an I-don't-buy-that-for-a-second grin, then took her hand to his mouth and kissed it. "Let's do this. Move your cute ass."

They opened their car doors and jumped out of Cash's new jacked-up, black Rubicon. She liked it. It fit his personality. He said it'd do in a pinch, whatever that meant. The tires practically came up to her hip bone, and she stared at the front one until he came around the hood and took her hand in his again.

Roman's truck was parked at the top of the driveway. *So he was here first. Good.* If they were angry at her, he may have calmed them down. *How would I feel if my daughter walked away for ten years?* Anger might be tops on that list, but when she'd talked to them on the phone, they were anything but angry. More like better than thrilled. *Happier than elated. So why the butterflies?*

Each step toward the imposing front door felt heavier than the last. She couldn't breathe. She needed to practice that whole inhale, exhale thing, maybe sit on the front stoop, trying to re-master that skill set. But her parents were expecting her. Hell, they'd expected her since she called home to explain she'd been swept into witness protection then the CIA.

And here she was, on the front steps, unsure.

The red door swung open. Her beaming mom—with teary eyes and a smile spread wide across her face—had her arms outstretched. Dad stood close behind. He was still huge and commanding, with warmth plastered on his face that made Nicola cringe in an emotional ache.

Nicola's feet stopped moving. Her legs were made of cinderblocks, her arms cemented in place. The only things she could feel were pain and shame and... Cash's hand. She couldn't focus. Somehow Cash moved them toward her parents, and they took over.

Hugs and kisses. Words, certainly, but she couldn't make heads or tails of them because of the fierce sobs racking her body.

"I'm so sorry." She repeated it over and over, feeling less like a woman in her thirties and more like a child.

Wrapped in warm arms, one of them smoothing her hair, another holding her tightly, the pain began to ebb. There was shushing and murmuring. But the only thought she had was how strong their love was. Their forgiveness, too.

She wasn't worthy.

But everything they did communicated that was exactly what she was. *Worthy.*

Blinking and wiping away the tear streaks, Nicola took a deep breath. Then another. Until she could inhale and exhale. Her chest felt lighter. The weight of her ice-cold guilt melted.

Her mom grasped her by the shoulders. "We love you."

"And we understand," her father tacked on.

All she could do was nod, knocked over again by the emotional blow. The tears started again. Her sight blurred.

"None of that now. This is a happy day," her mom said, wiping at her eyes. Her dad nodded.

They smiled. Really, truly smiled. She couldn't feel any hatred toward their lying daughter. She didn't see it in their expressions. They simply held her.

Roman walked outside, stood next to Cash, and she tried for a weak smile. It came easier than she'd expected.

"Why don't you bring this whole thing inside before the neighbors get too nosey," Roman suggested, then laughed. "Nic always could make a big entrance."

Then she did smile without having to try, and she laughed, loving her brother more in that moment than she ever had.

"All right. In, in." Her mother shooed everyone in the door, keeping an arm wrapped around her, directing her to the living room. "I hope you're hungry, angel."

Angel. She'd never thought she'd hear her mom call her nickname again.

The house smelled delicious and familiar. Nicola sighed, sitting on the same couch in the same spot as always. Cash settled down beside her, an arm thrown over her shoulder. For a second, her stomach jumped. Her parents didn't know about her and Cash. Not before, and she wasn't sure how to define them now, other than that they were a *they.*

Her overprotective father didn't bounce a sideways glance when he kicked back across from her.

In the background, she heard Roman rifling through the pantry, asking their mother where the snacks were. It all felt so normal.

Mom brought dad and Cash beers and Nic an orange juice, knowing that she would need her odd comfort drink. She'd drunk gallons of OJ with her mom over the years, rehashing teenage drama.

"Thanks, mom."

Roman walked in, beer and dip in hand, potato chips under an arm.

"So CIA, Nicky?" Dad always called her Nicky. Drove her crazy until right now. He looked proud.

Nodding, she tried to think of what to say. "Yeah—"

"Little sister's a spy. Who'd a thunk it?" Roman laughed, stuffing chips and dip in at the same time. "And from what I've seen, she could give James Bond a run for his money."

"Double-Oh-Seven here can shoot and fight with the big boys," Cash said, giving her a squeeze.

The guys were bragging on her. Not what she'd expected and her cheeks heated.

"Well, as long as you're safe, angel. That's what I tell the boys as well. The three of you are safe out there, right?"

Roman, Cash, and Nicola all nodded some version of, "yes ma'am, yes mom, you got it." Mom smiled ear to ear.

"Dinner's ready in twenty minutes. Roman, don't ruin your appetite. Nicola Beatrice, would you join me in the kitchen?"

Uh-oh. Breaking out the middle name. She was in trouble. No one else seemed to notice as a football appeared out of nowhere, soaring across the living room, and her mom didn't give her a chance to wiggle out of that request. Nicola walked the familiar path to the kitchen, hearing the same floorboard creak as it had so long ago.

"Why don't you make the salad?" Her mom pointed to everything lined up on the counter.

"I can do that." This had been planned, but she was okay with it. The lineup of incoming questions made her nervous, but better to stay busy with her hands than fidget with her shirt.

"Thanks. So I'm going to skip all the boring and sad stuff and skip to you and Cash. That okay with you, angel?"

Nicola choked, spilling all the cherry tomatoes she had lined up to split, salt, and pepper. "Cash?" Her voice squeaked. *Yeah. That's not a dead giveaway of anything hot and heavy.*

Rolling her eyes, her mom laughed. "All right. We can dredge up years of missing—"

"I can talk Cash. I ran into Cash and Roman—"

"Angel, I know that already. You think either of those boys can keep a secret?"

I guess not.

Her mom smiled. "The more I feed them, the more they talk. It's the only way I've stayed sane knowing what they run all over the world doing. I've also known the two of you have circled each other from afar since you were—honest to God—believers in cooties. And now, he's holding your hand. Arm around the shoulder. Clearly, cooties aren't a problem anymore."

Nic knew her cheeks blazed bright pink. "You noticed?"

"I notice everything. Mothers always do."

"What about fathers? Do you think dad, um, noticed?"

Her mom laughed. "Maybe. Do you like him?"

"Of course I like him, mom. It's Cash."

"Do you love him?"

"Mom!" Nic's eyes bugged out like she was in the twelfth grade again.

"You know, before everything happened," her mom gestured to the window. Her dad, Roman, and Cash were outside tossing a football with one hand, nursing their beers in the other. "Cash had called your father. Wanted to talk to us. Without Roman or you there."

Silence. *I had a ring.* His voice echoed in her head. She hadn't doubted him when he threw that jab at her, but—

"Know anything about that?" Her mom cocked an eyebrow, smiling like she knew a secret. "Keep chopping, angel. We have hungry men to feed."

Nicola stared out the window instead and let her mom remove the knife and salad makings. She watched them in the backyard. Laughing and roughhousing. Cash threw the ball, spun round, and caught sight of her through the glass.

They locked eyes, and her stomach jumped when his half-grin and a half-nod were directed her way. He'd been her best friend her whole life. He was more gorgeous than any man walking the face of the Earth. And here he was, making her tummy flip.

The football hit the side of his head, and Roman cheered his direct hit. She laughed. Cash laughed before he turned and speared her brother, football in hand. Dad laughed. Everything felt like it should.

The doorbell rang. Somewhere in the background, she heard her mother fussing for a hand towel, wiping her hands on the way to answer the front door. Nicola was mesmerized, watching her family. Being home—

Chk-chck.

And just that fast, the unmistakable sound of a pump-action shotgun dumped an ice bath on her warm-and-fuzzy worldview. She palmed a steak knife from the kitchen island, slid to the wall, and listened.

A floorboard creaked. She knew that floorboard, knew every one that creaked and groaned, thanks to years of sneaking out with Cash and Roman. Nic looked out the window. The men were back to their casual game of drink-and-toss, shooting the shit.

She rounded the corner and knew that knife wouldn't be worth the silver it was plated with if her hearing was right. And she had no doubt it was. Tucking the steak knife into the back of her shorts, she had only one more corner—

"Jackson?" She was struck completely dumb.

He turned toward her, pivoting *her* Remington 870 Super Magnum pump action away from her mom. *Thank God.*

"Nicola, I've been looking everywhere for you. You haven't been home in days."

Jackson looked delirious and smelled like booze. His eyes were red-rimmed and glassy. He hadn't shaved in at least a day and his clothes were… tactical.

"Here I am, Jacks. Why don't you slip the safety back on that baby, and we can go for a walk?"

"Not yet. Is Cash here?" he asked, so calm and casual that the hairs on the back of her neck did the wave.

"I think this is between you and me. Whatever it is—"

"This is your mom?" He sounded desperate and distant.

How to answer this one… "Jackson, listen to me—"

He swung his gaze to her mom, but thankfully kept the shotgun aimed at her. "I'm Jackson Dale. You must be Mrs. Garr—" He took a step from her mom and sliced a glance to Nic. "Wait, I don't even you know your real last name. How is this possible? How could you do this to me?"

Her mom spoke up. "You can call me Janet."

Jackson smiled at her, but his eyes didn't focus. "It's nice to meet you, Janet. You have such a lovely house."

"Thank you, Jackson," she said, her face pale and eyes wide. "I'd love to have you join us for dinner. But I do have a strict no guns in the house rule."

"Nic and I aren't staying."

Good. She could get him the hell out of the house and that gun away from her mother. "Jacks is right, mom. We've gotta go."

The stench of sweat and liquor overpowered the room. He lowered the weapon slightly but kept a finger on the trigger. She knew how ultra-sensitive that trigger was. A slight breeze on the right setting would slip it to fast action.

"Let's go. Nice to meet you, Janet."

The back door opened and slammed shut. Grumbling and laughing male voices overwhelmed the house.

Damn it, she was so close. "Jacks. Come on."

Roman called out from the kitchen, cabinet doors opening and closing. "Mom, we're starvin'."

Jackson's eyes darted toward the voices. His voice slurred. "Who's that?"

"Just my family, Jacks. No one who needs—"

Cash and Roman both rounded the corner and cursed. Her dad slammed into the twosome when they pulled up short.

Jackson leveled the shotgun on the men and pleaded. "He's here. Nic, you didn't say Cash was here. Nic, why didn't you tell me? Nic?" With a pendulum swing, Jackson swayed unsteadily, the shotgun now aimed at her. "Nicola?"

All hell is about to break loose. She could feel it. She didn't know which way it was coming from first, but they all teetered on the edge of disaster and watched to see who jumped first.

Nicola drilled her eyes to Jackson, mentally pleading with him. In her peripheral vision, Roman, Cash, and Dad flicked glances past her and Jackson. Another round of hair-raising gut instinct took over.

Crash.

The rush came before she even heard it. Nic wasn't sure what her body was doing, but trusted her training. Everything else was in slow motion. Glass shattered from the windows. Roman grabbed their mother, tossing her to Dad. Cash grabbed Jackson. Nic jumped out of the way but was knocked down. Definite yelling, definite firings. The sting and burn of glass exploding scrambled her senses.

And when she tried to look up, she saw the red. Everything burned. Her nose ran, eyes running. Cash had her on her feet now. *What the hell is going on?* But she couldn't stand on her own, that much she knew. Her face. Her arm was on fire. *Help me.*

CHAPTER THIRTY

Everything burned. Nothing made sense. The only thing that kept her from screaming was that *she* was hurt. Not her parents. Not her brother. Not Cash. Nicola could deal with her pain. *No one else's though.* She'd brought enough hurt home already.

Hands touched her face. *Damn it.* "Stings… Burns." *And smells?*

"Get her to the bathroom." A woman, not her mother, ordered.

The dizzy spin in her head was confusing. Who all was there? Cash's strong hands lifted her. She knew the feel of his touch, the definition of his chest. Even if she couldn't open her eyes, she knew Cash's arms.

"What is that stuff?" Now that was definitely her mom. She sounded concerned, not hurt. But damn if she didn't want to concern her mom ever again.

Her dad mumbled something.

The snap of her mom's voice followed them. "Obviously, not the blood. That stuff. It's everywhere."

A cold cloth pressed to her face, wiping over and over. Slowly, the boiling sensation on her skin plateaued. Didn't stop, but became bearable.

"Drink this." It was Cash. He held a glass to her lips, then spoke to someone else. "No. Don't call for an ambulance. I'm driving."

Her vision wasn't what it should be. Her lips burned. Water would be good. Accepting the glass, the cold—

Ick.

Not what she was expecting. She spit it out. "What is that?"

"Milk. It'll help."

What the fu—

Oh.

"Cayenne shells," she mumbled again. "He hit me with—"

"I know, sweet girl. Beth told us."

"What? Beth?" It was all she could manage and it did nothing to ask the important question like when did she get there and why? Cash wiped her face, then her arms. It helped some, but only for flashing cool moments.

"Beth shot out the window. Glass hit you. The shotgun fired, not a direct hit thanks to Beth. But you got up close and personal with an exploding twelve gauge pepper blast. Bet all this pepper stings like a bitch."

She nodded, curling into his arms. Her ankles hit the bathroom vanity. They had to be sitting in the hall bathroom, with her in his lap. "I mess everything up."

"Nah. You're enough to drive a man crazy. Any other lunatic ex-lovers I should know about? They'll be gone before dawn." He repositioned her. "Can you open your eyes?"

She shook her head a tiny bit, feeling like a baby. "They burn. I don't want to."

"All right. That settles that. Don't try in case there's glass in 'em. You're going to the ER. No idea how I'm going to explain this though." Cash paused, leaning out the door. "Your mom is cracking me up. I'm pretty sure Beth gave up and okayed the use of a vacuum, even though a cleanup team is on the way."

"Is Beth still here?"

"Yeah, Roman's trying to hit on your girl, but she's having nothing to do with it. And Beth may be on an adrenaline high."

Nic laughed, then stopped short, her lips stinging anew. "Ow." She ran her tongue tentatively over her lip and tasted her blood. "Don't make me laugh. What about Jackson?"

"We'll deal with that later." Cash called over her shoulder. "Hey, Beth. C'mere."

Nic heard Beth bounce into the bathroom, her mouth running highway speed before she could make out the words. "—believe that? I just knew it. And how much did I save your life with that cayenne shot. I told you, pack the pepper. Next time one of those boys shows up, knocking each other out—no offense, Cash—you can put them in place. When I gave you that box of ammo, it was a joke. A joke. And then those creepy-assed, drunk calls from Jackson. My timing pretty much rocked—"

"Beth." Cash coughed to hide a laugh. "Take a breath girl."

"How did Jackson find me?" Nicola asked Beth.

"I don't have all the details, but Jackson found out that two Titan guys disarmed a bomb at your parents' house. I don't know. Maybe the bomb-disarming crowd likes to chat? And from all Jackson's ramblings, I'm pretty sure he'd triangulated your burner phone and monitored your location. That's how I found you. Throw that thing away. You sure as hell don't answer it. I called you a million times today."

"You're the best, Beth."

"They should put me out in the field. I'm a rock star."

Nic smiled again, ready for the sting. "I know. I love ya, you know that?"

"Of course. God, Cash. She looks awful. Take her to the doctor."

If Nic's eyes had been open, they would've rolled. Cash threw Beth some version of, "yes, ma'am." Nicola seriously loved both of them.

"Angel?"

"Nicky?"

Her parents replaced Beth who left, babbling. Nicola felt like a blind spectacle, but didn't shy away from her parents. "I'm sorry."

"So it goes." Her dad clapped Cash on the back. "Roman's got your vehicle ready and running. Nice looking car, by the way. Is that new?"

What a week.

Her mom smoothed her hair. "We'll see you two here for dinner again soon. I packed a bag of food. You both need to eat. Had Roman put that in your car too, Cash."

Cash lifted her up, they said their goodbyes, and she was in the passenger seat of his car again.

The door was still open, and Roman walked up. She knew him by the cadence of his gait. "You know how to make an entrance and exit. Don't ya, Double-Oh-Seven." He had stolen that from Cash, but she still loved it. "Anyway, Jared just called me back. He said if she could stand the extra thirty-five mile drive, he'd take care of everything through Titan's docs."

She shrugged.

"I got the feeling he wanted to talk to you two," Roman continued. "Prepare yourself for the dickhead version of Debbie Downer."

Roman shut her door, patted the outside twice, and Cash backed out the driveway. She didn't need to see to know he flew down the highway, passing cars right and left.

"I'm not dying, Cash. No need to get a ticket."

"Sweet girl, unless the speed limit is enforced by sniper fire or an air assault team roping down from a screaming helo, we aren't slowing."

Dr. Tuska waited for their arrival and had her with a surgical ophthalmologist and ocular trauma specialist doing a thorough onceover before she could shrug them off and ask for a saline wash.

The nurses marched into action, cleaning her up. All in all, Titan's medical team took an hour and fifteen minutes to get Nic seeing again. *Not bad.*

Now, she waited. No had one checked her in, per se, so she didn't know what else to do besides wait for Dr. Tuska's discharge instructions and the tube of antibacterial ointment she was promised.

The room looked normal enough, but the sheets weren't standard hospital linens. They were smooth and felt like high thread count. Even the pillow was soft, given that it was probably one of those plastic, liquid resistant types. But it was still a hospital bed, and the place still smelled like cleaner. She hated hospitals, and the only reason she didn't push the button to call her nurse was Cash. Leaning up against the bed, he calmed her with his large hand covering hers. Despite the trauma and drama of the evening, she relaxed against him.

Dr. Tuska rapped on the open door and joined them. "Jared just arrived. I can hold him off if you need time before you see him." He chuckled, flipping through her chart. His knowing smile spoke volumes. "Like I mentioned before, dab this in your eyes three times a day. Any other scratch, give a smear of Neosporin. You're good to go. Want me to tell Jared you're tied up for a few more minutes?"

The doctor was quickly climbing the ranks of Nicola's favorite people, and definitely worth his weight in gold. Dr. Tuska must know how *pleasant* Jared could be when things didn't go according to his plans. Nicola laughed to herself. She was getting to know the old bastard. Jared wasn't actually much older than Cash. He just acted like it.

Nic shook her head, laughing despite her stinging face. "I'm fine. But thanks."

Boots clomped down the corridor. She could almost feel Jared's ever-present attitude problem.

"Here we go." Cash chuckled.

Jared slammed into the room, eyed them both, and squared off his stance. "Princess, I need a word with you. Cash, out."

Cash tightened his hand on hers, and she sensed he was ready to tell Jared to go to hell.

"That's fine," Nic said, preempting their battle.

Cash didn't move, and she patted his hand. He couldn't be seriously concerned that Jared would yell at her. Or worse... what would be worse? Racking her brain, she came up with nothing. Jared was harmless—to her at least.

Clearing his throat, Cash squeezed her hand again and stood. "Don't be an asshole, boss man."

"Out." Jared harrumphed.

Cash kissed the side of her forehead. "I'll be in the hall. Yell if the jackass gets too nasty."

"Make sure you shut the door on the way out," Jared grumbled.

"All right, guys. Enough." This wasn't what she needed right now.

Nic and Jared stared at each other for a long minute, and Cash slowly walked out the door, letting it click behind him. Jared paced the length of the room twice.

Paused.

Then did it again.

"Do you want me to apologize?" she asked, getting annoyed. "I didn't need to come to your special doctors if you didn't want me to. But they were very good, so thank you."

Two steps and he was in front of her, growling. "Let me ask you something, princess."

Oh shit. This couldn't be good. "Okay."

"Your file says you're smart. True or false?"

"Don't know what it says. I haven't seen it. But, yeah I am."

He studied her, unblinking. "Still, you fell for Cash. That can't say much about your intelligence."

She furrowed her brow at him, which stung despite the low-level painkiller they'd given her. "Jared—"

"I need another man on my team. Chick. Lady. Whatever you are." He crossed his arms over his chest. He looked like a bulldog, broad, muscled, and barely fitting in his black shirt. "What would it take to steal you from the CIA?"

What the hell?

"Excuse me? Are you offering me a job?" She couldn't wrap her head around his question. She closed her eyes, opened them, and he was still there, looking annoyed she hadn't given a good enough answer yet. "I have a contract with the CIA. They own me."

"I couldn't care less about stupid government paperwork. I can have that cancelled with a text message. Here's what I'm offering: no double agents, no bullshit games, and me. I'm the toughest boss you'll ever have. Smartest asshole you'll ever meet. And I'll pay you more than you've ever dreamed."

Her mind ran a million different ways. Questions bubbled and excitement coursed through her veins.

"You have three seconds to accept the job, princess, or I'll deny it was ever suggested."

"I'll take it."

"Maybe you are as smart as your file says. Your contract's sitting on Cash's doorstep, waiting for you to sign it. God, that'll fuck with him. He hates when I get through his security." Jared turned toward the door, then looked over his shoulder. "By the way, you should check your personal bank account. A nice six figure signing bonus posted this morning."

Her jaw fell open.

Jared smiled. "What, princess? You think I didn't know what your answer would be? I just wanted to be sure about the phrasing. The sooner you figure this out, the better off you'll be: I know everything. I see everything. And I am everywhere."

Jared went out the door, and Cash came in.

"What was that all about?"

"Can I see your phone?"

He looked puzzled. "Yeah, sure."

She took it from his hand, opening the web browser and pulling up her bank account summary. "Oh my God. That crazy bastard."

"What's going on?"

Nic handed the phone to Cash. "Look at that. Deposit made last night. Posted today. Description: Merry Christmas in July, princess." She pointed. "Do you see all those zeroes? Do you see that? I'm going to pass out."

Cash wrapped an arm around her. "Well, well, Double-Oh-Seven. Congratulations and welcome to the team." He kissed her lightly on the forehead. "That's freakin' awesome."

"Are you okay with it?"

"Me? Are you kidding? Nic, you saved my life at that warehouse. You're good—like you said—better than good, and you've proven it. Are you excited?"

"I never would have... God, yes. This rocks. I need to call Beth. Oh wait. *Beth*. We've been together since day one."

"Well, she was your handler. You guys weren't actually together in the field. You were all phone calls and meetings. Right? And she's close. It won't be different. Just like you're on assignment, but you'll get your jobs from dickhead, not communicated from Beth. Besides... " Cash scrolled through his phone. "I just got this."

He handed her back the phone. It was a text message from Roman. *Dig for me, bro. What's the deal on this Beth girl?*

"Are you serious?" Her jaw dropped for the second time that night.

"You didn't see that coming? Anyway, let's get out of here. You've got to be ready for bed."

She nodded, cuddling into his chest. "Totally ready to fall asleep in your arms."

He laughed. Scooping her off the bed, Cash whispered in her ear. "If you think you're sleeping anytime soon, you're mistaken."

CHAPTER THIRTY-ONE

Nicola slept all day, and Cash had spent most of it watching her in his bed. She was a vision of sweet beauty: tousled hair, peacefully closed eyes with feathery eyelashes he simply adored. Warmth spread in his chest each time she gave a sleepy sigh, unconsciously snuggling against him.

Minus a few hiccups, loving this woman was the easiest damn thing he'd ever done. He twirled a piece of hair around his finger as she stirred again. She blinked awake, and his throat constricted. God, when she smiled, his world stalled. Years of training and control were gone with the bat of her eyelashes.

"Good morning," she murmured, all sleepy and cute.

It killed him how adorable and innocent she could look, knowing she was a trained killer who had spent most of last night at the hospital after an attack. No red eyes. No telltale signs of a night gone wrong, with the exception of a few cuts and scratches. She didn't smell like a pepper grinder anymore, only her lavender shampoo. Man, he loved the scent of lavender.

Bright sunlight poured into his bedroom. "Try, good afternoon."

He leaned over, kissing her forehead. Nicola burrowed further into the crook of his arm. Her naked shoulder fit perfectly, as if their bodies were made to fit together. The soft caress of her skin drove him delirious with the need to kiss her again. He did, long and tender, consuming her.

The vivid nightmare of a shotgun pointed at her the night before made him want to retch. He'd be angry enough to kill Jackson if the bastard hadn't already been dead.

It took hours of watching Nic sleep for Cash to realize that not once had he wanted to beg her away from Titan, from the CIA. No, he'd been scared of losing her again, but he hadn't been scared of her working a job. If anything, he was excited she'd joined the Titan team. That realization solidified the decision he'd already made. They were going to be together forever.

His girl, a Titan chick. *Now, how badass is that?* He broke into a grin, pulling her deep against him. "I love you."

Her chocolate brown eyes danced, and she gave him a look that made his soul beam. "Sorry I slept so long. Must've needed it."

She probably needed food too. Something quick would have to do. His mind raced through everything they could do, everything he wanted to say.

"What do you say we get your Titan contract signed and sent off, then grill up some burgers?"

"Perfect. I'm starving."

Cash watched her pull from his arms. She drew her long legs away, then stepped out of bed naked. His stomach swam in circles remembering last night, how he'd kissed every inch of her and made love until he couldn't think anymore.

Now he could think. Hell, he couldn't stop thinking. Nicola *Garrison.* It sounded so right.

The charcoal grill burned off, and the sky was turning from orange to purple with the sinking sun behind a canopy of trees. They were stuffed and lounging on his deck with Nic propped against his bare chest. Her fingers trailed on his jeans, snaking designs, and that was quickly becoming one of his favorite ways to relax.

"Want to go for a ride?" Cash shifted her to face him. "I could show you around the property."

"I'll   go   anywhere   with   you."

He locked a forearm around her chest and squeezed, trying both to hold her close and make sure his heart didn't explode. No better time than now to go for their drive. "Let's go."

Throwing on his t-shirt, Cash took an excited breath. Taking her hand, he led her to the Rubicon. His chest felt tight. The flare of excitement licked his senses, and he was hyperaware of every glance and move she threw his way.

There was no tour, just a scenic drive. With more than a few acres to choose from, he had one area in mind. It could be seen out his bedroom window, the perfect place to create a memory. He slowed to a stop and idled.

"Pretty." Nic looked out over the rise of the hill. "Want to get out, walk around?"

Hell yes. Did he ever.

High grass waved in a summer's breeze, its sweet smell permeating the warm air. The western sky still held a touch of orange. In the disappearing late summer light, everything was cast in a light purple hue. Fireflies floated and swirled low across the hill, surrounding them in gold bursts of light.

Nic didn't walk anywhere but into his arms. They stood and swayed on the sloped field. Her arms draped over his shoulders as they slow danced to nature's symphony. With her head pressed against his chest, his strong heartbeat reached for her.

"I need to show you something," he whispered, breathing against her ear. She pulled back, and even in the cascading shadows, her brown eyes melted through him. "It's my secret, and I need to share it."

His hands slowly ran up and down her back, as if his fingertips were on a mission to scan and memorize. A breeze whispered by, and their hands found one another, fingers entwining. "C'mere, sweet girl."

He led her to the back of his Rubicon, popped the hatch open, and stared at Miss Betty's case. For years, that gun had gone almost everywhere with him.

"Your secret is your rifle?" Nic teased and leaned into him, kissing his bicep. "It's not a secret. I know what you do."

He didn't say anything, just stared at the gun case, searching for the right words.

She stepped closer, two fingers grazing over his cheekbones. Her fingers drifted across his skin, leaving a trail of heat, and stopped over his lips. "You don't have to tell me if you don't want to."

Cash kissed her fingers and turned them both toward the case, clicking it open. He pulled the rifle out, cradling it as he had a thousand times. "Have you ever heard the Rifleman's Creed?"

She shrugged. "Probably. I'm not sure."

"*This is my gun. There are many like it, but this one is mine. My rifle is my best friend. It is my life…* That's how it starts. The whole Creed isn't important, but its symbolism is." He took a breath, turning to her. "Before you left, I wanted to marry you, but life changed in ways we couldn't control, and my rifle became my world."

"You're a sniper. I understand how important your weapon is to you."

He stepped closer to her, needing to press against her. "I still had your ring, and you were my best friend. You were my life, my whole world. I graduated college, and before I knew it, I had a rifle that kept me alive. That I chanted about day in, day out. My best friend. My life."

Nic started to say something, but he took her index finger in his and smoothed it over the trigger. "I didn't know what to do with your ring after you were gone. And this gun was with me everywhere. This is what I did: the trigger's gold plated. I couldn't get Roman's tattoo. I couldn't scream from the rooftop that the woman I loved was gone. But I could have this with me, no matter where in the world I was."

"Cash…"

He looked at her in the dark, trying to make out her features and read her mind. "The Creed goes on to say *My rifle, without me, is useless. Without my rifle, I am useless*. It just fit. You'd always been with me. And somehow, thinking about us together in spirit, trenched out in the hellholes and kill zones I'd been sent to, it was nice to know you were in my foxhole. And Nicola Beatrice became… Miss Betty."

She paused, then her voice was strong and powerful. "I love you, Cash. And I love that you did that."

"Miss Betty kept me sane. Safe. I talked to her. Trusted her. She defended my life, my country. But it was always you, and I've always loved you."

Nicola palmed his face. She drew him in for a kiss that warmed his soul, reinvigorating his belief that no woman on the planet was more perfect than her.

He placed the rifle back in its case and put it away. Crickets chirped, and a night owl sang. Taking care to remember every moment, he turned back to her, and a smile curled his lips.

"I love you, Nic. But gun, or no gun, I want to spend the rest of my life with you. I loved you years ago, I loved you when you were gone from me, and I love you still. Always have and always will." He slipped a ring out of his pocket and took her left hand in his, sliding it onto her finger. "I've grown up with you, fallen in love with you, and I want to marry you. I hope to God you want the same thing." He cupped her face in his hands. "What do you say, sweet girl? Think Nicola Garrison could be more than just a name on paper?"

A smile so bright he didn't need the sun blossomed across her face. "Of course I want to marry you. That's my dream come true. I've wanted to since the first day I met you."

With her in his arms, with those words, life was perfect. She softened into his embrace, pushing into his kiss. This was more than a dream come true. This was his woman, his life, molding into what it should've been.

"It's a new house, but if you don't like it, it's on the auction block tomorrow."

"I love it."

"Good. Though I do have a lot of rooms that need to be christened."

"I'm pretty sure you have a big new car that hasn't been..." She pulled him toward the passenger door, giggling.

"Hot damn, I love you, woman."

EPILOGUE

Somehow Cash should've known that sporting a tux was part of the deal. Can't have a wedding without a tux. *Well, you can.* But that's not what Nicola wanted, and what she wanted today was priority number one. The tux could be considered mission critical.

He tugged at the black silk bowtie. Not his style. And standing in front of God and everyone, grinning like an asshole, it made him more than a little self-conscious.

The church doors flew open. The dramatic organ notes bounced off the cathedral ceiling, filling the room with the powerful processional they'd chosen. The most gorgeous vision of beauty and white lace emerged, rendering him love-struck all over again.

Yeah, for Nicola he could sport a bowtie and monkey suit. Hell, he'd do a top hat and a cane. Anything to get to, "I do."

The walk down the aisle was almost too much. How the hell was he this lucky? The only thing Cash wanted was Nicola in his arms. But her slow procession had a payoff. Her hand landed in his, and everything felt perfect.

The preacher droned on, talking to the filled church pews. Cash wasn't listening, totally entranced by his bride. Love swelled, thumping loudly throughout his body, and an excited constriction struck his throat. The only thing he had to do, other than stare at Nicola, was recite his vows. He'd easily agreed to write them without thinking over the consequence of that decision. Could he put into words his dreams of the future?

His promises to take care of her, partner with her? Hell, worship her for the rest of their lives?

And then the preacher's eyes were upon him. *Show time.* Cash unfolded the paper with his neatly printed vows. If he thought his smile couldn't get any bigger, he was wrong. And then it was just them. He saw no one else in the church besides Nicola Garrison, his soon-to-be wife.

Nothing he wrote would do justice to what he wanted to say. *Screw it.* Crumbling up the paper with his vows, he shoved it back into his pocket and clasped her hands in his.

"Hey, sweet girl." He thumbed the tops of her knuckles.

"Hi," she whispered, smiling. "I love you."

God, did he love this woman. Needed her too. And no pre-written vows, no matter how authentic, could encapsulate how he felt in this moment. Cash cleared his throat, pressed her knuckles to his lips in a kiss, and breathed out.

"Nic, my farthest reaching memory is you. My farthest reaching dream is this: marrying you. Promising my love, honor, and faithfulness until I take my last breath... Whether that's from old age or from my enemy's bullet, whether we're on opposite sides of the world or working in the trenches together, know that you are my best friend, my truest love, the center of my existence. Every day I have with you is a gift.

"I vow to be your partner, to always have your back. I vow to hold your hand when no words are needed, hold you tight if you need comfort, and kiss your lips just because. I've always been yours, sweet girl. And I'll always be yours. Today. Tomorrow. Forever."

Nicola wrapped her arms around his neck and kissed him. A soft chuckle ran through the church, reminding him that they weren't really alone. But he didn't care, and she obviously didn't either because they weren't anywhere close to, "you may now kiss the bride."

Somewhere behind him, the groomsmen were getting rowdy. Someone let out a, "hooyah." And Beth—he was sure of it—*aww*-ed. Loudly. But they all faded away. Nic's lips were on his, and the kiss reached into the depths of his soul.

Nic drew back from their too-hot-for-church kiss. "My turn." She held out her small white paper, then ripped it, tossing the paper pieces into the air like confetti. Another chuckle ran through the church. "Here I go… Cash Garrison, I took your last name when I never thought I'd see you again." Pain flashed in her eyes, and he caressed her hand until she smiled again. "It was the saddest of consolation prizes, but I clung to it because you were my world. I love you. More and more each day.

"I promise my heart, my soul. I promise to always trust and love unconditionally. I will follow you to the ends of the Earth if you need me. I will be your faithful, loyal wife to come home to, knowing you are forever my partner. Yes, in sickness and in health. But also through the hell of radio silence and undercover operations. I am yours, as I always have been. I vow this to you today."

Cash had her in his arms the second she stopped speaking. He snaked his fingers around her veil, into her hair, and dipped her back, kissing her again in front of God and guests. *Screw the reception.* He was ready for the honeymoon suite.

Behind him, the preacher laughed. "The rings are just a formality. Skipping right along, I now pronounce you husband and wife."

Cheers and claps echoed around them.

Husband and wife. Cash and Nicola Garrison. For real. He whispered into her ear. "How long do we have before the reception?"

She giggled. "I don't know. Why?"

"Because I'm down to start the honeymoon before champagne and cake."

"You're going to make the best husband ever."

ABOUT THE AUTHOR

Cristin Harber is an award-winning author. She lives outside Washington, DC with her family and English Bulldog, and enjoys chatting with readers.

Facebook: https://www.facebook.com/cristinharberauthor
Twitter: https://twitter.com/CristinHarber
Website: http://cristinharber.com
Email: cristin@cristinharber.com
Newsletter: Stay in touch about all things Titan—releases, excerpts, and more—plus new series info. www.CristinHarber.com

Did you like Cash and Nicola's story? Pick up the next the novel in the Titan Series:

WESTIN'S CHASE (Jared's story)

And for sexy, quick reads, check out two Titan novellas:

GAMBLED
CHASED

ACKNOWLEDGMENTS

Thank you to everyone who feels the Titan love!

Karen Allen, you are a dream editor. Lynn McNamee, thank you for the editorial support. You two are amazing.

I can't thank you my critique partners enough. Jamie Salsbury, Nicola Layouni, Victoria Van Tiem, Andrea Bramhall, Claudia Handel, Kaci Presnell, and Sharon Cermak. You ladies are writing gold. Love your thoughts, nitpicks, and every biznatchy comment that made us throw CC stars. Amy Anhalt and Racquel Reck, you're lumped in with them, even if we didn't cross writing paths when this was a WIP.

And, tons and tons of thanks goes to my husband. XO.

FIRST LOOK AT WESTIN'S CHASE

He saw no point in being the leader if he couldn't guide his men home at the end of every job. His team. His operation. And right now, his disaster. Fire exploded around Jared Westin as he rolled for cover. Gravel dug into his cheek, and branches scratched at his eyes. Acrid smoke billowed, leaving the bitter taste of accelerant on his tongue.

Radio silence was a bitch. He was fine. He would survive, despite the bite of the bullet in his calf and the shrapnel in his shoulder. His men and the rescued hostage were his concern.

Stuck on the side of a mountain in Afghanistan, he saw that his only way out was through a hostile mess of turbans and firepower. Not the best strategic position. Jared's only comfort was knowing the released American would soon be on their helo and out of enemy fire. Rocco and Brock had hustled the guy down the side of a cliff toward the pickup zone before the firefight got bad.

Thump, thump.

The enemy's aim was blind, but close enough to cause harm. Dirt and rocks flew at him each time the bullets found groundcover instead of flesh.

Popping up his head, Jared eyeballed the area. He had a third man in this melee. Roman remained somewhere nearby, drawing enemy fire. A flash of a grenade hit ten yards to Jared's right, followed by Roman's return fire. *He must've had the same damn thought. If I'm going to die on a cliff in Afghanistan, let me do so in a pile of empty brass shells.* There was no way either of them was dying without a fight.

Jared checked his super-mag clip—full, with lots of potential. Plus he had a Sig Sauer strapped to his thigh. It had a solid reputation of accuracy, and he needed those bullets to hit their mark.

Fire burned through the brush nearby, and he caught sight of his man. Roman's shadow danced in the fiery glow cast against the rocky mountain. He was hunched against a boulder, reloading.

Jared reached into the gear pack strapped to his back. He needed something explosive. A bloody distraction. In the background, the *chop, chop, chop* split the night as the helicopter neared the landing zone. It was right on time, and he needed to get a move on. If not, they would be on their own.

Moving too quickly, his head spun. *Blood loss must be worse than I thought. Spectacular.* Jared rifled through the bag. More ammo. Two knives. And… thank the gun lords above, a handheld grenade launcher and two big-ass rounds.

Palming the launcher, he recalled the sexy woman he had to thank for this beauty. She went by Sugar. He had no idea of her last name or her real name, but, damn, he loved working with her. She handed out grenade-launching hand cannons as gifts. *Now if that wasn't a turn on…*

And if this thing saved his life, he would have to come up with a decent way to say thanks for the cover.

He snapped the metal handle into place, loaded up the first 40 mm grenade, eyed Roman, and shot out a blast. The explosion ripped open a possible escape route. Jared slammed the second cartridge into place. *Locked and loaded.* After a nod to Roman, saying this was their chance, he let it rip.

Jared covered his face and ran toward the hellfire with his super mag firing. Brass casings spurted from his weapon, leaving a trail behind him. He pushed through the burn in his body and the pain in his leg and shoulder, ignoring the heat that seared his clothes. When his magazine clicked empty, he tossed the piece into the flames.

Behind him, pops of firepower said Roman was behind him. Jared took a harsh breath. The smoke burned his throat. Gun pulled from the holster on his thigh, he pivoted and picked off enemy tangoes. They hit with bull's-eye precision. Sig Sauer deserved a thank you when this shit mission was done.

Their chopper hovered two hundred yards away in the pitch black night, hanging motionless off the side of the mountain. Roman was fast on Jared's heels, and the two of them beat feet as quick as they could toward the bird.

As Jared closed in, Rocco and Brock became visible, hanging from the opening, providing cover. Bright explosions ripped through the night as bullets rained down behind them. Two rappelling ropes blew in the violent mountain wind. *Hell yes!*

With no time to overthink his moves, he launched over the edge of the cliff and into the inky-black abyss. He crawled through air, reaching for a lifeline. The seconds took too long. Without the ropes, he knew death was certain. A free fall down into the rocky mountain spikes meant lights-out for good.

Gravity took over, and momentum lost. Jared's weight began a rapid descent. His skin prickled as he splayed his fingers, reaching—hoping— for success.

One hand fisted the rope, his wounded arm taking the brunt of his body and gear poundage. With a grunt and heave, Jared growled up to a second handhold. He had two hands tight on the rope, and Jared looked over at Roman. Swaying in the obsidian night, Roman screamed, "Hoorah!"

Crazy bastard.

His heart screamed, punching his bruised ribs. The jump was the best damn adrenaline rush he'd had in a long time. Jared took a painfully deep breath as the helo pulled up hard and swam off into the sky.

The devastating sound of the chopper leaving brought tears to her eyes. Gunfire and battle cries in a language she didn't understand screamed into the chilly night. Her saviors had come for one of them, but not both. It didn't make sense. They hadn't tried to find her. She heard them show up, create hell, and leave after finding her counterpart—the only other American in this camp.

They have no idea I'm here.

That was worst case scenario because that meant they weren't coming back. Big time bad news. Maybe she should have listened, stayed stateside, and handled her *work* headache differently. But, no, she needed an adrenaline rush. Needed to get her mind off everything at home that she wanted to avoid. And when a Middle East gun-tracking assignment popped up through black-op back channels, she'd hopped on a plane without even telling her friends.

Not that they would let her pull a stunt like this. Because... well, she would've been captured.

Hanging out with the elite gun-slinger types was problematic. Even if she was decent on the trigger, she wasn't elite or even as good an operative as she thought. Her background was intelligence gathering. She was only a *former* ATF agent with a desire for something bigger and too much time on her hands. *Pathetic.* All she had was an ego that rivaled the size of this goddamn mountain, and—

Sugar. Shut. The. Hell. Up.

She shook her head, then rubbed her eyes. "You *will* survive. You *are* that good. Who the hell needs a military rescue?"

It'd been more than forty-eight hours since her dumbass partner had stumbled into enemy hands and she'd tried to rescue him. That hadn't worked out according to plan, and she was tossed into a makeshift cell and given nothing more than dirty water and rock-hard bread. As a foreign woman, they could've done much worse to her—and that threat still loomed. *But I can handle this.* She could kill each one of her captors and walk off that mountain before she had any more woe-is-me thoughts.

Jeers came her way from her captors who'd survived the rescue operation, and her cage allowed no escape. She stepped away, feeling the earthen walls at her back and the lump at the back of her throat. She laid her palms flat against the cold dirt and dug her fingernails in. Two men approached, shooting into the night like it was Mardi Gras. *Celebrating? Oh, yeah, because they still have me.*

Made in the USA
Lexington, KY
14 June 2014